S E O U L E S S

SHAYNE MEISSNER

This is a work of fiction. Names, characters, places, and incidents either are the product of the author's imagination or are used fictitiously. Any resemblance to actual persons, living or dead, events, or locales is entirely coincidental.

First Printing, 2020

ISBN-13: 978-1-8381532-8-1

ISBN-10: 1-8381532-8-4

For Nala Quinn,

my continual source of inspiration

Acknowledgements

Starting this book was easy. Finishing was another story altogether. Being that this was my first novel, I underestimated the undertaking it would become, and have found an incredible respect for all those who have had the determination,(and perhaps madness) to go through this time and time again.

It goes without saying that I could not have done this without some very special people in my life, but I'll say it anyway.

Thank you to Wing-yi, without you here to support me, being captain of our ship at times when I hid myself away to work, as well as giving me a much needed kick up the arse every now and then, this book would not have existed.

Thank you to Ryan Colley, for leading the way, and being an incredible resource every time I felt lost or overwhelmed.

Thank you to Jordan Greaves, for being there for me to bounce ideas off for the last 18 years, critiquing them to make them stronger and inspiring me with your own.

Last but not least a big thank you to all my family and friends, you have all helped bring this book into the world, however indirectly.

In other words; this is your fault.

Contents

죽음

Part One

Death

The streets of Seoul blurred in and out of focus beneath his feet. Jong-sup had never considered himself scared of heights, but standing fifteen stories above his demise he had to admit that he was finding it increasingly difficult not to empty his bladder where he stood.

Did deciding to end his life make him weak? He certainly didn't think so. Personally, he felt it took a will stronger than most to be able to look the ultimate fear in the face.

For death really was the greatest fear of all. Other fears were symbolic of death; spiders, snakes, heights or small spaces. It wasn't the thing that frightens people, but what the thing represents. When people stood in a cage of snakes or held spiders, on-lookers will herald them as brave. So why doesn't this title apply to a man who has the courage to skip the subjectivity of fear and delve straight to the object itself.

Why was he hesitating? Was this doubt? Did he have something more to live for that he just wasn't seeing? Jong-sup quelled the thought as quickly as it had come and pushed it to the back of his mind. No! He was a lot of things, many not good, but he wasn't a quitter, once he had set his sights on something he bull-headedly charged at it until he had either decimated his target or over shot it and crashed in to anything unlucky enough to be behind.

The view from this high had a kind of neon beauty. Seoul being a city of lights meant that the sky was never truly black, it had a kind of orange-yellow haze that outlined the tall concrete giants that were littered around the landscape. He was in no mood to appreciate scenery; the subject of his attention was vertical. The streets below could just be made out. Small pools of vomit were blemishes on the otherwise spotless pavements; evidence of escapades that had happened just a couple of hours before.

He ripped his vision away from the spiralling view of the ground and leaned back against the waist high wall behind him, picked up his bottle of soju and downed the last measly dregs of the fiery liquid. Holding the empty bottle at arm's length and closing one eye, he squinted through it. It was possible to make out 'ROTTE' emblazoned in big red illuminated letters in the top left corner the building athwart him. He turned the bottle, bending and distorting the glowing word when something caught his eye.

Just above, there was a dark silhouette that was hard to fixate on, it flickered as if made up of gas. It seemed to dance ever so slightly left and right like a flame and it entranced Jong-sup and for a brief moment his current predicament seemed far away, until it took the form of something familiar; the figure of a person.

Jong-sup spasmed in shock at the embarrassment of somebody seeing him in this state and dropped the bottle, but the instant his view was not obscured by the clear glass, the figure had vanished. His heart was in his throat and he could feel his pulse in his ears. Feeling foolish he peeked over the edge of the hotel and could just make out that the bottle had shattered and layered a portion of the street in glass. Luckily, no one was around in these early hours of the morning; he didn’t care for their well-being, only was relieved that he hadn't drawn any attention to himself from any nosey do-gooders.

He slowly squatted and put his weight on the small wall that separated him from the maze of ventilation shafts that made up the domain of the hotel rooftop. Clutching at his heart as its beat gradually returned to normal, he felt at once his mortality. No longer young at forty-five years old and not taking care of himself for more than ten years it took time to settle in his chest. With the adrenaline no longer circulating his system in such great amounts the feeling was starting to return to his body. With this return of sensation came the realisation that he had now indeed emptied his bladder. He could smell the putrid odour of the dark wet stain; it filled his nostrils and made him gag.

‘Damn it!’ he spat through gritted teeth and kicked out at nothing; flailing his arms in the air. This was his favourite suit, he wanted to go out dressed in his best, to keep an ounce of his dignity when they scrape his mangled corpse off the pavement. After a moment, once calm had returned to him, he chuckled lightly. This is how it should be, he thought to himself. Nothing in life had ever satisfied his expectations; why should death be any different, and with that he began to rummage around in his trouser pockets and pulled out a business card; his business card.

It was ivory white with gold lettering that spelled out PARK JONG-SUP, just below was written KSI technologies. He built a scenario in his mind of his fellow board members finding out about his untimely and unfortunate death. He played with different outcomes. Sorrow, tears, guilt, laughter, celebration. He scowled at the thought and spat on floor beside him. God how he loathed that company and everyone in it. He bent the card and flicked it, watching it disappear over the edge.

In the peripheral of his vision he could have sworn he could see the dark flickering figure again. Rubbing his eyes, he found that it had gone. What was wrong with his eyesight? He knew he needed glasses but refused to wear them, they made him feel weak. Had he drank too much? Yes, he had drunk too much but he could normally handle his alcohol.

That irritating woman he had left in the room would be getting pretty worried now and might even start looking for him. Her name escaped him. The only remarkable aspect of her personality that he could conjure was how unbelievably mundane she was. For a moment he wondered if she would miss him; silly thought, she barely knew him. Would anyone miss him? He filed that thought to the back of his brain where he stored all useless notions.

At last deciding that the procrastination had gone on far too long he, using the wall for support, stood up and dusted himself off. Jong-sup turned away from the street and spread his arms out wide as if in vain of Christ; he did always have a high opinion of himself.

Tasting one last breath of air he leaned back.

Just then the air all around him fell still, the breeze had halted, and the distant sounds of the city were muffled. Static seemed to emanate from his body making the hair on his arms, legs, and the back of his neck stand-up. He could feel an immense surge of power pulsating from just to the right of him he could feel it in every fibre of his body. He forced his head to rigidly turn to face the unknown presence.

The sight of it made his eyes widen and turn red with bloodshot immediately. He felt ice shoot up and down his spine and he scurried away from it never averting his eyes. He did not scream out; no breath would come. His heart pounded against his ribs to the point of pain. It was hard for the eyes to understand; it was at the same time there and not. Gradually the shape appeared clearer and becoming increasingly more so. He recognised it instantly, the dark cloak from which underneath now slid two pure white skeletal arms had been stitched into his memory since seeing it illustrated in a book as a child. Nothing could be seen under its hood only a void that appeared darker than the night that surrounded them.

Finally Jong-sup couldn't take any more of its silent looming presence.

'What are you?' he squeaked pathetically but he already knew the answer.

I am Death came the reply, the sound didn't seem to come from the spectre, rather was whispered loudly in his ear. The confirmation gave him no relief instead making his body tense up to levels he had never before felt; like his tendons would tear in two. Then the realisation came to him that the voice wasn't at all what he had expected. Ancient and husky sure, but unmistakably female; almost recognisable but he couldn't place it. With the acceptance of this observation he steeled himself, and his next sentence was spoken with less stutter, cowardliness nevertheless shining through.

'You're a woman?' after momentary silence.

I am Death came the reply. The voice, still terribly close to his ear and just as terrifying, had a lesser effect now, diluted by Jong-sup's old-fashioned and stubborn ideas. Would the important job of overseeing the end to all life be assigned to a woman? he doubted it. He had obviously gone mad under the stress of the situation; he'd read of such things but didn't think that he would be one to suffer anything similar. Honestly, he was disappointed in himself, he thought he was stronger.

'So, I'm hallucinating,' he said defiantly.

No

'Any hallucination worth its salt would say just that,' the tremor now hardly detectable in his throat, 'then why would you appear before me in this westernized form,' he said with an almost mocking tone. Though he sounded confident, and in truth he was, he still could not bring himself to look at the apparition directly, since to do so still froze up his muscles and locked up his throat.

I do not appear said Death, I am only perceived

'So you're saying this is my doing?' he spat.

What was he doing arguing with nothing? He thought to himself, he really was insane. 'I'd love to stay up here talking to myself, but I have other arrangements. So, goodbye, figment of my rotting mind.'

Jong-sup, without hesitating, stepped on to the edge, hung one foot over the fifteen story drop and-

Stop came the voice; and stop he did, although he did not know whether through choice or not. The tone in Death's haunting voice had not changed but he felt something was different.

Anger.

It was felt rather than heard and it was suffocating. Jong-sup forced his neck around once again. Death was advancing slowly closer. There was no sign of movement from beneath its tattered black robes, it was simply drifting. When it had reached him, it stepped off the edge but didn't fall, just hung in the air. The physics of our tangible dimension were unknown to Death. It moved around until it was about ten feet in front of him. It regarded the mortal in front of it for a brief moment, standing there, his mouth stupidly agape.

Death hesitated for a second and wondered of the consequence of what it was about to do. Its skeletal arms disappeared beneath its cloak for a second and returned with a yellow deteriorating scroll in one hand and a long silver deadly-sharp scythe in the other.

Park Jong-sup son of Park Duk-jae and Hong Sun-hee

Father to none

Cheater

Gambler

Thief

Adulterer

Jong-sup was shaking, still not taking his eyes away from the dark void from under the hood. The voice was painfully loud, and the judgements were stabbing at his eardrums.

Murderer

'I haven't killed anyone!' the shock of the accusation had lessened the muscle constricting terror and made it possible to squeeze out his defence.

The innocence of indirection does not exist

'What are you talking about?!' Jong-sup cried.

Silence and he was. You, who have hurt many, physically, mentally, emotionally, are under the impression that you can go through life without retribution. However, your crime is having the ego to believe that you can decide when your time has run out, you have imitated my work for long enough, Death is master to all life, in time you will understand that

Death raised its scythe above its head and held it for the briefest of moments, Jong-sup's pupils narrowed with terror as Death brought it down swiftly into his skull. Issuing a disgusting gurgle from his mouth, he gazed cross-eyed at the blade sticking from his head, and then it was gone.

In an instant the breeze returned, the rumble of the city vibrated in his ear canal once more and the static that filled the air was but a memory. Jong-sup quickly felt for the gored split in his skull but could feel nothing. No gash, no pain, nothing. He let out a sigh of relief. His knees buckled as his strength left him, dizzy, he fell forward. Off the ledge.

Finally completing his goal, he tumbled as he faded in and out of consciousness, his vision kept going black and, on each return, he was further from the ledge or closer to the ground. It took longer than he thought it would, in fact, it reminded of a recurring dream in which he would trip over and fall through the darkness. He was half expecting to suddenly wake up and still be lying next to that tiresome woman. This was no dream however, instead of bursting awake and alert; he hit the pavement. Hard. He didn't bounce, rather, he kind of splayed outstretched in a contorted fashion. His brain slammed against his skull turning to mush and every bone in his body shattered. Blood was running from his ears, his eyes, his anus. The pain was like nothing he had ever felt. Mercifully, consciousness did not stay with him long.

Jong-sup didn't know how long he'd been out. It couldn't have been long as darkness still covered Seoul. The pain was still present but was incomparable to before. Forcing his eyes open, the light from the streetlamp stung, a shape slid in to view granting him some shade. A face, a young man, multiple faces, four in fact; all hovering over him. The muffled noises he hadn't realised he'd been hearing until now started to become clearer.

‘H........at.......e....................hey........................me,’

‘Hey mister, look at me ....that’s great, you're doing great, are you okay?’ said the young man closest to him with a look of concern on his face that was sickeningly sincere.

'Can you tell me your name, sir?' said a woman with a moon face, sporting cherub-like cheeks. Jong-sup found that he could move his arms and legs slightly and so tried to achingly sit up.

'No sir!' yelled the young man 'You have to stay down until the ambulance arrives,' and laid his hand on Jong-sup's chest.

'Get your hands off me!' Jong-sup growled. The young man released him in shock as if almost bit by an aggressive dog. To the protests of the small crowd, Jong-sup stood up and pushed his way past them, ignoring their pleas. He was limping quite badly and on one hand all of his fingers were bending in unnatural ways. Pain still seared through him but he couldn't process this right now, not with quarter of his brain still mush against his skull. He marched forward without granting the strangers so much as a thank you.

If he would have looked back, he may have seen a tall thin man in a scruffy green cardigan pick up his business card and slip it into his pocket. He didn't.

Jong-sup was going home.

수락

Part Two

Acceptance

1

Still limping heavily, pain racking his body Jong-sup finally laid eyes on the concrete eye-sore he called home. Alpine view was an apartment complex for the elite, the famous, the wealthy. When he had bought this apartment more than twenty years prior it was a classy place; at least in his estimation. Now though, after several renovations it was a tacky monument to the gods of modern art, clashing colours, warped furniture in the lobby and photos of stars lined the walls of the corridors that he couldn't recognise.

He never socialised in the clubhouse anymore, he felt uncomfortable, and as out of place as an antique lamp would have looked in this building. Nowadays he much preferred to walk briskly to the comfort of his own home and today wasn't any different, just far less brisk. The automatic doors slid open for him and ignoring the 'Good morning Mr Park' from the lobby receptionist, he made straight for the lifts. The doors on the central lift were thankfully already open which would save the possibility of any idle chit-chat or questions about the state of his attire. Pressing the button to the twenty first floor the doors closed over.

'Good morning Mr Park,' said a sweet voice cheerily. Jong-sup flinched round startled to see Mi-na; the young girl who lived next door. Mi-na was an adorable child, almost ripped from the pages of a child's clothing catalogue, at seven years old she was short for her age and had long hair down to her hips that was today tied into two braids separated by a blue ribbon. She bowed politely and he tipped his head in return.

'Are you alright Mr Park? Your clothes are torn,' she inquired in a soft voice that fit her ever daydreaming expression perfectly.

'I had a fight with a dog,' he lied in reply and gave an ugly smile.

'Oh no, that must have been scary!' she said with genuine concern.

'No, not really. It's dead now,' he replied, not really knowing himself if he was trying to upset or entertain the poor girl; he never was any good with children.

'That's sad,' she said with her usual glazed over expression 'but I'm glad that you were not hurt.'

Jong-sup grunted in reply.

There was an awkward silence for a moment till Mi-na broke it.

'Did you know, Mr Park? My dad is running for Mayor of Seoul,' she said without a hint of gloating. He knew, of course he knew. The posters were plastered all over the damn place, he couldn't go a day without being reminded by the white of her father's perfect teeth. 'if he wins, we probably won't be neighbours any more Mr Park,' she said her voice trembling slightly as if sad.

'Your father won't win,' he laughed.

'Why not?' she asked in interest not offence.

'Nobody likes him,' he replied. The conversation was interrupted by the lift doors opening. In the hallway directly opposite the lift was Mi-na's apartment. The door was open and standing in front of it was her father and subject of conversation, Dong-wook. He was smartly dressed and groomed as always. He was the current District Councillor of Gangnam-gu and Jong-sup despised the attention he got from everyone on the complex; always kissing his ass. He stood in the hallway talking to two cheaply dressed men who gave off an aura that they were looking for trouble. One turned to look at Jong-sup and smiled cockily. He had a gaunt face and hair badly dyed an off-orange. It looked more like a stick-up than a conversation. Mi-na squeezed past them and walked into her home.

'Good morning,' said Dong-wook. Jong-sup nodded slightly in return and turned left out of the lift and walked down the hallway to his own apartment. He thrust the key into the door, it beeped and then opened. He knew immediately that the cleaner had come, as the pile of sick he had left on the floor had disappeared; and he had no dog. This was some relief at least.

The apartment was spacious and decorated with simplicity in mind. The walls were cream and there hung no pictures nor decorations of any kind. A large window acted as the far wall and in the left corner stood a bar now clean and topped up with full bottles of whiskey, soju and wine. The lack of furnishings in a room this large made it look empty, especially now the clothes that were normally strewn everywhere were now folded neatly in the closet. It would take a couple of days to return to its usual state.

The only other rooms were the bedroom and the bathroom. He kicked off his shoes by the front door and headed to the former. The bedroom was around half the size of the living room and in the centre was the sleeping mat. He craved to be taken by sleep and if he never awoke that would be just fine by him. Not bothering to take off his clothes he flopped onto the hard floor covered by a thick blanket. His answering machine was blinking so he haphazardly reached for it and pressed play.

'YOU HAVE ELEVEN NEW MESSAGES,' beeped the machine.

Groaning loudly he slammed his finger on the stop button. He'd check them tomorrow if he was unfortunate enough to not suffocate in his slumber. He rolled over so that he was lying on his back. The mat was firm and level, just how he liked it and he had no trouble drifting away from reality and into the solace of dreams.

2

Later that evening Mi-na was sat at her dinner table having just enjoyed a large meal. Her housekeeper and almost full-time carer; Carina, was busy wiping the table in front of her. Her parents weren't home, of course they weren't, they rarely were. She was staring off into nowhere as she often did, pondering.

Although her parents didn't have the time to spend with her, she understood that she really was lucky. She looked around at the luxury her parent's lifestyle had afforded her and she felt sad. Mr Park was always alone. She couldn't recall a time when she had seen him have a visitor. Some of the other children that lived in the complex had once told her that Mr Park had a wife and child in the past, but he had murdered them. She didn't believe them; they had a story like this about everybody who seemed a little off, but Mr Park seemed the primary target of their tales.

'Carina?'

'Yes honey?' replied Carina in English, her accent distinct.

'Are there any leftovers from dinner?' said Mi-na, her English wasn't perfect but still of a very high level.

'Oh my! Are you still hungry? You are going to get fat,' said Carina poking Mi-na's belly and smiling lovingly. Mi-na giggled and wriggled around; she loved her housekeeper.

'No! Not for me,' she smiled 'for Mr Park.'

'Why? He is a mean old man,' said Carina not really surprised, she knew very well the kindness of this girl she had almost raised herself.

'He's not mean, he's funny,' said Mi-na defensively her bottom lip protruding slightly.

'I don't know honey; your parents might not like it,' said Carina.

‘If he doesn’t answer I’ll leave it by the door, I promise,’ she bargained.

Carina considered it for a moment.

‘Okay but don’t take too long,’ said Carina; she always caved.

Mi-na jumped out of seat and hugged Carina tightly. Carina gave her a pinch on the cheeks and went to fetch the leftovers. She returned from the kitchen with a transparent plastic container that was now full of bright red-orange kimchi and chicken.

Taking the container in hand Mi-na left her home and turned down the corridor towards Mr Park’s place. She felt slightly nervous as you could never really predict his mood. The best possible outcome was a grunt and a smile, for Mi-na that was enough. The more likely result was that he would scold her for not minding her business.

Reaching the door, she noticed that it was open just a little. She knocked anyway.

‘Mr Park?’ she announced, ‘I’ve brought you something, Mr Park?’

She received no reply. Putting her ear to the door she could swear that she could hear something. He might be in the bathroom she thought. Considering leaving the food by his door an idea struck her. Mr Park was old. Perhaps he had fallen over and needed help. If she left now without checking on him and he’d been hurt, she would never be able to forgive herself. Slowly she pushed the door open enough to squeeze her head through. Peeking in revealed that nobody was in the living room. His place was much smaller than hers she noted.

‘Mr Park? I have some food for you, are you okay?’ no reply came. She could hear some movement. Entering completely now and closing the door behind her she took off her shoes and left them by the door. Carefully and quietly she made her way to the first door on her right. Peering round the corner she found that this was the bathroom. Creeping in she put her hand on the shower curtain and hesitated, if

Mr Park had fallen in the shower, he would be naked and most likely angry. Steeling herself she pulled the curtain back quickly.

To her relief it was empty.

The only other door was right next to the bathroom. If he isn't here, he must have gone out she thought. The door was already halfway open, so she gave it a little push to reveal the bedroom in its entirety.

'There you are!' she exclaimed. Mr Park it seemed had been rather clumsy. Somehow, he had managed to have got his tie stuck on a hook in the ceiling, usually where you would hang the clothing line. He was now suspended in the air; his face was an awfully unhealthy shade of blue. There was a chair that had been knocked over on the floor. It was a good job she had come she thought, he could have been hanging here for ages.

Jong-sup was appalled to see the young girl in his apartment without invitation. He was trying his best to shout at her, but his windpipe was cut off and he was only capable of producing a slight groan. He was also relieved. He had been hanging here for almost three hours. The feeling had all but completely gone from his limbs, a gift compared to the excruciating first forty-five minutes.

She stared at him in her usual dream-like state.

'My dad has those boxers,' she mused. Now reminded that he was indeed indecently dressed in front of this child he felt extremely embarrassed. He expelled the loudest noise that he could possibly muster.

'Don't worry Mr Park, I'll help you down,' snapping out of her trance, 'I'll get Carina!'

Panicking he made another spluttering noise; he even made his body sway a little.

'Oh right! you probably don't want any ladies to see you in your underwear,' and she disappeared from his sight. He could hear her searching around and making noise, then a crash and an 'Oh no, sorry'. Jong-sup went through a list of things in his head that she might have smashed. Please don't let it be the soju he pleaded.

Mi-na retuned in a what felt like half an hour but in reality was no longer than a couple of minutes. She brandished a knife and a grin and he couldn't say which was sharper. Re-establishing the chair's correct position, she climbed it and held the knife out on a fully extended arm. The knife was carefully wedged between his tie and his flesh, which if he had been here any longer may have become one and the same.

'Sorry Mr Park,' she said as she twisted the blade to face the fabric of his captor. It was uncomfortably close to his jugular as she started to saw at the material. He could hear the fabric starting to tear until "SNAP" he landed on the ground with a thud. Unable to slow his fall he landed directly onto his face. Mi-na reacted quickly and turned him over which was no easy task.

'Why can't you move Mr Park?' she asked.

'Because my body is numb you stupid girl!' he barked making use of his now unclenched vocal chords.

'Oh, I see,' she said looking a little hurt. At the sight of her face he muttered a quick 'Thanks' and she lit up again.

'I'll wait out there while you put some trousers on Mr Park,' she smiled.

It took a little while for the feeling to return, as well as the ability to move but when he came into the living room Mi-na was waiting patiently cross legged at the table. With the addition of some trousers and a vest he sat at the table across from her.

'I almost forgot!' she gasped 'this is for you' and she slid over the plastic container. At the sight of the kimchi, Jong-sup realised that he was famished, he ripped off the lid and grabbed the metallic chopsticks that were lying on the table. Then he paused and cleared his throat.

'ugh, thanks,' he said almost shyly. He wasn't used to acts of kindness being directed at him and he still wasn't sure that he liked it. He then proceeded to shovel as much of the kimchi and chicken into his mouth as possible. It was grotesque to look at, and to listen to. The whole experience was unpleasant really, for most people that is but Mi-na just sat there and smiled.

'I'm glad you like it,' she beamed.

'It's alright,' Jong-sup grumbled.

'My housekeeper made it, she is a very good cook and even cooks Korean food we-'

'Do you mind,' Jong-sup interrupted, 'I'm trying to eat.'

'Sorry Mr Park,' and she bowed and smiled on just watching him devour the gift.

In between mouthfuls, Jong-sup had time to contemplate now that the blood had returned to his head. When he had awoke a few hours earlier, hot, stinking, ill-tempered and in pain he swore the whole ordeal must have been an alcohol induced fever dream. He wasn't a religious man nor a spiritual one, he didn't believe in anything. Only money, not because he was a man who was particularly materialistic but because money is numbers and numbers are about the only thing that you could rely on in this world. Sure, he enjoyed some of the finer things in life but that was a by-product of his old-school hard-working state of mind.

This however, was something different, after listening to his messages when he had awoke he was reminded of why he was finished with this life, and still trying to make sense of his apparent "dream" he set out to do what he had planned to last night. He started to think that something was wrong after twenty minutes. It was taking longer than it did in the films and the memories of the previous night were becoming clearer. Why didn't Death appear on this occasion? Could his ability to die really have been taken from him? Surely hanging for hours by the neck should have killed him?

No! He thought, how could this be possible. Out of all of the people on this whole planet why would death choose to pick on him, he wasn't evil, and he knew a few guys far worse than him who killed themselves successfully. It didn't make any sense, there must have been a reason, perhaps he didn't do it right. He had to know for sure.

He collected his thoughts and, reality returning to him, noticed that Mi-na was staring at him.

'Hey, you should probably go now, your maid will be wondering where you've been.'

'Yeah, I suppose so,' she said gazing at the wall but not attempting to move. Jong-sup was becoming impatient, so he woke her from her daydream with a loud clap of his hands and a clearing of his throat.

'Come now,' he said taking her by the arm and leading her out the door. 'and remember don't say anything to anyone about my little accident'

'Don't worry Mr Park we all fall down, but I wouldn't ever want to embarrass you,'

'Yeah, yeah, embarrass,' he replied absent-mindedly, his attention was on something else. Mi-na opened her mouth to speak but Jong-sup quickly shut the door in her face. She shrugged her shoulders, turned and made her way back to the comfort of her own home, skipping as she went.

Back in his abode Jong-sup was feeling desperate. He was worried that all that had happened was true and even more worried of what it meant if it weren't. He pulled at his hair turning around and around not really sure what his next move was. Then, an idea struck him, but he needed to be struck harder if it were to work. He ran to the wardrobe in his room and flung it open. On his hands and knees he chucked item after item over his shoulder as if digging a tunnel until he hit gold. Struggling much more than he had remembered doing so in the past he dragged the two twenty-five kilogram weights from their hiding place. Perfect! He thought, this will do the trick.

Jong-sup stood there waiting under his contraption, eyes closed and apprehensive. He had suspended the weights about three feet above his head using a blanket, the wardrobe door and the hook that had failed to strangulate him. All he had to do now was to close the door and he could test the theory of life after death. But he was scared, this might prove to be more painful than his preferred methods but what other choice did he have? he wasn't going to hang around and see those bastards at KSI tech grinning as he gets put away, most likely to the end of his days. The pain would probably only last for a moment until his brain switched off the nerves to his receptors he reasoned, not actually knowing if there was any truth in that at all.

He stared out the window at the beautiful shared garden he had never really appreciated.

'Come what may,' he exclaimed out loud in the tone of a man who had long given up hope. He exhaled a long and shaky breath. He kicked out behind him slamming the wardrobe door closed and released the blanket. The next milliseconds were drawn out and frames were stored into his memory, he wasn't sure but he remembered that he could see a dark patch, an abnormally dark patch, out in the communal gardens at the back by the trees. If it had a face no features were visible, but he felt that it was facing towards him.

Before he had any time to produce an entire thought, he heard a loud crack atop his head that echoed throughout his body. The pain was momentary but so intense that it might as well of stretched through eternity. All was black.

3

At three twenty-five in the afternoon the next day; Jong-sup sat impatiently waiting in the board room for the meeting to start. The top of his head was wrapped in white cloth as a makeshift bandage. Although the split in his skull had sealed over and the pain receded, he was paranoid that it was going to split apart again and his brain would come tumbling out. When he had awoken earlier, or risen, or reanimated, or whatever it was that happened to cursed creatures such as himself, he finally had to admit that what he had seen on the rooftop two days prior had been chillingly real and for the time-being at least, he could not die. Some people might have rejoiced at this revelation, but Jong-sup knew this for what it really was, torture. Death was playing some cruel game with him. Playing with him as a child might disintegrate an ant with a magnifying glass. Why then, would he drag himself to work? because he hadn't skipped a day of work in his life and he wouldn't start now. He wasn't a no-good layabout expecting everything to be handed to him like the youth of today.

Being situated on the top floor of the building, the boardroom offered fantastic views of Seoul. Right on the bank of the Han river the scenery was among the best in the city; the views from the other side of the room being that of your usual cityscape. The room itself was modern and cold, everything was metal, glass or tiled and he missed the times when things were wooden and more sophisticated, not this tacky rubbish that wouldn't stand the test of time.

This was an important meeting, well for him at least as he was hoping to find out how much help they were going to afford him, or more likely how much they were going to screw him over.

Finally, he was relieved to see people slowly start to fill up the room, there were ten board members in total and they were just waiting on one. The one that they all waited on. Jerry Moon. CEO of KSI Technologies. Jong-sup hated Jerry, always did, even before these latest events had come to light. In his opinion Jerry was a spoiled stupid American who had had everything handed to him on a silver plate. He didn't much like any of his fellow board members either, they too had their part in stabbing him in the back. Jerry might have plunged the knife in, but the others had twisted it and made sure that it had remained there.

He looked around at the lifeless faces that sat at the table around him. Not a decent man among them and the women, of which there were two, were just as bad if not worse. He didn't know who he liked the least or hated the most. They were all dressed as he was, though his tie wasn't as tight and one of his cufflinks was missing.

Every so often one of them would glance at the bandage wrapped around his head, Jong-sup would immediately catch the look with his own and they would divert their eyes in an instant. They seemed almost scared of him, not ashamed or regretful. They looked at him as though he was a dying, rabid dog baring his teeth threatening to pass on his disease.

At last came the main arrival, five minutes late but nobody would dare say anything. Jong-sup took care not to scowl at him as he made his way across the room and took his place at the head of the table. Jong-sup was sat in his usual seat at the bottom right. Jerry, after adjusting himself looked down the table at the people before him, making sure to look at Jong-sup last. When his gaze did fall upon him, he noticed the white cloth draped over his head but decided not to comment. He may of hated Jong-sup but etiquette was still an important part of Korean society, even if Mr Park didn't always seem to follow the status quo. He cleared his throat and began talking.

'Welcome, everyone,' although Jong-sup didn't feel included.

Jong-sup looked at the clock for what felt like the two-hundredth time. The hands of the clock weren't still but they sure as hell were taking their time. Why was it taking so long? Thought Jong-sup, they had been going over sales predictions again and the specifics of an upcoming investors dinner but they were taking a while to get to the most important issue, and he had a suspicion that Jerry was avoiding the subject. Jong-sup wouldn't let that happen. He considered bringing it up or asking to move along but decided against it, he needed this as much in his favour as possible. He would be on good behaviour for now.

Barely listening to the brain numbingly boring talk of figures, and occasionally stifling a scoff at the sound of one of his colleagues brown-nosing Jerry, throwing complements out or calling themselves stupid if Jerry didn't agree with them, he took the opportunity to enjoy the view opposite him. The sky was a lovely shade of blue today and the river didn't look as brown as usual. A dark smudge against the royal backdrop grabbed his attention but by the time he targeted it with his irises it was gone; or perhaps it was never there.

Jong-sup narrowed his eyes, he didn't feel fear but a burning anger and frustration. If he ever saw Death again he would give her a piece of his mind. How dare she take away the one true and last freedom a man has, all for what? He couldn't answer for the life of him, or preferably the death. He went over different scenarios in his mind of their next encounter, each depicting his victory over it or her or whatever.

In his swell of pride at conquering an imaginary Death he absent-mindedly slammed his hand on the table. He hadn't noticed the disturbance he had caused the meeting nor the sudden silence that had fallen until Jerry Moon cleared his throat loudly. His sudden realisation that he was the object of their attention made him look down in embarrassment.

'Yes, Mr Park did you have something you wished to share with us all,' said Jerry wryly.

'Uh, yes actually. I was wondering when we were going to cover the largest of our current problems,' said Jong-sup, he could hear that his voice sounded weak and he was ashamed, before this debacle and especially in his prime he was one the most outspoken and biggest contributors to the board. Since most of the original members that he had come up with had moved on or died, he was one of the oldest; only three of the people surrounding him were over forty. The younger ones were spoiled brats practically bred for these positions of power who didn't earn it as he did, yet his word or advice was no longer considered valuable. He felt castrated.

'I think you are referring to "your" problem, correct?' replied Jerry, cool and confident.

'What do you mean?' asked Jong-sup, though he already suspected where this was going.

'Ji-yeon, would you kindly explain to Mr Park the results of our Friday meeting, please?' said Jerry.

'What meeting? I wasn't informed of any meeting,' said Jong-sup his voice becoming harder.

'You see Mr Park, we have decided,' began Ji-yeon. Jong-sup hated this woman maybe more than the others. Maybe because she was, in his estimation, unfit for her position or maybe it was because he desired her and knew of her affair with Jerry as did most of the board. Her face was heavy with make-up in the current popular style, her nose was softly sloped outwards, this wasn't the nose she had when he had first been introduced to her and he didn't think it was an improvement. Her eyes appeared unnaturally large with surgery and contact lenses that made her pupils look fully dilated as if she was in pitch black room.

'We have decided that the reputation of KSI technologies is the most important factor in light of the current events, the company, as an organic being cannot afford to lose its head, I think you would agree,' He did not agree. 'in other words, it would be unwise for Mr Moon's involvement to surface,' Jong-sup looked at Jerry who pretended not to see him. 'of course when these things happen, and of course they will, the people, and more importantly our investors need to see some action. As head of the safety testing division its unavoidable that you may be put in the limelight, as much as we would all hate to see that happen,' her insincerity was obvious to all present.

'So what you are sayi..' Jong-sup tried to say but was interrupted by Ji-yeon.

'Luckily, Mr Park we all feel very strongly that we want to offer you all the help that we can. You will retire with all your benefits intact plus a nice sum under the table, we will also assign the best lawyer that we have at our disposal, you may not even see jail time.'

Jong-sup stood up suddenly. He adjusted his collar and sleeves and paused for a moment. The silence was agonising to everyone present.

'I just want to say thank you. Really, to all of you for all the years, the sweat, the sleepless nights and the sacrifice I have put into this company, thank you. Thank you for taking it all and burying it into my spine!' his voice elevated and his teeth bared he could see some of the people wincing as if preparing for him to strike out at them.

'Hey, hey let's not get upset OK. I perfectly understand how you're feeling,' said Jerry holding up his hands as if roasting them on the fire of Jong-sup's temper.

'Really, that's a relief!' said Jong-sup his voice now louder and to his shame a little higher.

'You've done great things for this company, we all understand that, but Park, people are dead, you need to understand that,' explained Jerry his tone still cool and collected. 'you're just lucky that the brunt of the bad press has been taken by Sundai motor vehicles or the mob would be after you directly. This is a win for everyone, the stocks will stabilize, the company will keep running and you get to retire a rich man.'

'Tell me, what good will money do me behind bars!' Jong-sup snapped.

'If it comes to the worst, and you do spend a little time in prison you'll be out before you know it and then it'll do you a world of good,' countered Jerry.

'Please,' Jong-sup's voice softened again 'why don't we do what I suggested before and push the blame on the factory in China?'

'Sorry Park no-can-do, you see the factory has been dissolved not a week after the first accidents were reported. Even more, if we are found to have used an unlicensed company to produce our breaks, the results would be catastrophic.'

'I can't believe what I'm hearing,' Jong-sup said defeatedly 'you all agreed that to save money, cuts to production had to be made, cutting the testing period wasn't even my idea.'

'But you signed off on the parts,' replied Ji-yeon.

'So did he!' shouted Jong-sup pointing an accusing finger at Jerry Moon.

'No,' said Ji-yeon coldly 'You forged his name, don't you remember?'

Rage that had been simmering at the bottom of his stomach was now at boiling temperature. His brain sent the signal to lunge at her, to tear off her head if he must, but before his muscles could act out their leaders wishes something froze them in place.

Two ivory-white, skeletal hands were slowly coming up from behind Ji-yeon and gripping her shoulders. Although it was obvious that she could feel nothing, Jong-sup could see it as clear as day. He pointed and let out a series of mumbles, his bottom lip shaking and causing an awful bumbling whimper.

The people viewing this awkward display quickly turned to see nothing but the corner of the room; but Jong-sup was now looking at the top of Deaths black hood slowly rising from nothingness behind her. It stretched out to full height almost touching the high ceiling and towering over the mortals. The light seemed to be being pulled towards the ghastly presence. Death released Ji-yeon's shoulders and made way around the long table towards the loudly sobbing man. Death moved closer and closer until she passed through him and for a second, he was colder than he had thought it was possible to feel. Coming out of the other side the once comfortable temperature of the meeting room was searing. His hands prickled as his blood boiled under the skin.

Death had gone as quickly as she had appeared, he could feel it, but her unwelcome manifestation was too much to handle on top of all of what had just come to light. The pressure found a release in the form of a stream of vomit springing forth from his red, straining face. It hit the shimmering glass table and splattered out in all directions, there were a few screams of shock and then silence. Jong-sup's groggy mind recuperated enough to see everyone glaring at him in disgust, except Jerry who was averting his eyes out of the window in refusal. Disgraced, he fled from the room not looking back.

4

Vibrations reverberated through the bus as it rumbled along at the usual break-neck pace of Seoul public transportation. Jong-sup dazed with his head pressed hard against the window making him look demented to any pedestrians that passed by. The bus whizzed by a particularly reflective window fast but not too fast for him to get a good picture of how he looked and it amped up the shame. The visit to the bar on the way home had helped, but the effects were quickly wearing off. He tore off the make-shift bandage and threw it roughly to the floor of the bus to join the ranks of the empty vodka bottle he had discarded earlier.

Upon further inspection of his dome he was surprised that there was no split in his skull, not a gash or even a scab. How was he healing so fast? Was Death healing him rapidly to stop him from passing away. Maybe that was the answer to his problem, maybe he had to do it so fast and certain that Death couldn't catch up. He thrust his fist into the air in premature victory so suddenly that the few other passengers along for the ride jumped. He hadn't taken the bus in years, usually when he'd visit the bar he'd get a taxi but for some reason today he felt compelled, perhaps it reminded him of a simpler time.

The other passengers didn't seem so thrilled at Jong-sup's trip through memory lane, they were used to the crazy on the bus of course, but they usually weren't wearing such an expensive suit and watch. Even the scheduled crazy guy looked uncomfortable and a little vexed that Jong-sup had stolen the spotlight.

Stepping off the bus and into a puddle, Jong-sup dragged his hand down his face at the sight of the person who had just spotted him.

'Mr Park, are you on your way home?' it was Mi-na. She was dressed in her school uniform of a green blazer and grey skirt and carrying a backpack that was heavy with books. Jong-sup exhaled loudly.

'Yes,' he replied.

'Great! That's early for you. Let's walk back together then. It's only around the corner,' she chirped. He replied with a grunt.

'I was thinking about...' she started. Jong-sup was about to ask her to be quiet when he was struck with an idea.

'Mi-na, how would you like to make a little pocket money?' he said, forcing his voice to sound as friendly as possible.

'No thank you,' she beamed.

'What! Why not?' he blustered.

'I don't need any,' she replied.

'You know why you don't need any? Because you're spoiled. How do you think South Korea became what it is today, huh?' he lectured 'it's because we worked for it, hard. We worked tireless so we could raise the standard of living, this isn't the Korea I grew up in, no way. Life was hard, so we did something about it, worked our asses off and for what? So your whole generation could lie back like lazy imbeciles,'

'Well, okay then,' she said and smiled right at him, immune to his rant.

Just before they reached Alpine Heights, they took a left down a narrow alleyway that lead behind the housing resorts and behind the garden of their luxury homes. They came out to a clearing; a small decrepit building was the centrepiece.

'What is this place Mr Park?' she said in a tone of awe.

'When I was a little boy this was a shop that I would come to every day to buy sweets with the money I had earned collecting tin,' he explained. The building wore its age expressively. It hardly resembled the shop built in his memories. Half of the wall on the left side had fallen, the door was missing, the windows were broken and the sign that hung over the now barren doorway was ripped in half. Jong-sup was sad to realise that he couldn't recall the name, but the brickwork, that he could remember vividly, was so distinctive of the time.

'Ah, they don't build them like they used to, family businesses like what you see here used to dominate, now they've been driven out by chains, American chains in most cases,' he said not even trying to mask his discontent.

Just as in his recollection, he was happy to see the huge, twisted, ancient tree that grew from behind the shop and arced over it.

'Just one more thing,' he said more to himself than Mi-na.

He entered through the front and was taken aback by how small it was, as if it had shrunk since he had last been here. What used to be decorated in bright, vibrant colours was now dull and slathered in graffiti. The shelves had almost all been pulled down and not one of the sweet jars that had once occupied the shelves lay intact.

He made his way to the back of the shop, past the counter to the closet door which was still locked. He kicked the door several times before the old wood snapped at the handle and flew open.

Jong-sup emerged from the hole on the left side, arms full and face showing genuine happiness at this turn of luck. He had all he needed. Two lengths of rope, different thickness but it would do just the trick. He laid them out on the grass beside the tree and proceeded to tie them together at one end.

'Not like that, Mr Park, it'll never hold, look let me show you,' said Mi-na. In the blink of an eye she tied them in a complicated knot with the proficiency of a navy seal.

'That's not bad,' he said, actually impressed.

'Thanks,' she replied 'learned that at guides.'

'The reason I asked you here, Mi-na' he explained slowly 'is, you see that tree? I'm too old and no longer strong enough to climb it, do you think you could climb up there and tie this end of the rope to the end of that long branch that stretches over the shop?'

'No problem, Mr Park' smiled Mi-na.

'OK, well then, get to it,' said Jong-sup relieved.

Mi-na climbed the tree with surprising grace. At the top she rested on the long arching branch and biting her lip started to shuffle along its length with the rope tucked securely under her arm. At her destination she tied the rope around the branch in the same fashion as before. Her job complete it was time to come down but to Jong-sup's astonishment rather than returning the way she had gotten up she hung from the rope and slid to the ground.

'You stupid girl! What if you had fallen? And hurt yourself, all for the sake of showing off!' he scolded.

'Sorry,' said Mi-na, not at all sorry.

Jong-sup's plan had nearly come to fruition and that thought soothed his anger, now he wanted her gone.

Pulling from his wallet a note for fifty thousand won he dangled it in front of her.

'Now, before I give you this, I want you to promise me that you will never come back here, right.'

She thought for a moment, considering the trade.

'Okay, I promise.'

Jong-sup pushed the note into her hands and told her to run along, he watched until she had disappeared into the lane and turned his attention to the mission at hand. Taking the dangling end of the rope, he made his way to behind the shell of the shop that had made his childhood a little less bleak. There was a rusted ladder fixed to the wall, it was wobbly and missing a couple of rungs, but he managed just fine, he was old, not weak.

The shop seemed a lot higher from up here. Having doubts about the length of the rope he decided it best to remove his belt and fasten it to the end. It needed to be just right, a long enough drop and a sudden stop. At last happy with the measurements he placed his head through the ring he had formed from his belt. Let's see you heal me now Death, he thought, how will you heal me with my head detached from my body. He laughed as a single tear streaked down his cheek and went unnoticed. Feeling that he didn't have time to reminisce about life for fear of Death showing up to ruin his plan he launched himself from the roof.

There was a loud crack that echoed through the trees and could be heard out on the main street leading to Alpine Heights. Birds fled their tree top homes in all directions. Disorientated by the change of surroundings it took a couple of seconds for the pain to hit him but when it did it was agonising. It took a little longer for him to realise what had happened. He began to panic and regret what he had done, he didn't want to spend eternity as a severed head in constant anguish but with the return of the world to its usual state the reality of the situation became clear.

His head was not detached at all, it was very much intact, it was barley even bruised. The appendages that were splayed on the ground, twisted and twitching, revealed the origin of the loud crunch. His legs. The rope had been too long. His no-longer young legs had taken the force of the fall and had splintered at the femurs. Had the addition of the belt been his downfall? Did Death have a hand in this? Could Death make ropes longer? Far from being one who would doubt himself over another he settled on the latter.

He writhed in pain; his torso still being held up by the belt around his neck. Unable to summon the energy to move his arms he shifted back and forth, left, and right until his head was released from its trap. He found his vocal cords were no longer being held and so he used them.

'Is this what you wanted to see, you sick bitch?! How are you any better than me, huh?' he shouted. 'I never tortured anyone, are you not supposed to be impartial! The punishment doesn't fit the crime! Come out you cowered! Face the consequences of your actions, old men lying broken, is that how you get your kicks you sadistic bitch!'

He was answered by a change in the air, a swell of power pulsed through him. Jong-sup looked towards the source and found himself looking upon Death once more. In the shadows of the trees, on the opposite side of the clearing from the insufferable cripple, Death said nothing. She had nothing to say that hadn't been said and didn't believe that this man deserved to hear it if there was. Death just stared, reminding Jong-sup that she was now, as she had always been, part of his life.

'OK!' he raged 'I GET IT! OK, OK!' he shouted until his voice wore out and was but a pathetic whimper 'I get it, I get it, okay,' he sobbed. He now understood that there was no way to escape Death's unjust punishment. Death would always be there and perhaps always had been. Jong-sup had no choice but to accept the fate that had been forced unto him. He sat there for a long while until the bones in his legs started to rigidly snap themselves back together.

재건

Part Three

Reconstruction

1

The next two weeks went by quickly for Jong-sup, he found that he could jump forward in time a little by finishing of a bottle of whatever alcoholic liquid could burn his throat and make his stomach acids spoil the most. He had taken time to grieve for the loss of his ability to lose at this game of life. He wasn't happy about it but the anger and panic that had initially consumed him had now reduced to a simmer of self-pity, for who else would pity him?

He scratched impatiently at the oak table in front of him and looked at his lawyer who was sat next to him listening intently to the judge. Every now and then he would turn his head halfway towards him and give Jong-sup a weak smile. Jong-sup looked at the feeble young man in disgust, he doubted, no, he knew that this wimp wasn't the best lawyer that money could buy. His suit was cheap and unfashionable, and Jong-sup was surprised that he had the spine to support his stooped posture by the way he talked; quivering and unsure.

He looked around court room in boredom as the Judge read off information that didn't concern him, just formalities really. He was sick and tired of formalities, it was just like the Germans of which Korea had based their legal system on, to create such a convoluted mess of procedure and bureaucracy, had a Korean created it from scratch they would of got straight to the point, no messing around, Jong-sup thought.

The stalls behind him were sparsely populated, save for a few representatives from KSI tech and SUNDAI auto-mobiles. Kim Ji-yeon was present, serious-faced and pursed-lips as always but Jerry was noticeably and intentionally absent.

Death was watching, she was stood behind the jury, obvious to none but Jong-sup. Her silent gargoyle-esc observing didn't bother him too much. He could still feel the strange tenseness of the air and the frequency that pulled through him and set his teeth on edge when she was around, but she had been appearing more often of late and he had learned to bare it. Whenever he hurled abuse at her he was granted no response, she would just stand and stare, her black cloak swaying in a non-existent breeze. In the end he reasoned that if he had cursed someone, and there were many people who were lucky that Jong-sup hadn't the ability, he would damn well sure he would be there to collect every ounce of suffering.

Exiting the courthouse Jong-sup found himself looking at a day that perfectly matched his mood. Grey. He trudged down the stone steps leading to the street his arms limp at his sides and his own posture beginning to mirror his pathetic excuse for an attorney. Death followed closely behind.

'Are you finally satisfied?' he asked to Death but also to the world at large. Death gave no reply as was usual. 'Isn't this what it's all been about? Getting my comeuppance? Well it's finally happened, I am done.'

There has been no sentence

'Park Jong-sup? Can you hear me?' came a voice from just to the left of Death.

'Oh Ms Kim. I didn't see you,' he said his voice cracking slightly which he covered with a coarse cough.

'I said, there has been no sentence, you're not "done",' she said.

'Were we not in the same hearing? That bastard judge called me a man of "questionable character" can you believe it?' he said.

'No, I cannot,' she replied, then under her breath but not unnoticed by Jong-sup 'there's nothing questionable about it.'

'Well I guess you and the board can start your celebrations early,' he said.

'On behalf of the board I'm offended. Was it not KSI who posted your bail?' she said.

Little blots of water started to patter on the steps as the dark cloud that covered most of the sky began to burst. Ji-yeon, pulled out and opened an umbrella above her head, big enough for two but not considering for a millisecond to offer Jong-sup some shelter.

'Look, I won't be here when your trial continues most likely. When was it? In a week? Regardless, someone from KSI will be representing,' she explained.

'Will it be Jerry by any chance,' he said mockingly. She glossed over this ludicrous question.

'Unfortunately, I am rushed off of my feet, or else I'd ask you to dinner,' she said, though Jong-sup knew better. 'so, I should be going now, goodbye Park Jong-sup,' then again under her breath but loud enough to be audible to Jong-sup 'enjoy your last days of freedom.'

She made her way down the stairs to the black car that had just pulled up awaiting her. Jong-sup weighed the pros and cons of kicking her down the rest of the steps in his mind. The rain became heavier but still he stood there long after she had gotten in the car and was far out of sight. His suit darkened as it absorbed the rain and his hair hung around his face.

Something snapped him out of his rage-induced trance, but he was unaware of what it was until it happened a second time. Then a third. The now glimmering, reflective building of stone and marble lit up in a flash. Was it lightning? No thunder was following in its pace, so he looked around for the source. A fourth time. This time he caught the direction from which it came. From the street, behind a wall on the left side of the entrance. A man with his face covered by a camera. A camera? A moment of panic struck him. Then once again when the man disappeared behind the wall. Jong-sup yelled after him and then sliding slightly rushed down to the street and around the corner.

He could see someone walking away from him at a quickened speed and sought after him.

How could this have happened? He thought. There was supposedly a gag order on the media. It must have been affective or there would be swarms or the parasites outside KSI at all times. This must be a "fresh out of university" cockroach trying to make a name for himself in the sewer that was the news media. He had to stop his name from being dragged into this. Any public outrage would serve him ill in the trial to come and his sentence would likely be much harsher.

The man probably underestimated how quickly Jong-sup could move if so inclined, that or he hadn't realised he'd been spotted but Jong-sup clasped him by the arm and swung him around. The man was tall. Much taller than him, and thin, ghoulishly lean. He wore jeans and a green knitted cardigan that was soaked a dark colour.

Before the man had a chance to say anything, Jong-sup snatched the camera from his hands. The man put up surprisingly little resistance. Jong-sup threw the camera to the ground; a piece of it flew off into the road. Then he proceeded to stamp heavily on it. Again, and again, till it was in several pieces. It wasn't until his energy was spent and his breath came hard that he realised something. The man hadn't even protested.

He looked up at the towering sickly man and was shocked by his expression; he was smiling, just slightly but enough to put him on edge. He wasn't intimidated or even mad nor did he seem at all bothered by the status of his camera or the pieces that were left.

Then he moved his arm upwards and Jong-sup flinched. No strike came however, the man was slowly reaching out to touch Jong-sup's face. He slapped the strange stringy man's hand away, but his expression never changed. He just smiled curiously at Jong-sup.

'What the hell is wrong with you? Are you some kind of retard?' he spat, but the man didn't react at all. 'Get out of here you crazy bastard!' Jong-sup raised his voice. When the man again didn't react, Jong-sup decided to take his own advice and he ran from the scene with as much speed as his lacking breath could afford him.

2

The Black Apple was Jong-sup's usual watering-hole so what better place for him to drink until the lining of his stomach was burned away, especially after that court fiasco. He liked this place, it was classy, old-school yet timeless, like him. He tipped his head back and drained the whiskey in his glass and slammed it down on the bar summoning the barman to fill him anew.

He didn't *know* this barman, he wasn't new; he'd been there a while now, but Jong-sup didn't know him. He had never had a conversation with this servant in front of him, man to man. He'd kept the relationship of provider-consumer and he didn't plan on breaking that tradition tonight. It made him reminisce though, of a time when he'd been sociable enough to get to know the staff as friends, to joke and laugh and share a drink or two. Sometimes they'd let him stay after closing and they would just talk until the streetlamp switched off and were replaced by a more natural light.

He had had some good times here. When he was supervisor for the testing division, he found the best way to finish off a hard Thursday's work would be to buy his team a drink and start Friday morning joking about the events prior. After all the good times he had shared here with various staff members he was surprised that he hadn't ever ran into any here. Wouldn't they want to indulge in some nostalgia of the wild nights at The Black Apple? Unless they wanted to avoid running into him? Maybe they weren't enjoying themselves as much as they let on? His mood turned dark.

This was also where he had met her. His mood grew darker still.

The light in the smoky room dimmed low, almost enough to his current state of mind. He felt the now familiar tenseness of atmosphere, but not the normal stifling that came with it and turned to his right to see an already fully formed Death sat on the stool next to him. Not staring at him as usual but instead facing the inside of the bar like him. Almost as an ethereal patron. Her attire still swung and rippled in the usual slow-motion, as if under water, and she had both of her frightening arms on the bar in front of her. Jong-sup was startled to see Death so casual but hid it well.

'What're you drinking?' he asked letting out a laugh that splashed the bar with spittle.

Death said nothing.

'Barman!' he called holding his arm up 'I'll have the same again for my friend here.'

'certainly,' replied the barman as politely as he could manage. He sauntered his way to the side of the bar where Jong-sup was sat alone and thinking he had misheard he began to awkwardly top up his glass.

'What, are you deaf?' said Jong-sup coldly. 'Leave the bottle and bring me a glass, I'll do it myself!'

The barman passed him a glass, left him the bottle, and returned to the more polite customers.

'This one's on me,' said Jong-sup filling Death's glass to more than half. Death did not react however, she just sat motionless and silent.

'Fine, probably for the best. This shit will kill you!' Jong-sup let out a huge guffaw and slammed his hand repeatedly on the bar. This caused some of the other patrons to take a break from trying to ignore the man talking to himself, drinking two glasses of whisky and stared till he had quietened down.

'Are you here to enjoy my company?' asked Jong-sup.

No

'Well, while you're here, fancy telling me at last why you chose me, out of everyone else who deserves it more,' said Jong-sup his voice slurring to the point of incoherence.

No

'I thought as much,' he said. 'Then may I ask you a question?'

Yes

Slightly taken aback by this unexpected result he fumbled to think of what he was going to ask in the first place.

'Is….is...there a life after death? Heaven or something else?' he looked down feeling that he'd displayed himself as vulnerable. Death did not reply, she just continued to stare behind the bar. He paused in hesitation in case he would interrupt her, until it was obvious that he would be receiving no reply.

'Hey! You said that I could ask you a question,' he said offended.

And you did, I never said that you would receive an answer

'Fine, be like that,' he sneered.

They sat in silence together for a while, Jong-sup finished about half the bottle before he spoke again.

'I don't suppose you have a family do you, we're alike in that way at least. I used to want a family, you know, a long time ago. Right here, me and my team would have such a laugh and I would often wonder if that was what it was like to have one. Then I met someone, right there,' he pointed over to a booth in the corner, but Death didn't move an inch to look. 'She showed me what it was really like to have family, she took pity on this old street dog. You see, I never knew my parents. They died in the war. Can't even remember their faces. I don't even miss them "you cant miss what you never had" is what the matron at the orphanage where I grew up used to say, she was such a bitch!' He was talking to himself more than to Death. These were the thoughts that only seemed to creep back into his mind after it had been drowned in alcohol.

'Do you know when people are going to die?' he asked.

Yes

'Everyone?'

Yes

'So, what about me,' he probed.

You will not

He tensed up upon hearing the reply but decided it unwise to react with Death so unusually open to dialogue.

'What about him?' he pointed over the bar at the barman.

Tonight

'What! Really? Is that why you're here?' he asked feeling slightly betrayed.

Yes

'Oh, I see, I thought you might have been here to see me,' he said.

Why would I?

'I don't know! you're the one who's always stalking me!' Jong-sup's voice was becoming louder now, but he was distracted by the fake smile of the barman who had walked over to him.

'Hey, just to let you know it's last orders, can I get you anything sir?' he said politely though nevertheless obviously wished that he wasn't held by the tight constraints of etiquette. Jong-sup gave a grunt and shook his head, he was restricted by no such constraints. This guy, he thought, has no idea what's coming to him, lucky bastard.

Jong-sup decided to leave this once beloved establishment and was surprised to see that Death was following him; backwards. Death never took her gaze from the barman but floated an inch from the ground in reverse. Jong-sup stopped to observe. Death overtook him and carried on till she reached a public bench on the opposite side of the road. Jong-sup, with nothing better to do, decided to join her. The bench offered a decent view of the premise. It was dark, but the front of the bar was lit up in the eery glow of the streetlights.

Jong-sup sat in silence and searched his thoughts for any questions that he could pull some useful information from the mostly quiet and unhelpful Death. Nothing was coming to mind when he felt a tugging at his trousers; a cat, black, patchy and ravaged by mange. He flung out his legs to dissuade the filthy creature but every time it would move away it would stop, turn around and come back to resume its molestation of Jong-sup's expensive trouser leg.

'So, what time is it going to happen?' he inquired, hoping it wouldn't be too long a wait.

Death remained silent. 'Is it set in stone? I mean is it one hundred percent unchangeable?'

That depends

'On what?'

You could stop it she replied if you chose to

Jong-sup paused for a moment.

'Nah.'

A slight shift in the tenseness of the atmosphere told him that Death was surprised or disappointed or something; although she showed no outwardly reaction, she merely continued her vigil.

'Unlike you,' began Jong-sup, his tone viscous and condescending. 'I don't meddle in the forces that be, I won't ruin this guy's chance to see out his fate,' and with that he stood up to leave, quite happy with his dramatic exit. The cat followed suit.

Jong-sup was no more than ten steps away when there was a loud noise of a door slamming and the jingle of keys. The barman had finished closing up at last. Jong-sup's attention was drawn to the man in intrigue, until it was stolen by the decrepit feline pushing itself on its hind legs and rubbing its face in one long stride up towards Jong-sup's knee. He shuddered slightly, feeling the sticky film the cat had left on his attire. This was enough to fire up the furnace of his temper.

'Fuck off!' he growled, and he swung his foot out at some speed, catching the cat under its ribs and launching it into the middle of the road. The next events happened in the blink of an eye though they seemed elongated and clear to Jong-sup's adrenaline fuelled mind.

The cat had landed on its feet but now one side of it was highlighted by the bright glare of an oncoming vehicle. The cat froze in fear. There was no screech of brakes. The car had been coming too fast. Jong-sup saw the cat's eyes close in a flinching motion as if accepting its fate. The car didn't hit. The driver must have noticed the cat at the very last moment and swerved right and on to the pavement. There was a deafening crash and smoke billowed from the engine. A horrified scream echoed out and down the street as the driver; a young woman, realised what she had done. The car had crashed into The Black Apple.

The scene was obstructed by the smoke so Jong-sup; his mind still slow and trying to register the goings-on of the last few seconds, jogged over to the point of impact. The woman was hysterical, clutching her face and circling in place, he reasoned that she was beyond help and pushed past her. Close enough now for his eyes to see through the thick gas issuing from under the car bonnet, he saw the result of the chain of events that he had put in place.

Lying on the pavement in front of the vehicle, his stomach squashed and torn, some of his intestine poking out from the gaping wound; was the barman. Jong-sup's mouth hung open, he didn't want to stop this man's death because he didn't feel it was his business, now he had made it so and this was entirely different.

The barman's chest was heaving up and down and his heavy breathing was drawing blood from one or more of his crushed organs as it spilled from his mouth. He spluttered and shot a stream of the dark-red life fluid down himself.

'Are you here for me,' he managed, barely audible. Jong-sup couldn't form any words and just pointed at himself, but the barman's eyes were looking past him. Catching on Jong-sup turned to see Death looming behind him. Death moved through Jong-sup, entering his back and leaving home with that spine-chilling cold that he had hoped to never experience again. Death approached the dying man and crouched down beside him. The driver could now be heard dialling the emergency services, but she was having trouble being understood between her cries.

'Are you here for me' repeated the barman, Jong-sup noted that he didn't sound anywhere near as scared as he would have thought.

Yes, I am here for you replied Death her voice soft and unfamiliar to Jong-sup. There wasn't an ounce of malice or coldness coming from her. In its stead was a sort of comforting warmth that even Jong-sup could feel from where he was standing, and he craved it. He moved closer to bathe in Deaths loving radiation but found that he could move no closer than a few feet away. He pushed out with his hands but there seemed to be an invisible bubble surrounding Death and the dying, malleable but uncompromising. He surrendered to Deaths will and decided to watch the events unfold.

Death reached out and stroked the barman's face in vain of a mother and child, but most shocking to Jong-sup was Death's arm. Gone were the white bone, devoid of flesh appendages pulled straight from western mythology. In their place were the wrinkled but kind hands of an elderly woman. He wanted answers, he needed answers. What was she really? Why the preferential treatment for this nobody with a dead-end job? It wasn't fair that this punk who could barely scrape together decent customer service was welcomed by the loving gaze of a grandmother, when he had to stare into the empty abyss beneath the hood, the very symbol of death and decay. He pushed again at the invisible wall that defended his persecutor from his wrathful interrogation, but it wouldn't budge.

'I'm scared,' said the former barman.

You have nothing to fear my child said Death, her voice sounded as though whispered in his ear and he felt comforted, more comfort than life had ever granted him.

'There is still so much that I wanted to do and see and taste.'

I know Death sounded genuinely sorrowful but it is time for a new set of wonder

Death reached down to the torn man, grabbed him by the shoulders and effortlessly lifted him on to his feet. She then put one hand on his lower back and took his hand with the other, she led him to the wall of the bar, and they passed straight through.

Jong-sup who had been leaning against the invisible barrier fell forward as it was removed from reality. He looked down at the now completely still and mangled corpse of the man who had earlier served his drinks. This wasn't his fault, if the cat had left him well alone none of this would have happened. If Death didn't want this man's soul, she needn't have been so cryptic about his part in it. Then his rapidly sobering mind found conclusion. If Death hadn't have come to the bar he probably would have left earlier, in fact it was her that led him to the bench by peaking his morbid curiosity. That cat wouldn't have been bothering him, he wouldn't have kicked it, the barman wouldn't have died. She was trying to set him up, to tarnish his soul. The death of this man; lies with Death.

The sound of approaching sirens was Jong-sup's cue to leave, he didn't need the trouble of being questioned. He pushed past the traumatised woman and fled in the opposite direction of the on-coming sounds. He did not stop until he could no longer hear the commotion.

3

The following Monday, Jong-sup sat in his office going through a report on a new stronger material still in alpha-stage. He was heavily squinting, trying to make out each word and checking twice to make sure no mistakes were made. His office was not small, but it wasn't as big as his last office or the one before. It seemed every time the office was rearranged, he ended up with less space. Behind where he sat at his desk, there was a large window with a nice view of the Han, which he liked but facing him was a glass wall with a glass door, which he hated. It didn't offer any privacy, and that meant it didn't offer any respect. People further down the pecking order ran to-and-fro with papers in hand, distracting him occasionally.

'Mr Park, can we talk in my office?'

Jong-sup looked up to see Ms Moon Ji-yeon standing in his workspace, he hadn't heard her come in.

'Shouldn't you knock?' he grumbled, trying his utmost to conceal his hatred for this woman.

'Don't keep me waiting,' she demanded, ignoring his question. She flicked her hair, exposing a neck that he would have enjoyed throttling and walked out. He sat back in his chair and exhaled. He collected his thoughts and tried to take reign of his temper. When he had calmed, begrudgingly he pulled himself from his chair and made his way up to the floor above where Ji-yeon's office was located. He arrived at her door and thought about barging in but decided against it, he didn't need the stress. He bit his lip hard and knocked.

'Come in,' she called. Jong-sup shuffled in and stood there without saying a word, she left him hanging for a moment, she enjoyed flaunting her dominance whenever possible.

'Mr Park, do you not listen to your voicemail?'

'What voicemail?' he knew exactly what voicemail.

'The ones stating that it would be better if you didn't come into work for the duration of your trial.'

'I guess not, why wouldn't I come to work? I go where I'm needed.'

'With all due respect, you're not needed,' she said, not a hint of respect in her tone 'for now anyway. And anyway, the stress of the trial must be wearing you out, go and get some rest.'

'I don't need rest, this is how I earn my money,' he said, his voice defiant.

'You needn't worry, you'll be getting paid anyway, come now,' she put her hand on his shoulder to turn him around, in her mind the conversation was over.

'Take your hand off me!' he snarled. She wasn't startled or intimidated by his outburst, she had predicted it, so she calmly removed her hand and sat back on the corner of her desk. Jong-sup took note of how her skirt hugged to her hips and thighs, how he hated her but also craved her and this made him hate her more.

'I don't want to be paid for work I'm not doing. I will not shirk my responsibilities like one of you would, my generation built this country if it were up to people like you we'd all be living on the streets still!' his voice was elevated now.

'I admire your passion Mr Park, but you are simply of no use at the moment,' she said still cool and collected.

'No use?! The work I do in this company is a cog, that without, this clock would not be ticking!' he shouted.

'No your rusted and notched, and it looks bad on the company to have someone so negligent as you still working here!' she raised her voice in rebuttal.

Jong-sup went quiet, what had become of his beloved country where he could be spoken to in this way, and by a woman his junior. His hands were shaking. He couldn't make eye contact. Fine, he surmised. If they want to play a game, he would play and when he out-plays them, they'll wish they had never taken part.

‘I’ll go and collect my things and be out of here,’ he said feigning defeat.

‘It’s the best thing for everyone,’ she said feigning sympathy.

The next morning back at his home in Alpine Heights, Jong-sup awoke with renewed vigour. Something felt different, fresh, exciting. He had a plan, a goal to achieve, something he had not had for a long time. The last few years had been an exercise in the drudgingly stale taste of repetition. Being forced to remain home, or more likely the injustice of which has caused this situation to unfold, may have been the kick start he needed. He was going to take back the hold that Jerry and Death had over his life and steer himself with the ambitious drive he had had in his younger days.

If he was going to win his freedom, he needed resources. If he was doomed to live forever, he’d need enough money to sustain himself. Jong-sup, through hard work and immense sacrifice had lifted himself out of the horrors of poverty a long time ago. If he wasn’t cursed, he would have more than enough to last to the day of his last breath were he to retire now, however that money would be no good in prison. The thought of prison sent a shudder down his spine, he was afraid, not of the violent criminals that made their home there but of the lack of control. He wasn’t going to prison though; he would not allow it.

On the way home from KSI the night before, he had stopped by the bank. He wanted to withdraw all his money. He marched straight up to the premier lounge where the wealthy enjoyed privileges not shared by the common folk but was shocked to find that he wasn’t allowed to withdraw any amount exceeding a hundred and twenty million Won. He could not believe the audacity of the bank; it was his money! Apparently, this was standard practice and any amount greater had to be ordered and would be delivered to the bank in about a ten days’ time. Whilst an annoyance it gave him time to prepare.

He sat at his dinner table in the living room and pondered over the details of his plan. There were a few loose ends he needed to manage but he felt that everything would work out just fine. With no need to go to work and no meetings or anything of any official importance to attend to he had resigned to wear a simple t-shirt and jeans, it was uncomfortably comfortable, he had worn a suit or at the very least a shirt and tie every day for years. It didn't really feel right but he thought it better to get used to it.

At that moment he heard a noise, he paused, turned round, and paused again. He had fully expected to see Death stood somewhere in his place; she was long over-due a visit. He hadn't seen her since the night in the bar. Surely it didn't take this long to escort someone to the underworld or wherever the spirits of the dead go. Then it struck him, he had heard that someone dies every minute, how then would she have the time to torment him? Was she neglecting her other duties?

It was the noise again, this time its origin was clearer, a light tapping from the door. Jong-sup crept over to the door and peeped through the spyhole. He couldn't see anyone.

'Who is it?' he barked gruffly.

'Mr Park, it's me,' came the soft voice of Mi-na.

'Go away you bothersome child!' he replied callously.

'But I brought breakfast,' Mi-na waited a moment staring at the door and was delighted to see it creak open.

'Well, you'd better come in, but don't get too comfortable you can't stay long, I'm a busy man.'

Mi-na skipped in airily and kicked of her shoes at the door. She was wearing denim dungarees and knee-high socks; her long hair was fastened in a ponytail with a pink hairband. In her arms she was carrying a similar container as last time, but this time was filled with rice, scrambled eggs a small side of kimchi and a separate smaller container of soup.

Jong-sup took the food from her without a word of thanks and made his way over to the table, he pointed at the seat for her to sit down and she took it gladly. He ripped open the lid and started his devouring. Mi-na watched in silence for a while. Jong-sup hadn't realised how hungry he actually was, his recent experiences with pain had made him rather numb to it and so hunger felt like a slight dull ache.

'So,' she said finally 'how come you aren't at work?' Jong-sup looked up; kimchi hanging from his lips but gave her no answer.

'My dad says,' she continued 'that you have been fired, is it true?' Jong-sup issued something that Mi-na couldn't quite make out. He swallowed his mouthful.

'No, it's not true! I'm just on holiday, your dad should keep his nose out of other people's business,' he lectured, pointing his chopsticks at her rudely 'anyway, shouldn't you be in school?'

'I have the day off,'

'Why?'

'I'm ill,' said Mi-na

'What?!' he exclaimed, spitting out some of his soup 'you come to my house ill, have you no consideration for the elderly? You want to make me sick?'

'Don't worry Mr Park, I'm lying,' she said sweetly.

'Why would you do that?'

'Well I heard that my dad would be home today so I wanted to spend time with him as he's been really busy with his campaign lately and so I told my mum that I was too sick to go to school, but when I woke up he wasn't there, so I thought I'd come see you,' she smiled but her eyes didn't match the happiness of her expression. Jong-sup made a noise of affirmation and did something that surprised even himself, he reached out and put a hand lightly on her shoulder, only for a second before becoming uncomfortable and quickly removing it.

He noisily slurped down the remainder of the soup and pushed the container away from him.

'Sometimes I think that my dad cares more about becoming the Mayor than he cares about me,' Mi-na looked unsure even as she had said it, she was perhaps scared of how Jong-sup would react. Jong-sup felt that it was inappropriate of this girl to enter his home and take advantage of him in this way, he wasn't some shoulder to cry on and he had plenty of problems of his own to deal with. However, she had brought him breakfast so he thought he would indulge her this one time.

'Your dad isn't so bad, I guess. Well he's not lazy like many of his generation that's for sure and I'll be honest with you, he's not my type of guy, a little feeble and too well-groomed. Anyway, what I'm trying to say is that he may be a weak man, but it takes a strong father to work as hard as he does to provide for his family,' he looked at her cautiously, he had done his best but was afraid of her reaction, had it not had the effect desired.

'Thank you, Mr Park,' she beamed, and she reached out and grabbed his hand giving his finger a little squeeze. Jong-sup felt something at this gesture, something new and unknown, he didn't like it and pulled away from her. His reaction seemed to go unnoticed by her.

'Did your dad work a lot, Mr Park?' she inquired.

'I don't remember,' he replied.

'What did he do for work?' she inquired deeper.

'I don't know,' he replied.

'How can you n-'

'He died in the war, when I was very young, so I don't remember much about him or my mother.'

'Mr Park, I'm so sorry I asked.'

'No no, it's okay, it doesn't rub me sore any more. "you can't miss what you never had" as sister Hye used to say, the mean old bi-uch, I mean witch.'

'That's awful.'

'No she was right, eventually you realise you are pining over something that no longer exists, that crying is a waste of time, teaches you to be strong. Besides, I wasn't alone, my story was an all too common one. Many children lost their parents in the war and so St Mary's was full to the brim, there weren't nearly enough beds for everyone.'

'I guess, I'm very lucky.'

'Lucky? you're a spoiled brat! No offence, you're no different from any other kid nowadays. I used to feel relief that I wouldn't live to see the state of my beautiful country in the hands of the ungrateful youth, though I guess I'm no longer eligible for such repose.'

'What do you mean?'

'Nothing, nothing, you ask too many questions, girl.'

'I've been told,' she blushed.

'Yeah, well, it's an irritating habit.'

'Sorry Mr Park,' she said looking at her feet.

'It's fine, the inquisitiveness of youth I suppose.'

Now that he had finished eating, he felt the urge to get on with his organising.

'I think you should probably be getting back now, go get some breakfast or something.'

'That was my breakfast.'

'What! Why didn't you say anything?'

'You were obviously very hungry,' she reasoned.

Jong-sup made a muddle of irritated noises and reached into his pocket for his wallet. He pulled out twenty thousand Won and held it out to her, Mi-na put her hand up in protest but he grabbed her wrist and forced the note into her hand. She gave a low bow in thanks.

'Do you need any help today, Mr Park?' she asked.

'No need, I have big plans, not for the minds of young girls,' he grimaced.

'What plans?' she asked, her eyes full of wonder.

'My revenge,' he smiled cruelly tapping the side of his nose. 'keep that to yourself.'

Mi-na nodded in affirmation. She opened her mouth to sift out more information but was interrupted by a loud knock at the door. Jong-sup walked her over and she put on her shoes, he looked through the spyhole to see Mi-na's mother looking aggravated. He swung open the door exposing mother and daughter to each other. Mi-na's mother was quite beautiful if not a little thin, she was tall with a pretty face and long hair like her offspring. Her attractive features were pulled in concerned fashion that badly concealed her anger.

'Mi-na! What have you been doing?'

'I-'

'That's enough, we'll talk of this in private.'

'but-'

'Don't talk back to me,' she demanded. She grabbed poor Mi-na by the ear and dragged her to her side.

'Apologise to Mr Park!'

'Sorry, Mr Park,' she winced, her eyes watering. Jong-sup bowed his head very slightly. Mi-na's mother dragged her to their home down the hall where they disappeared from sight. Jong-sup grabbed his keys put on his shoes and headed out. It was time to prepare.

4

Jong-sup looked at the abandoned shop behind his apartment or as it now was in his mind; his base of operations. It was run down but it had all he needed, shelter and ever more important, privacy. As he approached the ruin, his mind drifted back to the many times he had enjoyed hanging around outside here with an ice cream in hand. He was happier then, as hard as things were, he was still naive to the cruelty of men.

He ducked in through the doorway and scoured the interior with his eyes. There was quite a bit of work to do here if he was to be comfortable for a while. He may have to cover the space of missing bricks somehow if the wind comes from that direction often. Moving to the back of the shop to the closet where he had found the rope before he pulled the door open, it was stiff as the wood had swollen with its exposure to the elements. He peeked inside; it would do perfectly. Nobody was coming here he thought, at least for the time he would need this space.

Jong-sup froze, there was a scraping noise coming from somewhere in the building, rats perhaps. Then a loud bang as something fell to the ground behind him. He did not turn around immediately; he slowly twisted his body preparing himself for whatever it may be. He was not prepared enough though.

A man stood opposite Jong-sup with his back to him, wearing a dirty yellow polo shirt and a green apron tied around his waist. He seemed busy sweeping the shelves paying no mind to Jong-sup at all. He had not heard him enter but that was the least of this strangers oddities, the man was stood suspended in air, the appendages that should have been supporting him; his legs, were torn roughly from the rest of him, along with his lower abdomen. There was a steady patter of dark red droplets of blood dripping from his intestine which swung gently in the air.

Jong-sup stood very still, like a mouse who has seen a cat and has yet to be spotted. The floating man turned in the air and moved to the fallen wall, Jong-sup could have sworn that as the man had moved their eyes met for a brief moment. The legless man then started picking nothing off of the floor and laying the invisible objects onto the bottom of the space in the wall, he appeared to be trying to rebuild the collapsed wall; but was making zero progress.

Jong-sup cleared his throat loudly, 'Excuse me!' There was a tight silence as the legless man paused what he was doing and cocked his head to the side. Jong-sup blinked and in the time it took for his eyes to reopen the legless man was stood two feet in front of him. Jong-sup clutched at his heart in surprise but he didn't utter a noise.

'Excuse me, I'm very sorry but we're closed right now for some, rather extensive, refurbishment,' said the legless man, his voice seemed to echo slightly but it was unmistakeably cheery. Jong-sup was relieved, being stalked by Death herself meant that he no longer scared easily but he didn't need to be attacked by any other manifestation of the paranormal.

'Who are you?' asked Jong-sup, still keeping his guard raised just in case.

'What's gotten into you? Don't play up just because the store is closed, here' the legless man flittered very quickly to the shelves on the far side and back again and handed Jong-sup nothing. He accepted the nothing cautiously.

'There you go, your favourite, you can pay me back tomorrow, okay?' said the legless man brightly, a wide smile on his face 'Now run along Park, I'm sure you have to get back before Hye gets angry.'

Jong-sup shook his head in disbelief as if to shake the sentence he had heard back out of his ears in rejection. He started to exit the long-gone store still clutching nothing in his hand, then it came to him. He knew this man. Mr Lee, the owner of this most cherished of places. He turned around to face this ghost from his past.

'Mr Lee?'

'Yes boy?'

‘What happened to you?’

‘What ever do you mean?’

‘Mr Lee, look at your feet,’ said Jong-sup, his voice uncharacteristically sympathetic. Mr Lee followed his instruction, gave a high-pitched squeak and retreated inside. Jong-sup followed to find Mr Lee leaning on what used to be the counter of the store.

‘I’m dead, aren’t I boy?’

‘I..I...think so,’ replied Jong-sup.

‘It’s coming back to me. I’m sorry I must have given you quite the fright, my brain isn’t what it used to be, now that it doesn’t exist, that is. Seems to be harder and harder to hold on to myself, I guess seeing you in my shop again messed me up some, I do apologise boy. Here have some sweets on the house,’ Mr Lee went back to the shelves and picked up a handful of more nothing.

‘Mr Lee, look around. The shop is derelict, there are no sweets,’ Jong-sup’s little patience was wearing thin. Mr Lee looked at his hand.

‘Oh yes,’ said the deceased man ashamed of himself ‘It’s not so easy you know, all this. It’s difficult to separate reality from memory when all I am is a memory of someone gone.’

‘It’s fine, I always wondered what happened to you. How did you die?’

‘I can’t really remember but I guess this must be a clue,’ he said gesturing at his non-existent legs.

‘A fair chance I would imagine,’ the novelty of being reunited with the man who had made his childhood that little bit easier was wearing off.

‘Anyway Mr Lee, I’m here because I need a space to store something rather important, would you mind if I used your closet?’ asked Jong-sup, knowing fully well that were he denied use of the closet he would have done so anyway, but formalities were semi-necessary for someone he had respect for. At least as much respect as Jong-sup could manage to muster.

'I'll do you one better, lift the panel under the bottom shelf at the back,' Mr Lee instructed. Jong-sup did so and was rewarded by a small ladder that lead into a cellar beneath the store. Perfect, he thought.

Later that same day Jong-sup roared down the road in his black, 1973 Sundai, a company car of some luxury. Sat amidst the beige leather interior he kicked away an empty can that was obstructing his access to the pedals. The car was littered with papers, receipts and a couple of bottles. It was a worthy example of the care he took of his belongings, particularly ones that were being lent to him.

He rolled down his window and spat out onto the tarmac, then he proceeded to honk his horn impatiently at the car in front of him who was taking much too long for Jong-sup's liking. He was on his way to an important appointment. It was time to plan his funeral. It was about a forty-minute drive to Suwon in the Gyeonggi-do province just outside of Seoul city.

The drive offered some beautiful views of the countryside of Korea, but Jong-sup had long halted his appreciation of nature. He kept his eyes on the road and his goal in his mind. His vehicle was dwarfed by the giant hills that speckled the landscape of the province. The colossal stone walls that surrounded Suwon signified his arrival as he passed by them. He had arrived with time to spare.

A bell chimed as he entered the funeral home and he was greeted immediately by a young man who bowed politely and showed him to a chair to wait. He was brought a cup of coffee but not five minutes had gone by before he was called into the office at the back.

Entering the office, he found himself having his hand vigorously shaken by a weedy, balding man with glasses and a wide, crooked and yellowed smile. The plaque on his desk read Nam Byung-chul.

'Mr Park, thanks for coming, you're early, that's good,' said Nam 'Now, please tell me how we can help you.'

‘I’m looking to organise my funeral, I...ugh….just want to make sure everything goes smoothly and stress free,’ said Jong-sup.

‘Yes, yes you’ve come to the right place then,’ smiled Nam. Nam then reached under his desk and revealed a hefty folder. ‘Right, let us get started then.’

Jong-sup listened to Nam go through package after package, deal after deal for close to thirty five minutes. He wanted to get this over and done with but didn’t want to be perceived as rude; he needed this snail of a man to be cooperative. After he had selected the cheapest coffin available and the package that included no food nor drinks for the attendees Jong-sup was becoming ever more irritable.

‘You see, Mr park, our mission in life is that you keep all your self-respect and dignity in death,’ grinned Nam sounding almost convincing.

‘How about we cut the shit shall we,’ snapped Jong-sup. Nam was taken aback; he was sure his full-proof sales pitch was working. ‘I mean no disrespect, but I’m a man who holds particular and private religious beliefs, and if you mean what you say, I take it you’ll help me leave this world satisfied spiritually.’

‘Are you Muslim?’

‘No!’

‘Jehovah’s witness?’

‘No! listen, I just have particular tastes,’ said Jong-sup. Nam sat back in his chair with a concerned expression stretched across his face.

‘Look, I could have gone to any cheap shitty parlour in Seoul but I drove out here because I heard a while ago that you were a man who could get things done,’ said Jong-sup. Nam reached into his pocket and pulled from it a pack of cigarettes.

‘Do you mind?’ asked Nam.

‘Go ahead,’ replied Jong-sup.

The next Tuesday, a couple of days before the deadline of his preparations, Jong-sup waited on the street next to the lane that lead to the old store. The sky was a beautiful shade of blue and he was feeling optimistic. Earlier that day he had run by the bank to collect the money he had ordered. The bank wanted to fill in an interrogation form about where he was moving the money, so he had filled in a bunch of nonsense, it mattered little. They also tried to push him into agreeing to be escorted home by armed guards, he kicked up a fuss till they let him leave. It wasn't really that much money, he still had plenty tucked away at the bank; or held at ransom depending on how you looked at it.

At last came the object he had been waiting for, brought to him in a van by two gruff looking gentlemen. One of the men exited and came round to lift Jong-sup's delivery out of the vehicle with a small metal cart. He told the man he didn't need any assistance taking it to his home. When the man looked unsure Jong-sup asked if he could buy the cart and slipped him more than enough money for it. He waited for the delivery men to be out of eyesight before turning on his heels and heading down the lane.

The package bumped and rumbled on the dirt track, Christ, it was heavy. He pushed with all the strength he could muster and before long he was coming into the clearing, the shop now visible under the enormous tree. He looked down at his shoe for a brief second to dislodge a stone. When his eyeline was level with the world again he was greeted by the all too familiar black cloak of Death. He looked straight into the black void beneath the hood, freezing his facial muscles with all his might to hold back from wincing. He noted that Death's arms were back to being devoid of flesh as normal.

'Haven't seen you in a while. Now, if you'll excuse me,' he said trying to sound calm.

What are you planning Park Jong-sup?

'Nothing, now I must be going,' he replied defiantly.

I saw you at the funeral parlour, what are you planning?

'That's none of your business I'm afraid,' he said smugly.

Death is my only business! And it is my business alone! Death's voice practically screamed into Jong-sup's ear battering his eardrum, although her tone was the same as always there was undeniable anger. Well if she was angry then he must be doing something right. Resolving to show no fear he dared not remove his eyes from her. She maintained her gaze in return and without uttering, if Death did utter that is, she started to become translucent before completely disappearing. Jong-sup looked around to check if she had simply changed her position but upon realising that she was gone, more from the change in his senses other than sight, he felt a rush of pride at a battle won.

'What a bitch,' he huffed under his breath as he pulled the heavy load into the shop.

'Who's a bitch? And mind your language boy,' said Mr Lee.

'OOAHH!' shrieked Jong-sup 'Don't sneak up on me you lingering fool!'

'Sorry, but watch your tone young man,' said Mr Lee 'anyway, who are you talking about?'

'Death,' replied Jong-sup.

'Ooo is he here?'

'You're out of luck I'm afraid, just left,' said Jong-sup. Mr Lee hung his head in disappointment and seemed to hover a little closer to the ground. 'Why? Did you want to get a hit in now you're as spectral as she is?'

'Why on earth would I do that?' asked Mr Lee.

'I assumed she was the reason you're still here, forgot to collect you or something,' said Jong-sup.

'No no no, this was my idea sadly. You see, I wanted to meet my child, my wife was pregnant at the time, I told Death that I wouldn't leave, I half expected him to get angry, me denying his purpose and all but he was ever so courteous.'

'Why do you keep saying he?' asked Jong-sup.

'Well, he's a man, isn't he?' answered Mr Lee holding his chin with his thumb and forefinger as if doubtingly searching his memory. 'Or whatever he is there are some things that are not meant to be known by men.'

'Whatever,' dismissed Jong-sup.

Mr Lee floated across the shop leaving droplets of blood like a bread crumb trail wherever he went. Jong-sup pulled the cart over to the closet and wiped the sweat from his brow.

'What's in the box?' inquired Mr Lee.

'My new safe, do you mind if I store it down in your cellar?' asked Jong-sup.

'Go ahead boy I'm not exactly using it,' replied Mr Lee.

5

The following Friday Jong-sup sat on the sofa in his living room sweating profusely. His hands were shaking, he had never done anything this calculated in his life. He wanted a drink. He needed a drink. But to pull this off he wanted to make sure that his mind was not left muddled by fermented liquids for once.

He had gotten ready way too early in anticipation and was now watching the clock's hands crawl their way around its face. A few times he was certain that time had stopped, could Death kill time? Probably not. Maybe Death was time. Useless thoughts that made time drag ever more slowly. His eyes frequently moved from the clock to the intercom, it would not be long now before his guests would arrive. Every so often he would look over his shoulder out of the large window to check for Death. Death was the last thing he needed at this social gathering.

Jong-sup sniffed at the air; he could smell something. The chicken was burning. He raced to the oven slid on his knees and pulled open the oven door to reveal a plume of thick smoke. The chicken was a little too cooked but presentable enough, besides, he cared little for how much they would enjoy his cooking.

At that moment, his hands still full of chicken, the buzzer sounded on the intercom. He shoved the chicken onto the side, let out a stream of swearwords and ran to the source of the irritating sound. A screen in the centre displayed his honoured guests. Ji-yeon covered the majority of the image with her best fake grin, in the background Jerry was visibly checking his watch counting down the minutes till it was socially acceptable to make an excuse to leave.

'Evening Park, we brought wine!' screeched Ji-yeon holding up a bottle to the camera.

'Okay, I'll let you in, just a second,' he pressed the button, there was a loud beep and then Jong-sup ran around making sure everything was in place. He put on some light jazz music and set the glasses on the table. He felt strangely nervous as if he actually cared about what they thought of his hospitality.

Within minutes there was a knock at the door. Jong-sup answered to a finely dressed and more handsome than ever Jerry and a scantily clad Ji-yeon.

'Hey,' beamed Ji-yeon uncharacteristically; she was quite the actress. Jerry smiled weakly from the side of his mouth.

'Come in, come in,' Jong-sup ushered grinning unpleasantly; he could also act. Taking Jerry's coat and hanging it on a rack behind the door he led them to the table.

'I'm sorry for the state of the place, I don't have guests often, I'm sure you understand,' he explained.

'Completely,' said Ji-yeon.

Jong-sup took, rather more roughly than necessary, the bottle of wine from Ji-yeon and filled a half glass each. He noted that the wine was a cheap variety, an obvious attempt to disrespect him. It wouldn't work, not tonight.

'Please, make yourself at home. I'll go and dish up dinner, its almost done,' said Jong-sup. Ji-yeon sniffed at the air and wrinkled her nose. Jerry sipped at his wine and gazed out of the window. Jong-sup returned promptly holding a plate of chicken and blackened vegetables in each hand and one on his wrist. He placed them carefully then turned around to fetch four small ceramic bowls, each containing a different type of kimchi. He passed a pair of metal chopsticks to each of his guests and then took a seat opposite them. Ji-yeon had an amused expression painted on her gorgeous face, anticipating one of the many scenarios she had imagined no doubt, like a sadist viewing a suicidal person fling themselves onto train-tracks.

Jerry looked bored.

'I have to say, Park, that I was quite shocked that you had organised this little get-together. I had assumed after your last outburst you wanted nothing more to do with our large family at KSI. I appreciate the invitation all the same,' said Jerry. Ji-yeon leaned forward slightly in her chair.

'Well, I uh, I was upset at first you see. I wasn't quite seeing the bigger picture, you might say. I was thinking only of myself but when I thought about it properly, I'd been working at KSI for so long it was almost like family, and what sacrifice wouldn't you make for family, eh,' explained Jong-sup, he played it off so well he had to remind himself that it wasn't true.

'We are so glad you are seeing it our way,' said Ji-yeon.

'Yes, I hope you know this was the last outcome we wanted but we have to make the best of a shitty situation,' seconded Jerry.

'Completely agree,' Jong-sup smiled, well, the corners of his mouth lifted at least. 'anyway, let's not fuss over the past, let's enjoy the now. Drink up you two.'

After they had finished their meal and some surprisingly pleasant conversation, Jong-sup poured them another glass and asked to be excused for a moment. He strutted over to the bedroom closed and locked the door then picked up the telephone from the side. He collected himself for a moment then preceded to dial in the number.

'Police, this is Park Jong-sup. I've locked myself in my bedroom, my boss and co-worker are trying to kill me.'

Jerry sat calm and relaxed at the living room table, he had to admit that coming here was a good idea. The less resistance this old fool gave to going to jail the better. He took this moment of alone time with Ji-yeon as an opportunity to start caressing her knee. She stared into his eyes intently and moved his hand up higher between her thighs.

'When the fossil finishes taking a shit, let's make our excuse to leave,' he said.

'Why? Not enjoying yourself?' she giggled.

At that moment they heard a loud thud coming from the bedroom. They did not move, just listened carefully. Again, another thud, louder this time. Another accompanied by a barrage of swearing. They rose from their seats and stepped a little closer to the door, Jerry pulled Ji-yeon behind him.

The door was roughly flung open, smashing hard against the wall and springing back. It was broken at the lock which now lay on the floor. Ji-yeon let out a squeal and began to jump up and down.

'WHOA! Sorry about that,' Jong-sup grinned, for real this time 'didn't mean to scare you.'

'What's going on?' demanded Jerry.

'Damn lock was jammed, had to kick my way out,' explained Jong-sup.

'Why didn't you just call for help?' asked Ji-yeon.

'My way was faster. I can solve a problem on my own, I'm not that old,' he replied.

'You scared, Ji-yeon that's all,' said Jerry, his voice shaking slightly.

'I'm fine, I'm fine,' interjected Ji-yeon.

'No you're not, listen thank you so much for the dinner but it's getting late now and I think Ji-yeon needs some time to calm herself.'

'You're not going anywhere,' said Jong-sup, his voice low and dark.

'What?' they asked in tandem.

'Without your dessert I mean,' replied Jong-sup.

'No no...' began Jerry.

'I insist, I went through all the trouble of buying it, least you could do is take a slice of it home with you,' insisted Jong-sup.

Jerry looked at Ji-yeon who nodded.

'That's settled then. Jerry, be a gent and grab that knife from the table and I'll grab the dessert,' commanded Jong-sup. 'No, the long one.'

Jong-sup walked over to the fridge, opened, and pulled from it a dark chocolate cake. He placed it on the counter.

'Looks wonderful,' said Ji-yeon, her voice noticeably shaky.

'You do the honours Jerry, cut as big a slice as you want,' said Jong-sup.

Jerry cut into the cake, he felt inhumanly uncomfortable, Jong-sup was being nice enough, but something was wrong, he could feel it.

'That's not right Jerry, let me show you how it's done,' Jerry held out the knife to him but Jong-sup grabbed Jerry's hand instead and clasped his fingers over his, holding them to the knife.

Jong-sup was staring menacingly into Jerry's eyes.

Madly.

Jong-sup's grip was tight around his hand to the point of pain. Jerry felt the need to let go but he could not, some fear was making him weak. The knife hung suspended in the space between the two men.

Before Jerry's mind could even recognise what was happening, Jong-sup flung himself into Jerry thrusting the knife into his own abdomen. Jerry squealed pathetically and tried with all his little leftover strength to unclasp the knife, but Jong-sup's grip was iron.

The apartment was then filled to bursting with the hysterical screaming of Ji-yeon who rather than try to help, ran into the bedroom and closed the door, which did nothing to filter the terrible noise emanating from her.

'What's the matter Jerry?' as Jong-sup opened his mouth to speak, blood gushed from it pouring down his chin and covering both of their shirts. 'too used to stabbing me in the back? Does your betrayal look different from this angle?!'

Jerry began to splutter inaudibly in shock, his eyes never leaving Jong-sup's.

Jong-sup pulled himself from the blade, wincing only slightly, before plunging it back into his cascading wound.

'Forged your signature did I?!' shouted Jong-sup. Jerry was bawling now still trembling too greatly to fight back.

Jong-sup removed the blade before creating a new hole in his stomach, sending blood splashing from his mouth unto Jerry's face.

'Too important to the company to take responsibility, huh?' Jong-sup's voice was barely understandable between the coughs and splutters. He was feeling faint, and fainter still with each passing second. Had Jerry been at his normal strength, Jong-sup wouldn't have been able to hold on.

This was it. Time for Jerry to get his comeuppance. He freed Jerry from his grasp, who dropped the knife, fell backwards and scurried away from him. Jong-sup bent over, picked the knife from the ground and stood up straight as he could manage. Before the dizziness could claim him, he held the knife to his throat.

'Enjoy prison, you slimy cunt!' he yelled, and in one quick motion he ran the serrated blade along his neck from apple to jugular. He was conscious of each sinewy fibre snapping apart. He could feel his heart paint the walls red with each beat.

The last thing he saw, was Jerry's terrified, blood-soaked face on a backdrop of cream and red.

Jong-sup was satisfied.

상향 회전

Part four

The Upward Turn

1

He did not know how long he had been in darkness. All he knew was that he was cold. Far colder than he had ever been. His mind was clouded, it took some time before the last events to cross his retinas were returned to him. With his awareness stitching back together, he tried to open his eyes, gently at first but proving more difficult than he would've liked he forced them open to reveal; nothing. All was as black as the inside of his eyelids. Was he dead? He certainly hoped so. Only to be quickly disappointed when his exposed toes rubbed against wood.

He had better not have been buried, he thought. He had made a deal and paid a lot of money to be disposed of in a more convenient manner. No, this was not a coffin, there was no lining of silk nor cushion at all. He seemed to be lying most uncomfortably on some small stones. Still, this was not what he had arranged and that weasel of a man better hope that this box is nailed shut and that Jong-sup never laid eyes on him again.

Summoning the little strength he had, he wiggled his body to discover that this box was a tighter fit than he had first thought. Claustrophobia swept over him and granted him some panic-induced energy. He kicked and lashed out and the top slid off with little resistance and immediately his wooden prison was flooded with light. It burned his pupils and he yearned for the darkness once more.

What he had thought were stones he discovered were ice cubes. No wonder he was cold, had he not been cursed, hypothermia most likely would have seen an end to him. The thought of death reminded him. He anxiously touched his throat. Healed. He sighed in relief and laid his hand to rest on his hip. He felt his finger slip into him. Into his lower body.

He looked down at the entry point and looked away instantly. There was a hole, about the size of his fist, bloody and roughly cut as if it had been gouged. He was missing something, he knew it, he could feel it. He wouldn't look directly into the wound to prove it, but he didn't need to. His kidney was gone.

He pulled at his hair and hit the wall next to him. He kicked out, splintering the far end of the wooden box. He grabbed a handful of ice and threw it. It went behind a curtain and hit something metallic. The ensuing echo silenced him.

He scanned his surroundings. The wall to the right of him was covered in white tiles and he could see about five meters in front of him ending at a brick wall. The view to the left of him was cut off by a curtain that spanned the room and looking up he could see that the ceiling was extremely high. Some kind of warehouse he thought. This definitely wasn't an official procedure; he wasn't a donor anyway.

Was he some sick freak's experiment? He wasn't about to stay around to find out. Fear was a hell of a motivator. Jong-sup pulled his naked body from the ice-tomb and fell over the side making a loud crash. He paused, hoping no one had heard. Whoever it was obviously wasn't around or was a deep sleeper. He pushed himself up onto his bare, sore feet and slowly crept around the edge of the curtain.

He braced himself for a moment, storing his courage and peered around.

The horror of the scene before him forced his bravery to abandon him. At least twenty naked bodies, blue with the cold, hanging upside down by their feet. Their organs had been removed evidenced by the slashes across them. Mostly men, but he could see a couple of women too. He had not witnessed such atrocities since the war.

He had to get out of here, he would not end up like one of them. He took a good look around the room from between the swaying corpses, he was definitely alone. The morbid puppet show of murder was situated in the centre of the room and surrounding it were various tables, boxes, crates and trays filled with sharp instruments of extraction.

He avoided the corpses as best he could and skirted the edges of the room. There was a large sliding door opposite where he had awoken and the light that peered through the lining hinted at freedom. The icy pain he felt throughout was beginning to thaw, and for the first time since his very recent resurrection he could feel a breeze coming from the space that parted the door and wall. It felt pleasant on his face, on his chest and, on his genitals. He was naked. This was a problem. There was no way Park Jong-Sup was going to go running around Seoul, defiling his city with obscenity. Plus, the police attention was the last thing he needed right now, considering he was supposed to be dead.

Jong-sup looked around for any clothes that may be discarded but to no avail, spying a crate near the door that was partially open, he pushed off the lid. It was filled with ice and empty space. Damn.

An unmistakeable but muffled noise sounded. Laughter, coming from the other side of the door. He tip-toed closer to see if he could get a peek at his captor. No luck, it was closed over completely. He stood back and scanned the wall meticulously and spotted a small hole. It was a little high, so he had to climb a crate to look through. He moved his face slowly, lining eye to the hole. The peep hole didn't offer him a very clear look at the next room but from his vantage point he could see a table at which five men were sitting. Looking at the men, all young and covered in tattoos he felt that he would actually prefer to deal with a serial killer.

'then she says she isn't in the mood anymore,' said the skinniest of the group, sporting a high quiff dyed an off-orange. It took a moment but Jong-sup recognised him as one of the men interrogating Dong-wook outside his apartment.

'So then what?' asked a shirtless muscular guy sat opposite.

'I told her what happened to the last person who denied me. Then I gave her a slap for good measure,' replied the orange haired thug.

'You are brutal, Young-jin,' laughed the man sat next to him. Holding out his fist to him, who bumped it in kind.

‘Well, a blowjob feels ten times better when the girl is sobbing,’ Young-jin then proceeded to mime himself twitching while ejaculating, this was met with a roar of laughter from the thugs.

‘What’s going on here!?’ a new voice, Jong-sup couldn’t see him, but the tone was obviously from an older man. Footsteps echoed around the instantly quiet room as the unseen man approached the group sat around the table.

‘Uncle Eung,’ said the group in unorganised unison.

‘I take it by the fact that you are all sat around bullshitting that all the work is done,’ said Uncle Eung.

‘Well, you see, Uncle,’ said the Young-jin.

‘Why am I not fucking surprised!’ shouted Uncle Eung.

‘We finished, but then that new guy got dumped on us last minute, so we made a start but-’ he stammered.

Uncle Eung walked briskly around to Young-jin and punched him in the mouth.

‘but what? Are you guys paid to think of excuses? Because that seems to be the only fucking thing you boys show any fucking skill in!’ Uncle Eung’s voice was a screech now ‘You are aware that we keep our most “sensitive” cargo here, so that means we move it in and out as quickly as possible.’

The shirtless thug stood up and bowed.

‘We’re sorry Uncle, we’ll get straight on it.’

‘Yeah you will. Now open that door, I wanna look at my cargo.’

These words bounced around in Jong-sup’s skull. He jumped down from his lookout point and hopped from one foot to the other in panic. The fight and flight instincts were battling for superiority in his mind, but their power was evenly matched. His decision was made for him when the noise of the door being unlocked reached his ears.

He opened the lid of the crate he was just standing on and hoisted himself into it, landing painfully on more chunks of ice. He thought quickly and used a small piece of ice to keep the crate propped open slightly, so that he could see.

Sitting in the corner of the box he noticed he had company. In the opposing corner, sat in the exact position as him, was a dried out, almost mummified body. He kept his surprise silent to avoid alerting the dangerous men who were now strolling into the room. Jong-sup couldn't tell the sex of the corpse not that it mattered. He or she had been dead a long time.

Peeking out from the crack, Jong-sup could see Uncle Eung clearly. He was about Jong-sup's age, wearing an expensive pink shirt, the sleeves rolled to the elbows and he wore some designer sunglasses on his receding hairline. He was walking leisurely between the harvested bodies; it didn't faze him at all. He stopped at a woman.

'Shame this one, pretty face and nice perky tits, could've made a good whore,' his tongue slithered 'wait! Why the fuck do the men still have balls?' He pulled a flick knife from his pocket and grabbed the inverted man closest to him by the testicles. 'Gotta do everything myself,' he grumbled sawing at the sack. Jong-sup could tell from the rigidness of Uncle Eung's arm movements that they were proving to be tough to cut through.

'Some sick bastard will pay big money for these and you're just giving em away!' yelled Uncle Eung holding out a handful of nuts to his subordinates.

'Forgive us Uncle,' said Young-jin with blood coming from his nose from previously being stricken.

'Once you've castrated these sorry lumps of meat, I'll think about it. Get to it!' At Uncle Eung's command the five thugs started to spread out between the victims and hack or slice away.

Jong-sup's attention was drawn away from the horror show outside his wooden sanctuary to the inside by the sound of movement. Scanning the bottom for mice proved fruitless but from the corner of his eye he caught his crinkly companion turn its head to face him directly. Jong-sup's hand shot to his mouth to avoid making any sound that would bring attention to his current whereabouts and opted instead for a high-pitched whine. The jaw of the zombie shook for a second before collapsing open.

What have you got yourself into this time, Park Jong-sup?

Jong-sup knew this voice all too well.

'Death?' he inquired, fully knowing the answer.

Yes came the unfittingly feminine voice of Death.

'What the hell is wrong with you, trying out new ways to make me shit myself?' he raged as close to silent as he could.

Can't you see how continuously avoiding accountability is a downward spiral? said Death ignoring his question.

'This has nothing to do with me, I've never even seen these men before,' whispered Jong-sup.

Reprehensible

'And you're a vindictive bitch!' snapped Jong-sup, forgetting himself for a second 'look, please do me a favour, since all this is your doing in the first place. Cause some kind of distraction so I can slip out of here,' said Jong-sup, sort-of asking.

No said Death. Then she was gone, Jong-sup could tell as the corpse looked somehow more lifeless. He mumbled some curses under his breath.

'So, where's the late comer? Finish him off so we can get this lot out of here,' demanded Uncle Eung from outside the crate.

'Of course, Uncle, over here,' said the shirtless thug. Together they walked over to where Jong-sup had resurrected and pulled back the plastic curtain.

'What am I looking at here?' asked Uncle Eung.

'I don't understand he was just here in the icebox,'

'Well, I guess he just got up and walked out,' said Uncle Eung with obviously demeaning sarcasm.

'Kim!' shouted the shirtless thug across the room.

'Yeah' replied the Young-jin.

'You move the old guy?' asked the shirtless thug.

'No, why?' asked Young-jin.

'Why else? the old bastard isn't here.'

'What! Let me see,' said Young-jin panicked.

'You idiots are the most incompetent lackies I've ever seen! Spread out and look for it!' screeched Uncle Eung. This was Jong-sups cue, it was now or never. He burst from the crate dived over the edge, rolled on to his feet and stood facing his captors, bullock naked. All present stood like statues in hesitation, nobody had expected this, and their brains were taking time to catch up.

Young-jin decided to take it upon himself to break the tension. He opened his mouth wide and screamed deafeningly. This had a domino effect on the rest of the men who joined him in choir. Uncle Eung was loudest and most feminine of all and led by poor example, hiding behind a nearby crate.

Jong-sup took this state of panic as an opportunity to make his escape and shot through the large open door into the room where they had been sitting at the table. This room was well lit and much smaller than the previous, equipped with all sorts of living facilities. He didn't stop to admire though but made his way, without pause, to a small door opposite. Flinging it open exposed a short staircase heading downwards. He hoped he was on the second floor, the last thing he needed was to end up running around underground. He considered flinging himself from one of the windows but decided against it and raced down the stairs three at a time.

Back in the large room, the screams were beginning to die down. Uncle Eung sprung up from his hiding place.

'What are you doing. You cowardly dogs?!' he screamed his voice still high pitched 'Go get that cargo!'

‘But Uncle, isn’t it bad luck to oppose a zombie,’ said the shirtless thug. Uncle Eung picked up a handful of utensils from a drawer and launched them at him.

‘He aint no zombie you fucking idiot, he just aint realised he’s dead, now get after him or you’ll replace the missing cargo yourself!’

At the bottom of the stairs, Jong-sup found himself in an office. It was horrendously maintained, and he couldn’t imagine ever leaving his office in this state, and he hated his workplace. The wallpaper was unravelling backwards down the wall, paper lay everywhere with no apparent method to the madness and cigarette butts were littered all over the desk.

To Jong-sup’s delight though, this office held some treasure. A denim jacket was hung on the back of a chair and a pair of blue work overalls were bundled in the corner. Finally, some luck. He was pretty sure he had scared the crooks upstairs enough to halt their pursuit at least momentarily but still he shouldn’t hang around long.

He threw on the mismatched attire and crept slowly to a blind obstructing his view through the window and parted it with his fingers. On the other side of the glass was a bigger warehouse still, though this one had a lot more traffic, bronzed men carried boxes and operated forklifts and at the far end opposite him was freedom. He couldn’t make out anything outside as the glare from the sun was too great. So, the room he had woken or risen or reanimated or whatever, was directly above this one. He wondered for a second if these workers had any idea of the horrors that hung above their heads at all times.

Footsteps. Heavy and becoming louder, someone was racing downstairs behind him. Perhaps he had not spooked them to the extent that he had thought. Acting on the first idea that came to him; he scurried under the desk and held his breath. Finally, the footsteps reached the bottom and the door was roughly kicked open. Young-jin ran in and without pause ran straight through the opposite door to the main warehouse.

Jong-sup couldn't hear any more footsteps and so with no time to lose he crawled out from his hidey-hole. Rearing his head, he noticed something plastered on the wall in front of him that hadn't caught his attention earlier. A banner of red, decorated with six black stars. He knew this image. It had been in the newspaper countless times. It was a bad sign. The Yuk Sung Pa were the most dangerous and deadly gang in Korea. He had figured that the men were in some kind of gang operating a black-market scheme, but this was the organisation that single-handedly ran the black market.

Jong-sup took another peek through the blinds like a nosey neighbour, only he was not suffering from paranoia. Young-jin was nowhere to be seen and the labourers continued on their tasks seemingly unaware of the current events that surrounded them. This was probably his best chance he thought. Pushing the door open just enough to slide his body through he ducked behind a pile of rubber tubing and scoped out his next waypoint.

An engine roared loudly as a truck began its entrance into the warehouse toing behind it a large luxurious yacht. The workers hurried over to the boat in unison abandoning their forklifts which gave Jong-sup a chance to run over and crouch beside one of them. Written on the side of the yacht in a fancy font was the name "Heaven's Brothers" in English. Jong-sup eyed the workers movements to check for any pattern which would allow him an unnoticed escape. One of them came close to the forklift so Jong-sup made himself as small as possible to avoid detection and prayed that the worker wasn't returning to his previous duties as it would leave him overtly exposed.

Luckily for Jong-sup, the man was only collecting a wrench before hurrying back to the object of their team effort. Jong-sup exhaled with heavy relief before searching his surrounding again. Over on the left-hand wall of the large open room was a huge piece of green cloth pinned up displaying in proud lettering "Yuk Sung" surrounded by six black stars.

So, these men were part of the organisation, or at the very least, they knew who they were working for. This complicated things further, since they were likely to try to restrain him if he was discovered. The time for hesitation was over, or more accurately, had been taken from him.

The very floor where Jong-sup stood began to quake and noise bounced around the metal shell of the building that drowned out the noise of the truck or the workers. Then the fount of the commotion became apparent. From the corner of his eye, descending from the room above, a platform, most likely used to lift cargo was instead carrying his furious hosts. He was directly in their eyeline. Before he even had time to ask himself if they had noticed him, Uncle Eung yelled a call to arms.

'Stop that fucking dead man!' The reaction was immediate, all present dropped whatever they were doing and picked up whatever could be used as an instrument of pain. The thugs surrounding Uncle Eung were brandishing knives and Eung a pistol, this didn't go unnoticed by Jong-sup who panic-stricken, jumped into the forklift that had been his shield and decided to instigate its other function, as a sword.

He put his foot down full force, intent on driving through the approaching workers but learned quickly that unlike his car, the back wheels of his getaway vehicle turned. He over shot it and instead of turning towards the open door he hurtled right towards the armed brutes that sought his organs. They dove out of his way like cheating pins at a bowling alley. Jong-sup learned quickly and narrowly missed the wall as he corrected his route to the exit.

'Close the damn doors you fucking idiots!' shrieked Uncle Eung. The worker closest to the control box next to the doors slammed his fist on a big red button and, after a short delay, the doors began to rumble shut.

Jong-sup leaned forward and crashed through a wooden crate sending wood and plastic flying through the air. His metal death-machine sped at the exit grazing the "Heavens Brothers" along the side letting out an ear-splitting high pitched sound that made anyone unfortunate enough to receive it want to crawl inside themselves, including Jong-sup. He gritted his teeth and bared through it before blasting through the nearly closed doors.

He tasted freedom, but he couldn't see it. Instead his view was obstructed by more warehouses, almost identical to the one he had just outmatched. Looking over his shoulder he noted by the large number painted over the, now broken, doors that he was being stored in number twenty-three.

To the left of him was an enormous shipping barge on a river which he had to assume was the Han, being the only river large enough to carry such a massive craft. Did the Yuk Sung really own this entire lot? They really were the criminal superpower the papers made them out to be.

Dock workers and thugs alike began to stream out of several warehouses that surrounded the concrete square that Jong-sup was driving in circles. They must have received word. Jong-sup played chicken with a few, driving at them, testing their will. They didn't budge, so Jong-sup had to, he didn't want to run anyone over. A body jamming his wheel would be the cherry on top of a cake made from bad luck.

After he'd patrolled the increasingly small area twice more there was a deafening bang, and the world turned on its side. Jong-sup wasn't aware at first that Uncle Eung had shot out his tyre, only that he found himself ejected from his seat and having a forceful reunion with the earth. He rolled thrice before shockingly, to all including himself, landing on his hands and feet. His palms bled with the introduction of gravel into them, but he ignored the stinging tingle and turned to meet the horde.

Around forty men formed a semi-circular flesh barrier around him. The thugs from warehouse twenty-three at the forefront and Uncle Eung nestled comfortably between them. There was a mixture of anger and fear in their eyes; a dangerous mix.

Water at his back and murderers at his front, he knew which he trusted more and made his choice accordingly. Jong-sup spun on his heels and made for the Han. The riverbank drew closer and closer.

Two gunshots sounded, the first went wide and the second worryingly close to his ear, the heat singed his lobe and he cupped his hand around it. Just five steps more befo-

He felt it before he heard it. Into his shoulder blade. The force knocked him off his feet and onto his face. As many people as he had pissed off in his life, he had never been shot. The films under-played it.

Writhing around on the ground Jong-sup discovered he had no use of his arm. Was this it? What would they do to him? Would they harvest him then chop the leftovers into pieces? Had death been an option this would have suited him just fine. Death wasn't an option however, she was a person, or being or whatever she was; she was cruel, and she would force him to live forever in as many pieces as they saw fit.

Two tattooed arms hoisted him up and flipped him onto his back to be confronted by Uncle Eung who put his boot on Jong-sup's chest and pointed his pistol in his face. Jong-sup knew that the shot wouldn't be fatal, but he twisted his face in the agonising thought of the pain.

'Enough!' came a deep husky voice from behind the mob. Uncle Eung removed his foot from Jong-sup, turned and bowed. He stayed in that position until the crowd parted to make way for a towering man with neat hair greying at the sides. His suit was something nearly out of Jong-sup's price range. In contrast with the rest of his smooth appearance was a noticeable scar down the left side of his face.

'This is the guy who's been causing all this fuss? When I saw nearly fifty of my guys surrounding someone, I thought for sure this guy must be some Taekwondo master on roids,' said the stranger his voice the very essence of calm. 'Instead I find that it took more than two of my well-paid men to take on this old man.'

'Sir,' said Uncle Eung still bent over 'if I-'

'You! Don't get me started on you!' interrupted the man 'What made you think firing a gun here was a good idea? Did you hear the hear the sound echoing off these walls? If someone were to call the police and I had to deal with an inspection, huh? Luckily, I pay them enough. Still it doesn't excuse your recklessness. Hand me your gun,' Uncle Eung let out an audible whimper. 'hand it over!' barked the man. Uncle Eung obeyed. 'stay where you are,' said the man.

Uncle Eung sobbed knowingly, his body bent over bowing acceptingly. The man held the gun by the barrel, the hilt pointing at the earth like an axe. The man's face was unreadable as he brought the gun down on Uncle Eung's skull. His body went limp and the sobbing was silenced in one strike, but the man wasn't finished. He smashed into the back of Uncle Eung's head another six times till there was a large dent from his crushed skull.

'Someone come clean this up!' he demanded. He came closer to Jong-sup, looming over him and blocking out the light.

'I've seen what this one's done to my boat; his organs are worthless to me. Let's sort this guy out old school. I want to see him suffer,' and for the first time, Jong-sup saw him smile.

2

How did it come to this? Thought Jong-sup. Of all the separate paths in life, were any darker and more unfortunate than this? He still had all his organs, that was one way of looking at it, naively optimistic though it may be. Well, at least the view wasn't too bad he levied as a fish swam close to his face. The water at the bottom of the Han was a lot clearer than he would have predicted. He was able to see all kinds of things as he slowly swayed left and right; starfish an octopus and all manner of sea life.

His surroundings would keep his brain occupied, which was more than he could say for his body. His arms and legs were bound by a heavy metal chain attached to an anchor that the ruthless man had gotten from his yacht. He said that there was something poetic about it before he ordered Jong-sup to be tossed from the bridge. Jong-sup didn't share his poetic insight and still didn't know his name.

The sensation of drowning was horrifying but had long worn off. The cold hadn't though, it still stung his skin. Once all the oxygen had left his lungs, he felt the need to inhale but couldn't, which induced a momentary panic. Now though, he had let go of the habit of breathing and found a sort of peace. There was something foetal about being underwater, your lungs closed and unable to struggle.

He was unaware of how long he had been down here, but the sun had set and come up again. Beams of sunshine were piercing the watery ceiling in long rays and bouncing off of fish scales and seaweed. At his back was the concrete wall of the riverbank and in front of him somewhere hidden in the murk was the opposite side of the river. He watched intently as a starfish made his way up the chain and began the ascent up his legs, it took most of the day and made snails look speedy by comparison. Surely the starfish would start to devour him little by little until he was nought but bone. There was no way his consciousness could continue while divided into thousands of miniscule digested pieces he thought. He hoped the starfish would hurry and bring his friends too.

Jong-sup didn't know that you could sleep underwater but discovered so when he awoke suddenly. After not sleeping for what must have been three days the sheer exhaustion must have forced him under. He looked around blinking in his usual waking up ritual, but it did nothing to un-muddy his vision.

Something was different. The sun was down but the moon reflected enough light to gift Jong-sup a couple of meters vision. There was no life. Anywhere. He looked down at his starfish companion to find it on the riverbed seemingly dried and shrivelled. What had caused this? His body started to tingle slightly and gradually intensify. The water around him began to bubble as if carbonated.

A short distance away, on the surface, an elongated silhouette moved slowly closer, obstructing the moonlight. Jong-sup couldn't make it out but the closer it got the warmer the water became until he started to suspect that he was being boiled alive. Then, there was a snap. It was so loud that it could be heard underwater, though muffled. Jong-sup looked around to find the source, but the answer came to him as he began to float upwards.

His limbs were still bound by the heavy chain, so he had no control over the direction. The dark silhouette came to a stop right above him. He discovered that it was made of wood when his face smashed against it before breaking the surface

Death was waiting. She stood in an ancient burned pile of buoyant wood that at one time must have been a boat. Now though, whole chunks were absent and the part that were present were riddled with holes. Etched into the gunwale was the word Styx. He could recall the word, but he knew not from where.

Death reached down and lifted Jong-sup into the boat by the chains. Where his bindings were touched, they dissolved before his eyes and he was relieved that she had not touched him instead. His arms and legs now free, he erected himself and looked upon Death.

Her image was as haunting as always, legs not visible nor her face beneath her black hood, only her skeletal arms slid out from her cloak, and her cloak was most unsettling of all; the way it swayed not in reaction to wind or any earthly force but at its own rhythm. Today she carried a long oar as she hovered at the stern of the decrepit vessel.

'So, should I take it that you are looking out for me?' asked Jong-sup, but no reply came even after several minutes, Death just continued to steer the boat up stream.

'I never asked you to help me out, so I don't owe you anything,' grumbled Jong-sup 'You hear that?' he wasn't anticipating an answer, and he received none. 'If anything, you owe me now! It was you who got me in this situation!' he spat 'and you can start by taking this fucking curse off of me!'

No

'Why? Why? Come on, why?' his voice turning to desperation in an instant. 'Those guys who tried to drown me, they're the ones you should be punishing. Did you see the organs they harvested? That's what real bad people look like!'

He was about to revisit his protest when he became aware that his feet were submerged in water. Then his ankles. Then his shins. The boat was going under fast. Jong-sup jumped overboard just before it completely disappeared. Death remained at her station and as a loyal captain went down with the ship without uttering a word.

Jong-sup splashed around trying to keep his head above water. He was a competent swimmer, but his muscles had been wasting over the last couple of days. With rare fortune he spied a maintenance ladder not far away and made his way to it. Using the very last of his strength he scaled the ladder and collapsed on the bank at the top. Looking back at the river he saw no evidence of Death's boat not even a ripple on the surface.

He would rest for a short while before attempting the long journey to where he had stashed his money, then he would start enacting his retirement plan.

It wasn't long before Jong-sup discovered the results of his scheme. With not even a single won to his name he was forced to make his way home on foot. Still wearing his mismatched clothing he had scavenged from the warehouse and barefoot; he decided to avoid all busy areas and stick to the backstreets. It was there that he stumbled upon a small news agent displaying today's papers on a rack out front. The face plastered on the front caught Jong-sup's eye and he plucked it from the pile and continued on.

Jerry Moon – Billionaire – Philanthropist – Murderer?

The people of Seoul were left with many questions last Friday night as Jerry Moon, CEO of KSI technologies, was spotted being dragged from a private resident's complex with his hands cuffed behind his back. Was it a lover's quarrel gone too far or something more sinister? A press conference was held this morning by the Seoul Metropolitan Police Agency that pointed to the latter. Though the details were vague and no date for trial has been released it seems that a murder was committed, and that Jerry Moon and a female employee were present. This news has come at a bad time for KSI as there has been speculation that they were involved with the SUNDAI auto mobile scandal that has left 14 people dead. Though KSI had so far avoided being dragged into the limelight, hiding in the shadow of much larger and more publicly known SUNDAI, after these new events stocks at KSI have plummeted and show no signs of slowing down. Stockholders are jumping ship.
Continued on Page 3

A cruel smile stretched across Jong-sup's face. Lizard-like, he licked his lips, finally things were looking up, he thought. His mind went back to the terrible ordeal he had faced the past couple of days and wondered if it had all been worth it.

Yes.

It was definitely worth it. He'd do it ten times over if he could be gifted a chance to see Jerry in person. After reading the article several times, something was bugging him. Victim. The tabloid had referred to him simply as the victim. Maybe they were trying to be respectful to the deceased, but Jong-sup wanted the injustices he had faced to be public knowledge. Not all of the details of course. Then the realisation came. Apparently, his funeral was being held today, so soon after a mere ten days. Surely the police would need to keep the body as evidence? He thought to himself. But they didn't have a body. He was the body. Jong-sup's face went bright red at his foolishness, and he looked around for anyone that might have been reading his thoughts.

The pilgrimage home was long and painful on bare feet. Jong-sup's soles were bloodied and blistered so he was allayed to finally reach the street of his old home. So close to the scene of his shenanigans, not even a fortnight past; he would have to tread carefully. Too many people around here may recognise him.

The distance to the alley leading to his hideout wasn't too far but he wasn't going to take any chances. He pulled off his new denim jacket and wrapped it around his face leaving only a tiny hole for his eyes. Perfectly aware that this made him appear mentally ill, he was quite satisfied. This was Seoul after all, people will generally go out of their way to avoid the crazy rather than stay and watch. It might as well have been a cloak of invisibility.

With disguise at the ready he charged down the street. Luckily, the time couldn't have been more optimal as it was still an hour till rush hour and nearly all of the residents in this neighbourhood were working professionals. Two elderly ladies creaked slowly down the road chatting as they went. Jong-sup didn't even consider slowing down and pushed between them knocking one almost off her feet. Her friend turned to hurl some abuse at Jong-sup but seeing his bare feet and questionable attire she decided against it and resorted instead to helping her friend regain her footing.

Jong-sup didn't spare a thought for the pensioners as he made it to the alley. His spirits, though, were sunk as soon as they had been lifted. Walking on the pristine concrete pavements had been hard enough but the walk to the abandoned shop was cluttered with small stones, glass and brambles.

Sinking vertically to coincide with his enthusiasm, he squatted against the brick wall to rest his poor feet before exposing them to such torture. After a minute or so an awful noise echoed off the walls. Crying, and not only regular crying, but bawling. It was coming from Alpine view and getting steadily closer. Jong-sup's view of the street was obstructed by a pile of black rubbish bags stacked four feet high and so he was safe from being spotted while he rested.

The wailing accompanied by two sets of footsteps continued its approach until stopping just around the corner from where Jong-sup sat. He froze to avoid any unwanted attention.

'Come on honey,' came a sweet caring female voice with an unfamiliar accent 'we're already late.'

'I don't want to go!' came the source of the crying 'he's mean.'

Jong-sup knew this voice, it was Mi-na, although she was sounding uncharacteristically spoiled for the chipper girl who had annoyed him on many an occasion.

'Don't talk like that about you papa,' came the other voice that Jong-sup had to assume was the helper Carina 'This day is important to him.'

'This day is important to me!' cried Mi-na.

What a spoiled brat thought Jong-sup. 'I want to go say goodbye to Mr Park!' she shouted and then howled with sorrow and hugged into Carina.

'I know darling, I know your father wanted you to go to the funeral, but he has no choice. It would look bad if his family weren't there to support him,' consoled Carina.

'I know,' replied Mi-na between sobs 'but I...I…I don't want Mr Park to be alone, what if nobody goes? What….what if he's scared.'

'Oh, my lovely, don't you worry. There will be lots of people there,' replied Carina.

'Promise?' asked Mi-na.

'Yeah….yeah sure,' Carina replied sounding uncertain 'and tomorrow I'll come with you and we'll buy some flowers, leave for him.'

'I don't think he'll like that' said Mi-na, her crying dying down to a sniffle 'maybe a bottle of soju?'

'Whatever you want, lovely.'

The triumphant feeling of achieving revenge seemed to wash away with Mi-na's tears. He had not for one second considered how she would take the news, and had he considered he wouldn't have predicted that she would have wept for him. Maybe she pitied him? That was most likely it. Either way, being witness to her emotional reaction had utterly deflated him. He wished he hadn't. Sprinting across the ragged and sharp ground of the path would have been preferable and he regretted his hesitation.

'Down that path, right at the end, is Mr Park's special place, Carina,' came Mi-na's voice from the other side of his rubbish pile blockade.

Jong-sup held his breath.

'Do you want to quickly have a look? Will it make you feel better?' Jong-sup held his breath tighter and suppressed the urge to run for it.

'It would,' said Mi-na.

Jong-sup's heart pounded as if in the presence of Death herself.

'but we can't.'

Jong-sup exhaled, slowly and quietly.

'Why not?' asked Carina.

Shut up you stupid woman! Screamed Jong-sup on the inside of his head.

'I promised Mr Park I would never go there again.'

'Okay, well then, can we leave now?' asked Carina.

'Alright,' replied Mi-na.

Once their footsteps were distant enough, Jong-sup returned to breathing normally. Was he really doing the right thing? He questioned himself. Jong-sup! He thought loudly in his head. What are you thinking? This is the best idea you have ever had! It was time for Jong-sup to start enjoying his hard-earned freedom of this, seemingly infinite, life.

3

Back at the shop, Mr Lee was sweeping nothing while holding nothing, but he was whistling away none the less. The sight of the grotesque trauma he had sustained to his legs still bothered Jong-sup and the blood trail that he left everywhere he floated didn't help, even it was only ethereal. He would have preferred it if the spectre moved on, either to the next life or at the very least somewhere else. Out of courtesy and a deep held respect for him he would keep his irritation to himself.

'Welcome back, young man,' exclaimed Mr Lee at the sight of Jong-sup 'I trust you were successful in your ventures?'

'Yes, a few bumps along the way but I think things should run smoother now, at least I hope so,' replied Jong-sup.

'Hope, hope is an important thing,' said Mr Lee.

'Well, I hope not to be here too long,' stated Jong-sup.

Mr Lee looked a little hurt at the thought of being left alone again after all these years.

'Where are you going?' asked Mr Lee.

'Well, I haven't completely decided yet but somewhere my money will stretch further than here. I was thinking Thailand,' replied Jong-sup.

'I've never left Korea,' said Mr Lee, his voice not envious but defiant as if he couldn't understand why anyone would betray their county by leaving.

'Well, before I do anything, I need to find someone who can make a new Identity,' said Jong-sup.

'Why would you need to do that?' inquired Mr Lee.

'It's not important, I'm going to take a nap downstairs,' said Jong-sup, ignoring Mr Lee's comment.

'Of course, thought I should let you know though, someone was nosing around here,' said Mr Lee.

'When?' demanded Jong-sup.

'Two days ago,' said Mr Lee.

'What did they look like?' asked Jong-sup.

'I couldn't tell. They didn't come in; they were just standing by the ally,' replied Mr Lee.

'Could it have been a child?' Jong-sup asked.

'Could have,' Mr Lee replied.

'Probably was,' said Jong-sup with a groan. He proceeded to open the storeroom closet and then use the hidden staircase to the cellar. He unlocked the safe and looked at the old purple binder full of KSI's secrets and evidence of involvement; both his and others in the company. He would save this for a rainy day. Printing this stuff out before leaving the office was a stroke of genius on his part.

He counted his money, smiled, and locked it away again and still smiling he wrapped himself in a dirty old blanket and huddled himself into the corner of the old dusty cellar. His decent into sleep was almost instantaneous, and for the first time in a long time, perhaps for lack of alcohol, he dreamed.

Jong-sup opened his eyes to a bright white room, he was led on a queen size bed with sheets that matched the walls. He was so extraordinarily comfortable. The sun was shining through the window from a pale blue sky. He rolled over to find himself next to a beautiful young woman, her eyes were closed, and she was naked under the sheets. Turning to look back through the window he discovered another girl of equal beauty lying the other side of him too. Wow, he thought, life couldn't be better than it is right now.

He sat up in bed and took a moment to soak in his utter contentment. Then the bed started to rock heavily; back, forth up and down but he wasn't afraid, he was enjoying the ride. The newly mobile bed began to move forward towards the bedroom wall but before reaching it the wall fell away to reveal beautiful tropical forest all around, filled with life and exotic fruits.

The white sheets that he lay under were pulled from him like a magician's table trick, but now he was fully clothed. The bed was no longer a bed, or it had never been one to begin with, it was now an elephant carrying him in a basket on its back. Jong-sup looked either side of him for his female friends but disappointingly they were absent. There was a driver straddling the elephant's thick neck and just as he noticed her, she turned and gave him a seductive wink. Jong-sup was glad to be finally getting what he deserved after his hard work. Maybe life wasn't so bad, he definitely wasn't thinking about ending it now that was for sure. If he had known that this was how life was out here, he would have moved ages ago.

Then the basket dropped, and as soon as it hit the ground it unfolded into a beach lounger. The perfect place to have one too as he sat facing the sea with palm trees arching overhead. He looked around but couldn't remember what it was he was looking for.

'Mr Kim!' came a voice from somewhere he couldn't quite locate. Who is Mr Kim? He thought to himself. The answer was right in his hand, he was holding his passport. The picture was him, but the name read Kim. Of course, Kim was his new name. He mustn't forget that again he thought.

The voice came again, this time from two gorgeous women in far too revealing bikinis for good taste. For some reason he couldn't recognise if they were the girls from the bedroom this morning or not, but it mattered little. They skipped across the sand towards him with an ice-cold beer in each hand. One of them flopped down next to him and nestled in the crevice of his arm. The other ran behind him and began to massage his shoulders.

The ladies were saying something, but he couldn't quite catch it, they sounded muffled as if underwater. The lady in his arms, uttered something incomprehensible and then began to unbutton his jeans, which he couldn't recall changing into. She started to move her head slowly down to his crotch area and Jong-sup looked on in awe. Before she opened his zip, she glanced up at him.

Jong-sup stomach sank. The girl had changed, or he hadn't noticed her getting up and this familiar face taking her place. Yes, he knew this face, it was her; the woman he really hoped he wouldn't see again. The scenery surrounding her shifted jarringly and now they were sat at a table in what Jong-sup recognised as the interior of The Black Apple, only the décor had reverted to its older style.

The woman whom he detested sat facing him and staring into his eyes she tucked her hair behind her ear and smiled. Jong-sup was instantly filled with warmth and then shame and self-hatred.

'How about you finish your drink and I'll show you' said the despicable woman. Jong-sup swallowed the saliva that had been building up in his mouth noticeably, then thrust his glass to his lips to hide his steadily reddening face.

Slamming his glass down on the table he took her hands in his. The Black Apple distorted heavily then contracted in on itself. Once expanded again he was still holding on to the woman only he was stood outside under a streetlight in the dead of night. Their outfits had changed, and she was wearing less heavy make-up. Jong-sup could feel his mouth opening against his will and his lips quivering pathetically.

'I…. I…. lo…… I.. love you,' the words hit his tongue and tumbled out of his mouth.

'I know you do, Park Jong-sup,' she replied, then she kissed him hard. Jong-sup's mind wasn't on the kiss however it was instead becoming heated.

You never did tell me, not once. How could I have been so naive not to notice? He thought. That's it! His body was acting on its own but he was going to steal back the reigns. He concentrated hard. The world around them was becoming fuzzy like the static on a television once the programmes had ended. He could feel his face becoming his own once again, and the second he was able he forced his mouth away from hers and bellowed loudly

'I wasted my life on you, you bitch!' his eyes were filled with tears and his face was twisted into a snarl. He raised his hand high over his head but before he could bring it down to strike his oppressor there was a loud hissing in his ear.

Jong-sup's eyes blinked open to the view of Mr Lee's ghostly face looming over him. He opened his mouth wide to scold him for his invasion of his personal space when Mr Lee put his cold translucent finger to Jong-sup's lips.

'Shhhhhhh!' said Mr Lee in an unnecessarily quiet voice considering Jong-sup was the only one able to hear him 'There is a man upstairs looking around.'

Jong-sup groaned silently, he didn't need this, his sleep had granted him next to no rest. It was probably a homeless scavenger who would vacate as soon as he found that the register was empty, and the produce all gone.

Still, Jong-sup wanted to get a look at the intruder. He could hear him walking around, picking up and placing back objects. Gently, almost feline, Jong-sup made his way to the opposite corner of the basement to where he had been sleeping, next to the wooden ladder that lead upstairs. Light was burrowing into the darkness of the underground through a crack in the panelling overhead. A shadow passed before it as Jong-sup placed his eye closer.

He could see a pair of white and green trainers and nothing else. They were scuffed and untidy so it might be a tramp as Jong-sup had suspected. The man stood in his spot and Jong-sup soundlessly pleaded for him to move back so he could get a good look at his face.

'Mr Park!' called out the man. Jong-sup didn't answer more out of shock than fear.

'Mr Park!' repeated the man 'I know you are here somewhere, please. I saw you come in and you haven't left, so please, have some self-respect and come out.'

Still Jong-sup remained, not wanting to accept the reality of the situation.

'If you don't come out, I'll come find you, so please Mr Park, I just want to talk,' said the man in a tone of finality. Jong-sup decided that there was no use in waiting it out, the stranger had quite obviously sussed him out. Now it was time to face up and assess the damage.

Climbing the stairs cautiously and tentatively opening the closet door, he came face to face with the man. He stood around a foot taller than Jong-sup but was not nearly as broad. His clothes were badly mismatched but what stuck out immediately though, was his dirty green cardigan.

'I've met you somewhere, haven't I?' asked Jong-sup.

'Indeed you have, though I must say I'm disappointed by the lack of recognition in your eyes, perhaps you see all others as beneath you,' said the man.

'What's this about?' interrupted Jong-sup.

'Then again, maybe your just getting old,' said the man wryly 'who knows how old you really are, Mr Park, a man who doesn't die could be a thousand years old for all I know.'

The man's words shook Jong-sup to the core, of all the things this stranger could have come out with he didn't even consider for a moment that it would be this. How did he know?

'Who are you?' asked Jong-sup.

'Who I am is irrelevant, Mr Park,' he replied.

'You're trespassing on my property! So, you tell me who you are or leave!' snapped Jong-sup.

'Oh, this is your home? You see as far as I knew your home is not far from here and is currently cordoned off by the police considering your recent and unfortunate murder,' said the man calmly.

Denial was no use. Somehow this man knew everything.

'What do you want?' Jong-sup asked defeatedly.

'Now, THAT is the right question,' said the man smiling cruelly at Jong-sup 'you've probably figured by now that I know much more than you had believed anyone did. You have been working tirelessly of late to establish some form of comfort for yourself. I have been watching.'

'Why? And for how long?' pleaded Jong-sup.

‘A long time. You see, you and the rather unscrupulous company you work for, had caused a number of people a great amount of pain,’ the man paused seemingly for dramatic effect. Jong-sup just glared at him. ‘A couple of the families who had loved ones so cruelly ripped from their lives weren’t satisfied with only a few people being held responsible as scapegoats and so put their money together and hired me,’ the man flamboyantly gestured at himself ‘for the first two weeks or so I thought this was another uninteresting job, company cuts corners and subsequently cut the strings of life from a meaningless number of consumers. There’s some bad press and a few lower down are sacrificed, until the whole thing blows over and it’s business as usual.’

‘What’s that got to do with me? SENDAI paid compensation to the families afflicted! What?! Was that not enough, they need to squeeze every last coin they can out of a bad situation?!’ yelled Jong-sup.

‘You see Mr Park, for some people money isn’t everything. Some people want justice. I’m not one of those people but some people, are. So, doing my job as well as I always do, I followed the trail of partner companies and found the origin of the “accident”. It was you, Mr Park, who signed off on those brake parts knowing that they were untested, knowing that the factory’s reputation was questionable at best,’ the man pointed an accusing finger at Jong-sup who writhed beneath it.

Mr Lee came into view through the floorboards hovering to the side of Jong-sup.

‘Is this true? It couldn’t be true, right?’ said Mr Lee, the disappointment obvious on his face ‘I don’t believe it, you were always a kind and gentle boy.’

‘It’s none off your business old man!’ Jong-sup snapped at Mr Lee. The stranger looked slightly taken aback by the “old man” comment, unable to see the floating half-corpse of Mr Lee and took it as a slip of the tongue. Mr Lee looked at the ground he hadn’t the feet to stand on and sank through it leaving the two men to their argument. Jong-sup's gut wrenched at the sight of Mr Lee's expression.

'I disagree,' said the man 'as long as someone is paying me it's as much my business as yours. And your business *was* boring. You were a walking stereotype, grumpy, miserable older businessman, there were a thousand more just like you in Seoul alone. That was until one night I decided to tail you and some cheap floozy back to your hotel. I waited outside for you to exit, and exit you did. From the roof.'

'I don't know what you are talking about,' proclaimed Jong-sup.

'Oh, I think you do, business man commits suicide in Seoul!' the man underlined it in the air with a hand 'Hardly front page news. I was just about to wrap up my investigation and go home when I heard a commotion and saw you scrape yourself from the pavement.'

'What?' Jong-sup laughed forcibly 'no one will believe that!'

'perhaps not,' replied the man 'but I'm not interested in that, I don't know how you did it, and I am not particularly interested, my interests are a little more…. material.'

He pulled from his pocket three polaroid pictures and spread them out at arm's length. 'This one is you coming out of the funeral home, the middle one is you coming out of the bank and the last one is you dragging a safe into this run down shit-hole. Go on, take a look.'

Jong-sup snatched them from him, took a quick glance and ripped them into pieces, threw them on the ground and spat on them. Then he grinned defiantly at the stranger.

'What year do you think this is,' he chuckled, 'I have photocopies.' Embarrassment glimmered in Jong-sup's eye for a second.

'There are plenty more, I am guessing that it's in your best interests that no one discovers your current status, right?' said the man, 'so I'm here to offer you a deal.'

'What do you want?' asked Jong-sup.

'I want the cash in the safe you're keeping in here somewhere,' replied the ruthless man.

‘How much?’ asked Jong-sup.

‘Mr Park, I want all of it, I’ve wasted enough time here so if you’d please get it all together, I’ll be on my way.’

우울증

Part Five

Depression

1

Winter came early to Seoul that year, Jong-sup had never felt the cold so close to his bones before. It hadn't yet snowed but there was stillness, as if the sky was holding its breath ready to burst. Jong-sup had little in the way of protection from the cold. He had sold his clothes that he had hid away a couple of weeks prior. It had earned him a meal and a few beers but hadn't served him well in the long run.

He pulled his coat tighter around him and shrunk himself into the corner of the box-fort he now called home. It was an effective shield against the wind and blocked out a substantial portion of the noise from the adjacent street. Less now though since the tarpaulin he had been using as a roof had blown away some days prior, he would have to replace it soon; before the snow came.

No other misfortunate soul shared this alley with him. It was Jong-sup's now, there was the occasional attempt to steal his territory, but they soon learned, Park Jong-sup was king here. This damp, stinking, dingy alley in Gangnam was his kingdom.

Gangnam, how Jong-sup hated this district. In his past life as an active member of society he had always made it his aim to avoid this place altogether. He was mostly successful too, except for the odd after-hours work meeting. Gangnam had changed so much, the faces that surrounded him were half his age and the streets were filled with children who couldn't handle their drink and had long forgotten social protocol. Now though, since everything in his life had been flipped upside down, so too was his detest for this place. The hustle of all the bodies in close proximity and the streets overflowing with traffic made this one of the warmest places in Seoul, far different from his previous residence in the suburbs where there were many more open spaces and so many more directions from which the icy wind could hit you.

From Jong-sup's squat in the corner he had a clear view of the opposing end. Apart from the exit onto the street, there was only one other way into the alley: a door from the kitchen of a restaurant. He was staring at this door a moment before it swung open. His internal clock was so accustomed to the routine of his surroundings that even with no watch (it too had been sold) he could anticipate the events of the day. For what seemed to Jong-sup the hundredth time, a short man in his fifties with a grease patched, white vest and shorts stumbled out from the door carrying a tub of dirty brown water. As usual he emptied it into the alley with little care for where it drained. Then, as usual he pulled a cigarette from his pocket and lit it, ribbons of smoked curled into the air. He turned to go back inside, his cigarette still lit, when for the first time in the last two months since Jong-sup had been sleeping here, he made eye contact. Jong-sup had been staring at the man in the safe knowledge that he would go unnoticed. Now having made contact with a living human for the first time in a while he felt, shame. He didn't want to be seen in his current state, ripped and patched clothing, visibly damp, his hair hanging greasy and unkempt and sporting unruly facial hair spotted with grey. In his past life he may have looked down on this chef, but now he felt as a peasant being unexpectedly noticed by a king. He wished his face would split open and crawl inside itself just to avoid his gaze. It was as if the chef was the gorgon Medusa and had turned him to stone, by the time it had worn off the chef was gone and the door was closed.

'Hey!' came a voice close to his ear. Jong-sup didn't react, it was Mr Lee, or the echo of what was once Mr Lee at least. His spirit was bound to his store it seemed; he could never go far from its walls. Jong-sup had taken with him a brick from the store, he wasn't sure what had given him this idea but it had worked, Mr Lee could travel to where ever he carried the brick and right now it was being used as support for his make-shift home.

'I haven't seen you eat in quite some time boy. I am worried about your status,' said Mr Lee concerned 'how about you get off your ass and find some food, yeah?'

Jong-sup didn't answer, Mr Lee irritated him to no end and he often visualised smashing the brick into pieces, but for some reason unbeknownst to him, he couldn't bring himself to do it. Was it loneliness? Surely not, he had been alone many years before he lost his home and all his worldly possessions.

'Come on, I would join you, but I haven't really the stomach for it,' said Mr Lee holding a handful of his own intestine in front of him. His cheeks filled with air and he burst out laughing, but soon trailed off when he failed to get even a smile from Jong-sup.

'I can't go looking through bins again, I won't do it,' protested Jong-sup.

'You'll have to, that or starve to death,' Mr Lee said.

'I already told you that won't happen,' countered Jong-sup.

His stomach gave out a massive growl as if on command. It was true though, even now as his body was most likely digesting his organs, he felt no closer to Death. The pain that had started off excruciating had numbed as long as his mind eluded the thought of food. Thirst was different, thirst never left him for a second, like the most loyal of companions.

'If I could bring some to you I would, I remember you always running into my shop, you'd never say no to a free snack back then,' said Mr Lee.

'And you'd never offer one,' said Jong-sup, Mr Lee looked deflated but didn't protest, he was right.

'Fine, I'll get going, if only to get out of ear shot of your yammering,' said Jong-sup.

He began to rock back and forth building momentum and then stood up with the vigour of a man half of his level of starvation. His knees and elbows crunched into position and he stumbled away without uttering goodbye.

The streets of Gangnam were almost empty, bar one lady mopping up a pool of vomit from outside her cafe, the youth were lousy drinkers and lacked consideration for the people who cleaned their messes. Not that Jong-sup cared much either, but the fact that they didn't irritated him none the less. He wandered aimlessly not knowing where to start.

He wasn't going to reach into a bin again; last time his hand had emerged cupping a bag of excrement, most likely dog. He really hoped it was dog. Besides, bins were few and far between nowadays, the people of Seoul were much too traumatised by previous terror attacks that they'd rather carry their trash home with them.

In a corner of a small square lined with bars and fried chicken fast food establishments, where the floor was littered with hundreds of cigarette butts, stood a low wall. Jong-sup sat upon it to preserve some of the little energy he had. By his feet he spied a half-eaten corn dog. He scooped it up eagerly only to be dismayed by the underside being soggy and dirt ridden. His stomach churned, he weighed it up in his mind. It may for the time being ease the pain but only if he could keep it down. His stomach decided for him as it shouted its opinion which echoed around the square. Jong-sup closed his eyes and forced the wet sausage closer to his mouth. His opinion was painted on his face in the shape of disgust. He stretched his jaw as wide as possible and held it in his mouth taking extra care not to touch the sides. Right before he introduced his teeth to the lump of processed meat and dough; he smelled something. It wasn't the repulsive thing in his mouth either. No, he knew this smell, noodles, hot, spicy and greasy. He threw the corn dog aside and rose from the wall his energy renewed.

Like a hound he followed his nose faithfully. It led him to a wide unfamiliar street that, when night fell, would be crowded with rowdy youth. Halfway down the street he could see the source of this heavenly scent. A small cart that looked hand constructed from rusted scrap metal with a woman, shrunken with age, frying the noodles. Smoke billowed out. Jong-sup cautiously approached the cart keeping his head down and purposefully staying out the elderly woman's eyeline.

'Good morning,' said Jong-sup.

'Morning,' came the croaky reply from the other side of the cart.

'A little early to be setting up shop, surely?' Jong-sup inquired.

‘Not if I wanna catch people on their way to work who hadn’t had time to have breakfast,’ she replied.

‘Ah yes, good thinking,’ said Jong-sup.

‘Can I get you anything?’ she asked.

‘Uh yes, can I get some japchae? Thank you. Spicy.’

‘It’ll be right about 3 minutes,’ she said, then meerkat-like she stuck her head over the counter and her sweet smiling face soured immediately upon contact with Jong-sup.

‘I’ll have to see the money first,’ she said barely hiding the disgust she felt at the sight of the ragged man in front of her.

‘Since when was that the way transactions are done?’ barked Jong-sup picking up on her tone.

‘Money first or no noodles,’ she barked back.

‘Just give me the fucking noodles you ancient bitch!’ Jong-sup’s voice bounced off the surrounding buildings. He snatched the plastic bottle of chilli sauce from the cart and drop kicked it across the street, then tipped over a small metallic table that was laid out for paying customers.

‘I’m calling the police!’ shouted the woman, her voice authoritative and not in the slightest intimidated by Jong-sup’s tantrum. Pulling from her pocket a big black object. It took Jong-sup a moment to realise that it was a mobile phone. She began to theatrically dial 112 making sure he could see her. How the hell could this woman afford a mobile phone? Jong-sup considered the risk and decided to betray his stomach in favour of not being discovered. He gave the old woman a rude gesture and turned on his heels and ran.

Once the ragged tramp was no longer in sight, she calmly placed the phone back into her pocket and began to put her cart back into order. She was no stranger to working this area and little events like this wouldn’t phase her. She didn’t live this long by being soft.

Jong-sup had had enough. Starvation was a small price to pay to avoid humiliation. To be overpowered by an old hag selling street meat filled him with shame. Normally, he wouldn’t give up the fight so quickly, but he had little fight left. Now, all he wanted to do was to crawl back into his crevice of boxes and dirt and wait for the flesh to rot off his bones and peace to find him at last.

Turning the corner to his alley brought him face to translucent face with Mr Lee, looking concerned.

'Good, right on time. There's someone over there,' said Mr Lee.

'Where?' asked Jong-sup.

'There, rummaging through your boxes,' said Mr Lee. Jong-sup squinted and peered through Mr Lee's chest, and surely enough the signs of movement were evident.

'Who is he?' asked Jong-sup.

'Stop looking through me boy! Have you no concept of personal space! Anyway, I have no idea, I haven't seen him before,' said Mr Lee.

'uh huh,' grunted Jong-sup.

'Homeless by the looks of it,' said Mr Lee. That relieved Jong-sup substantially. He could deal with the down-and-outs no problem. This guy was no different, he's soon learn that this territory was occupied. Jong-sup walked casually towards the trespasser, the closer he got the more dishevelled and lean the figure became. He wore a camo coat and a ragged green trapper hat, on his back was an old model military backpack. As Jong-sup approached silently he picked up a length of rotten wood that he had propped up on the wall.

'Hey! Thief! Turn around!' said Jong-sup authoritatively. He had meant to add on slowly and so was caught off guard when the intruder turn round with rodent speed, and upon the image of Jong-sup holding a piece of wood in striking position, let out a high pitched blood curdling scream. The noise pierced Jong-sup's ears and was amplified tenfold by the narrowness of their surroundings. Jong-sup reacted quickly and hit the man square on the nose. The wood, being as rotten as it was, snapped on contact with the man's face. He did not fall as Jong-sup had anticipated, but the force was enough to pop his nose. He crouched over holding his face as his nostrils spewed dark red blood.

'Please!' shouted the man, holding his hand out in front of him to ward off any additional blows 'I wunt stealin, I was mearly lookin about.'

'It's not yours to be looking through. What were you hoping to find? Food? Drugs? Get the fuck out of here before your nose is the prettiest part of your face!'

'No, no nothin like dat,' squealed the man, his eyes closed and his mouth agape displaying more missing teeth than present 'I'm lookin fer a buddy is all, a winter buddy.'

'I'm not looking for any friends, now I will not warn you again, leave!' yelled Jong-sup.

'I know you don't got one already, only one person been sleepin in dat bed, you won't survive the winter without one, surely you know dat?' said the scrawny man.

'I told you I aint interested!' Jong-sup gave his final bark.

'I gots food, I noticed you ant got any, we can share. I have enough,' he gestured at his backpack.

'I don't need..' but his stomach betrayed him, the thought of food had made it call out in desperation.

'I reckon you do friend,' said the man.

'We aren't friends,' said Jong-sup.

'Not yet maybe,' replied the man, 'they call me Pigeon.'

2

Jong-sup was still feeling unsure about this pact, and was weighing up whether or not to tell Pigeon to scram when the small scruffy man came scurrying around the corner with a tin dustbin in his arms and an ugly smile spread wide on his face. He nearly tripped a dozen times while power walking towards Jong-sup and skidded to a halt in front of him.

'You know for someone who aint used to livin rough, you must of picked the perfect spot for a squat, outta the way from prying eyes and these wall are tall enuff that noone will see the smoke,' said Pigeon utterly giddy.

'What gives you the idea that I'm not long homeless? Not that I'd want to be likened to your lot,' asked Jong-sup.

Pigeon picked up on the slight but ignored it.

'I've seen your lot before, business types, it's in your manner. Plus, those trousers have seen better days but I knows luxury brandin when I sees it,' said Pigeon 'so what was it? Alcohol or gamblin?'

'None of your business that's what!' snapped Jong-sup.

'Calm down sire,' Pigeon said mockingly giving a low bow 'I meant no offence, anyways, I got just the cure fer grumpiness.'

Pigeon reached into his backpack and pulled out a can of spam. Jong-sup instinctively snatched for it, but Pigeon's reflexes were animalistic and he pulled it just out of his reach.

'Don't be hasty, I know it's excitin but it's much better hot, jus you wait till I got dis fire goin.'

Jong-sup glared at the man but didn't protest, he lacked the energy.

Soon the fire was crackling from within the dustbin and Jong-sup and Pigeon were tucking into some glutinous spam. They had a can each, and while Jong-sup was tearing into his with ferociousness, his wooden fork practically a blur in the air, Pigeon was savouring each bite, rather gentlemanly. With the dull pain in his stomach receding and the warmth of the fire thawing his bones Jong-sup had to admit, if only to himself, that his mood was lifting. He finished much sooner than Pigeon who was alerted to the fact by the sound of Jong-sup scraping the bottom of his can.

'You aint still hungry is you? Well no more till tomorrow I'm afraid, gotta ration it out,' said Pigeon.

Jong-sup gave a sullen nod in understanding.

'Aw, go on then, you can have the rest of mine, I aint that ungry anyways.'

Pigeon held out the can and Jong-sup grabbed without hesitation, there wasn't much left but what was, was devoured in an instant.

'Glad to see that went down a treat,' said Pigeon.

'It was alright,' replied Jong-sup.

'Well, I'll tell you what, since we've just met, as a bit of a celebration,' and without explaining further he pulled out from his green coat a beautifully engraved silver flask and he shook it gleefully. Then, rummaged through his backpack and after a minute that seemed elongated well beyond sixty seconds he pulled out a shot glass.

He filled the dirty glass with a dirty brown liquid and handed it to Jong-sup who accepted it, the left side of his mouth curling slightly, which didn't go unnoticed by Pigeon, who had the vision of a hawk.

'Nearly gotta smile outta you dint I,' smiled Pigeon.

Jong-sup narrowed his eyes in return and scowled.

'Well, suit yerself. Only enough fer one I'm afraid, savin this fer a special occasion,' Pigeon then took a swig directly from the flask and placed it safely back into his coat 'Ahhh, American whiskey.'

Jong-sup followed suit and emptied his tiny glass. He held the whiskey in his mouth for a second attempting to savour the taste as it may be a while before he tasted it again. The burning of the lining of his cheeks forced him to swallow and he felt an inner warmth that complemented the heat from the fire nicely. For ten minutes, for the first time in a long time, all seemed right with the world.

'Alright then, better get some sleep, puttin the fire out soon,' said Pigeon.

'What?!' demanded Jong-sup.

'Puttin the fire out, while we sleep,' answered Pigeon.

'Yes I heard you, buffoon! Why?' said Jong-sup.

'You can't go sleepin with a fire burnin, this alley is a wind trap, imagin if it fell over, probably wouldn't, but if it did. I lost a friend that way before, don't wanna lose you just yet.'

'But it's freezing, I'll freeze!' said Jong-sup.

'You been doin alright so far ant ya?' said Pigeon 'Look ere, we sleep like this, back to back, that'll stop the cold from the floor getting to ya and we'll share body heat,' explained Pigeon.

'I do not want to be touching you all night!' said Jong-sup.

'You won't be, we'll put a blanket between us,' said Pigeon.

Jong-sup shook his head adamantly.

'Suit yerself, if you change your mind in the night give I a nudge, but I'm puttin out that fire. Now get some rest we got an early start tomorrow' said Pigeon.

'What do you mean?' asked Jong-sup.

'I'll let you know in the morning,' said Pigeon as he put out the fire with a bit of tarpaulin he pulled from his backpack.

Before even the sun had awoken, the two scruffy men darted in and out of shadows through the streets of Gangnam. One moved stealthily, the other much less so. One could not be heard; the other's groans were obvious to anyone still awake at this hour.

'You better tell me where we're going right now or I won't move another step,' groaned Jong-sup.

'No breakfast for you then,' replied Pigeon in an annoyingly chipper tone for this time of day.

'What's the point of keeping me in the dark? At least tell me how much longer it will take,' pleaded Jong-sup.

‘No time at all, we’re here,’ answered Pigeon and he slipped down an ally.

Jong-sup followed only to crash into the back of his putrid smelling companion, who turned and held his index finger to his lips in a childlike fashion.

‘We are right behind the supermarket, I comes ere often. It’s one of a few places in da area that has easy entry,’ he grabbed on to a maintenance ladder and began to hoist himself upwards but was snagged by Jong-sup.

‘You mean were going to steal?! I can’t afford to be taking risks like this you idiot,’ said Jong-sup.

‘Keep yer voice low. What risk? I does this all the time,’ reasoned Pigeon.

‘Can’t we just take what’s left over from the bin, surely the cans will be alright?’ asked Jong-sup.

‘fraid not, they don’t put any food goods in the bin any more, ter stop homeless from gatherin round their stores. Don’t reckon I’m the face they want representin them,’ Pigeon chuckled quietly and spread his toothless grin wide ‘listen friend, I respect yer moral outlook but we’re only gunna take what we needs, nothin more. Nothin noticable, that’s how you get yerself caught.’

Pigeon continued his climb to the roof and Jong-sup followed nervously behind.

The building was only two stories high and the roof was pretty bare except for a couple of ducts for the air conditioning. Jong-sup looked around at the buildings that surrounded and dwarfed them for any on-lookers but saw no signs of life.

‘So, are we going to enter through those ducts?’ asked Jong-sup.

‘You can if you want, but I’m ere fer food not air,’ replied Pigeon smiling but quickly stifling it at the sight of Jong-sup’s expression; he did not like to be made to feel stupid and the evidence was plastered on his face. Pigeon scurried across the roof and crouched down next to a low wall of the raised part of the building that formed the centre of the structure. He gestured for Jong-sup to come over which revealed a small door being made inaccessible by padlock. Pigeon wasn't in the least deterred by the sight of the lock and whipped out from within his coat a small hair pin, he held it skyward and it glistened in the city lights before he got to work like a master thief. Jong-sup was taken aback by the prowess shown by this lowly fool.

'That'll do it,' announced Pigeon at the completion of his task 'Okay, in you go.'

'Huh, me?' asked Jong-sup shocked.

'You aint gunna learn nothing waitin around up here, what would have been the point of you comin if not, eh?' explained Pigeon.

'What...what do I do?' Jong-sup asked. Although he had never lived this kind of life before and had no way of developing such skills, his lack of knowledge made him feel inferior; he didn't like it. Instead of looking up to Pigeon, he resented him for making him feel this way. Didn't Pigeon know it was his place to feel inferior to Jong-sup? Could he be living in upside down land?

'This door is fer access maintainin the lights and such. Lower yerself down but careful not to step on the ceiling panels; you'll fall right through. Instead place yer feet on the girders, the metal support beams; you'll see em. Then lift up one of the tiles; gently. Last but not least, grab some food but only what's on the top shelf.'

'Won't there be an alarm of some kind?' asked Jong-sup.

'Oh, right yeah, thanks fer remindin me. There are two motion sensors in opposite corners of the ceiling. That's exactly why we're coming through the rooftop. The sensors are pointin at a hundred- and thirty-degree angle more or less. So as long as you stay off the ground all's well.'

'And you're completely sure about that, right?' interrogated Jong-sup.

'As sure as I ever been about anythin,' replied Pigeon, cocking his head to and angle that accentuated the large space between his eyes, which did not make for a reassuring image. Jong-sup took a deep breath before lowering himself down into the darkness.

His eyes quickly adjusted to the low light of the inner ceiling of the store. The pain in his arms at holding his own weight was rising so he lowered his foot gradually down into it found purchase. Increasing the pressure of the surface found it weak; this must be a panel he thought. He spread his legs till they found much stronger footing simultaneously and not a moment too soon, he wouldn't have been able to hold himself a second longer. He relieved his aching arms and stood there, mid star jump position, collecting his thoughts.

Opting for the route that would require the least amount of movement he decided to lift the panel he had almost fallen though. He slid it back and was rewarded with a dizzying view of the floor, he wasn't high up, but the unfamiliar angle was disorientating. Either side of the square, that was his window into the empty shop, were shelves. Just his luck to be directly above the aisle.

It made sense that all the panels would be the exact same size and so it seemed all Jong-sup would have to do would be stretch his leg to his right at the same length they were stretched currently to reach the next girder. Using his arms, he pulled himself and adjusted his feet so that they were both on the same spot. The new height this gave him introduced his head roughly to the concrete above him. Dizziness returned to him without the aid of vertigo and he almost lost balance. To a normal person, absent of curses, the pain would have defeated him, but Park Jong-sup was no stranger to pain and managed to maintain his balance. The impact must have made some noise though as there came a muffled 'Mind yer head,' from above. Jong-sup grumbled in private response.

Finally, in position spread-eagle above what would hopefully be the shelves he reached down between his legs and with no little effort hoisted the tile out of its resting place. His stomach seemed to react before his eyes as it gurgled audibly. The part of the shelf the was presented to him was stocked full of tin cans. The contents of the cans were unidentifiable from this angle but at Jong-sup's state of starvation this was largely irrelevant. He lowered himself to sit on the edge of the opening; his legs dangling into the store. He leaned forward and outstretched his arm to its full length, but his fingertips could only just brush the cans. His stomach churned in protest and made his head light. Considering for a moment to give up and ask his ragged companion to do it, his long held and self-sabotaging pride kicked in and snapped him out of it. Pigeon was around his age yet had seemingly gone his entire life without accomplishing much at all. What could he possibly do that Jong-sup couldn't?

He positioned himself so that he was led on his front; his weight correctly proportioned to allow him to lean through without falling in. Reasoning that if he couldn't reach this time then he would simply give up all together. But reach he did. Only just though. He pulled the can up into the ceiling and for the first time in a long time he felt victorious. It was comparable to closing a deal with a new supplier. The dopamine rush made him yearn for his past life. After securing 3 cans he reached down for the fourth. From the corner of his eye a dark smudge faded into the room. He couldn't feel any change in the air but knew that void anywhere, though she hadn't appeared to him in a while. He snapped round pre-emptively, but there was no Death. Flitting his eyes around the store they halted on a moving object. The can he had been reaching for. He must have knocked it. It was on its side spinning slowly towards the edge of the shelf. Jong-sup lunged forward to stop it, but his old clumsy hands just pushed it further, sealing his fate.

The can hit the floor and though he couldn't see it he could hear it bouncing and then skidding across the floor. And then, nothing. Jong-sup exhaled a breath he did not know he had held. But his relief was unwarranted. His heart barely had time to settle when the alarm sounded. The noise was deafening and was amplified from his position among the metal beams. Between the wail of the security system he could hear Pigeon calling for him. So he put his bag on is shoulder and not before smashing his skull to the point of concussion again he made for the exit.

Pigeon was there to help pull him out and his expression surprised Jong-sup, he wasn't angry or scared but smiling.

'C'mon better run. Follow quickly!' said Pigeon scrambling to the ladder. They hit street level and without pausing for breath they fled through the streets. Jong-sup overtook Pigeon who didn't appear to be breaking a sweat.

'Come you fool!' yelled Jong-sup 'Hurry the hell up!'

'Calm down my friend, someone from the store will arrive shortly and turn it off and find a can on the floor. They'll think it was rats is all. You did remember to put the panel back over, right?' asked Pigeon but Jong-sup's face was all he needed for an answer. 'Well, no worries. We just can't go back there for a while. Got plenty of other places about,' and he gave Jong-sup a reassuring wink, who returned the gesture with a scowl. 'I don't suppose you managed to grab any supplies did yer?

'Three cans,' Jong-sup replied facing away in shame.

'That's great, you could've stopped there. Plenty fer now. Remember, don't want to take too much at a time, dats how you get caught,' explained Pigeon with an added slap on his back.

Jong-sup would never had admitted but this did make him feel better. He was the type of man who liked to succeed at everything he did. Failure was not taken lightly.

3

Later that very evening, Jong-sup sat basking in the warmth of the fire which was doing an excellent job at fending off the early onset of darkness and the chill that followed it. He was alone in the desolate alley in which Pigeon had affectionately, and Jong-sup hoped ironically, named Eden.

Jong-sup was less than fond of the name, not because it was so ill suited but rather because he despised the Christian faith. Although being raised catholic after his parents passed, his childhood had been made so miserable by sister Hye that he renounced the faith as soon as he had left the orphanage.

Movement drew his eye to the ground where droplets of blood pattered silently and then faded into nothing. Glancing up he found its ethereal source levitating three feet off the earth.

'Good evening, Mr Lee,' greeted Jong-sup.

'To you as well young man,' he replied, although after a delay of a few seconds.

'Where have you been?' asked Jong-sup.

'Back at my store of course,' he answered.

'You can do that?' asked Jong-sup.

'Why yes, when I distance myself from that brick you carry, I end up back there. Just the two locations and nowhere in between. My world has become a lot smaller,' A moment passed where nothing was heard but the crackling of the fire.

'May I ask you something personal?' asked Jong-sup.

'You have to be a person to hold anything as "personal" and I am not sure what I am anymore,' Mr Lee replied, looking down at his severed bottom half and internal and eternal bleeding.

'Is that a yes?' said Jong-sup. Mr Lee nodded solemnly.

'Why go back to the store? What made you refuse Death's offer?'

'Well, the obvious reason of course,' Mr Lee stated.

Jong-sup had nothing.

'I wanted to see my wife one last time, hopefully meet my child,' Mr Lee said in reply to Jong-sup's blank gaze, 'didn't I already mention that?'

He didn't know quite how to respond; he didn't believe Mr Lee's answer was obvious at all. I mean he understood the notion of what it was to love a woman but to risk infinite limbo was preposterous.

'I must not have been listening,' replied Jong-sup.

'Hmmm,'

'What happened when you saw her? Could she see you?' asked Jong-sup feeling unusually curious.

'I didn't. Otherwise I would have moved on or something, surely. Isn't that how it works?' he asked.

Jong-sup shrugged his shoulders.

'I sometimes wonder,' he continued 'what if she passed already and if that's true then does that mean that she didn't care enough to wish to see me as I did her?'

'Maybe she found someone else?' the words slipped out of Jong-sup's mouth and he knew it was distasteful. This was confirmed by Mr Lee's expression. He looked stricken.

'I mean, she's very old now and the thought of going down to the store where you two had built your lives together is probably too painful,' Jong-sup spluttered.

Mr Lee just nodded his head slowly, but his expression was less grim at least.

'I am sorry,' said Jong-sup.

An apology was uncharacteristic for Jong-sup and Mr Lee knew this all too well.

'Never you mind, no point dwelling on the unknown,' said Mr Lee.

Jong-sup didn't usually dwell on the sensitivities of others, but Mr Lee was an exception to the rule. He had got in early; when Jong-sup's heart was open and naive. He didn't grieve Mr Lee's passing, but he respected him.

'I've been wondering, why is it that I can see you. I thought at first that it must be because of the curse I must be in a state between life and death. If that was the only reason, then surely I would be seeing floating corpses all over the place,' said Jong-sup.

'Maybe, you can only see people you are connected to,' suggested Mr Lee. Jong-sup motioned in agreement.

'Does that mean I could see her?' said Jong-sup.

'Who?' asked Mr Lee. Jong-sup coughed, and his body language became defensive, even more than usual.

'Nothing, just, uh, never mind,' said Jong-sup.

Mr Lee gave a knowing expression and let it be, he knew not to push it. Jong-sup was not the sharing type.

'Who were you talking to?' came the voice of Pigeon. His face was red from the icy air and he had suffered a few minor scrapes and bruises since they parted in the morning, but his smile was ever consistent. Jong-sup wished it wasn't. He was tempted to pull out the few remaining teeth Pigeon owned so that he wouldn't have to stare at their blackened and cavity ridden state.

'Huh? I wasn't,' Jong-sup lied.

'I heard you, no need to be embarrassed I talk to me self all the time, staves off the loneliness.'

'I doubt we share many habits,' said Jong-sup.

'That's a shame, as I got a nasty habit of eatin and drinkin, got a good haul today and was considerin divulgin slightly.'

'Well, we aren't completely different,' said Jong-sup, his condescending tone had mysteriously disappeared.

'Why, thanks yer majesty,' said Pigeon giving a mocking bow. 'more the merrier, I got noodles and sausages and bread and a special treat, beef!' Jong-sup licked his dry bristled lips unable to utter a word nor hide the wild excitement from his eyes.

'Hang on, don't go expectin this all the time, chances are we won't eat like this again all winter,' warned Pigeon.

'I know, I know. How about we stop chattering and start cooking.'

'That's the thinkin' said Pigeon and he cackled loudly.

That night they feasted as kings, or so it felt. Jong-sup noticed that his stomach must have shrunken several sizes, as he felt as if he would burst at the seams. Neither one of them uttered a word during the gorging. Pigeon pulled from his disgusting coat his flask and offered Jong-sup a swig; he accepted gratefully. Leaning back, the warmth splashing across his face and the internal warmth from his belly, Jong-sup felt quite content and looking over at Pigeon he felt a slight camaraderie for the hapless soul.

'So, uh, Pigeon?' Jong-sup stammered.

'Yes? You need more bread?' replied Pigeon.

'No, no, thank you,' said Jong-sup. Pigeons eyes darted around cautiously, not knowing what to expect. It was unusual for Jong-sup to talk so courteously.

'I was just wondering, how you came to be like this?' asked Jong-sup, gesturing around with both hands.

'Like what?' asked Pigeon, still chewing on a sausage that was long ready for swallowing.

'Living on the streets I mean. Homeless,' explained Jong-sup.

Pigeon sat back and looked up and displayed an exaggerated look of pondering on his face, as if he had never been asked this before; and most likely, he hadn't.

'Well, I guess with all stories worth telling it starts with a woman,' he began, and Jong-sup was starting to wish he hadn't asked, he wasn't asking for dinner and a show 'originally, I'm from Naju. Lived with me mum and uncles. We were a farmin family but only a small one, so we weren't makin much. Anyway, I would sometimes go into town to sell milk. That's when I seen her. The most beautiful woman I had ever laid eyes on. She were studying at Dongshin university. She'd wander on by and buy some of me milk sometimes. Then one day I finally rustled up the courage to ask her on a date. One thing to led to another and we fell deep in love.'

Jong-sup exhaled a long and deep breath, this story wasn't interesting to him in the slightest.

'Our love was strong and fierce, and when she graduated, she got a job in Seoul. She moved away without even askin me what I thought.'

'Sounds like a woman alright,' interjected Jong-sup.

'No, it's not like that, apparently, she just didn't want to hurt me, and she knew I don't have the money to move.'

'Yeah they always find a way to twist it into their favour.'

'Such a cynic,' rebutted Pigeon. 'anyway, me family forbade me from goin as I had to help em look after the farm. After about a year I couldn't take it anymore and took the little money I had and made for Seoul.'

'Did you find her?' asked Jong-sup becoming more immersed.

'I did. Then I met her parents,' said Pigeon.

'And?' asked Jong-sup.

'Well, at dinner I said the wrong thing and it led to an argument with me and her father. Her father got injured pretty bad and I ran away. Tried to talk to her but she was having none of it.'

'Christ man, what did you say?' said Jong-sup shocked.

'I said I was sorry!' replied Pigeon.

'No! I mean, what did you say to her father to make him so angry?' asked Jong-sup.

'I just told him that my father was Chinese,' said Pigeon.

'And that was a problem?' asked Jong-sup, but he knew it was. The amount of pride running through the people of his generation and the one before him was enormous, and intense. The diluting of blood of one's grandchildren, even just a quarter, was enough for some to denounce a relationship. Jong-sup reflected for a moment if he felt different about his acquaintance. He did not. Most likely because he didn't think very highly of him in the first place.

Jong-sup sat for a while, turning over Pigeon's story in his mind. There must be more to his story. Why wouldn't he just return home? Why not find work in Seoul? There were too many questions and he couldn't decide whether he cared enough to ask him.

He opted for the choice of minimal effort and didn't delve any further. Something was persistently bothering him though. Why the lack of interest in Jong-sup's own story? He hadn't even asked, and Jong-sup felt robbed of the opportunity to shoot him down. He couldn't take it a moment longer.

'So, are you not interested in how I came to be in such a predicament?' Jong-sup asked gingerly.

'No,' answered Pigeon nonchalantly.

'What do you mean no?! Surely, the story of my fall from grace is of more interest to someone such as yourself,' said Jong-sup flabbergasted.

'I already knows your story. Or one of the many versions of it. Seen loads of yer type, no offence,' said Pigeon.

'I don't get what you are implying,' said Jong-sup.

'Look around at where we are. This is Seoul. For every winner at the corporate game there are a hundred losers. Best case scenario they return home. Worst case, they join our ranks. They don't often last very long either. Lucky for you, you got me,' said Pigeon, he gave Jong-sup a slap on the arm.

'I'll have you know; I was massively successful,' said Jong-sup.

'Hmm, it would appear so,' said Pigeon gifting another slap to the arm of Jong-sup who glared then shimmied out of arms reach.

'A series of bad luck is what landed me in your unsightly company,' said Jong-sup.

'Bad luck? No alcohol, drugs or women?' asked Pigeon.

'No, no, no nothing like that. I mean I had my taste of indulgence but nothing to cripple a man.'

'So, you've never had yer heart broken then?' asked Pigeon.

Jong-sup didn't answer. He dropped the conversation completely. Pigeon sensed that he had perhaps touched a nerve and for risk of being thrown out into the cold of the night, he too let it go.

Jong-sup looked up at the narrow strip of the sky that the alley granted him and reminisced about memories that he normally wouldn't allow himself; at least while the power of consciousness was in his grasp. What he found was that the pain was still very much fresh. He quelled the suspicion that his inability to allow himself to heal was the reason for this wound being still very much open. He swallowed, physically, mentally, metaphorically. With the trapped air that he forced down his throat so too were the painful memories pushed into his lower depths.

The sky was dark but as usual it was bordered by the orange-yellow glow that the city lights provided. Because of this, hardly any stars were visible. He could remember them though, from a time long past when he would gaze up at the heavens for hours. His vivid recollection filled in for the missing stars and it was as if they had returned and the space between them darkened until it matched, well, the only thing comparable would be the void beneath Death's ragged cowl.

With that last visage painted into his mind he was forced to look down, he felt as though he was looking directly at Death. Her stare crushing him with its gravity. Jong-sup's sudden distressed facial expression did not go unnoticed by Pigeon, who cleared his throat loudly. This seemed to work at pulling Jong-sup from whatever waking nightmare he was facing.

'I was hurt by a woman, once,' croaked Jong-sup.

'Uh huh' said Pigeon, afraid to say anything else that could throw Jong-sup off this train of thought.

'Her name was In-sook,' said Jong-sup.

Pigeon delved into his tattered coat for his rusty flask and handed it to Jong-sup; who took a large swig and winced expressively. 'She was beautiful. Absolutely beautiful. I thought I had struck gold,' continued Jong-sup, his face contorted as if he was trying to get rid of an awful taste or perhaps chewing off his own tongue. It was, frankly, a rather interesting spectacle from Pigeon's point of view. 'Turns out when you give your everything to a person, they realise you've got nothing else to give and so they go looking somewhere else; it's human nature.'

'What happened?' asked Pigeon unable to stop his curiosity from getting the better of him.

'What do you think?! She went looking somewhere else!' said Jong-sup.

'Like Busan?' asked Pigeon.

'Like into another man's arms you idiot!' snapped Jong-sup.

Pigeon's face was shocked as if he had never conceived of such an act.

'She would have denied it of course. Lied to my face, over and over.'

'Are you sure she would do somethin so unfaithful?' asked Pigeon.

'Of course I am! I saw her with my own eyes!' said Jong-sup fiercely, but then his tone receded 'I thought I would surprise her after work. She was a military nurse. Waited outside for over an hour just to see her exit with some guy. An American no less. When I saw his disgusting white hands all over her, I felt my heart stop beating and fall through the floor.'

'What did you do?!' begged Pigeon on the edge of his seat.

'Nothing,' replied Jong-sup 'I didn't want to believe it.'

'Where is she now?' asked Pigeon tentatively.

'She's dead,' Jong-sup's face was stone.

Pigeon didn't know how to reply and wouldn't have even if he did.

Jong-sup had never spoke these words aloud before; not even to himself. So, why would he divulge such deeply buried thoughts to such a hideous, pathetic excuse of a man like Pigeon. He must be becoming weak, or perhaps it was Pigeon who had somehow got under his skin and made his mind and his mouth loose. He looked over at

Pigeon scornfully. The decrepit man was preoccupied with rummaging through his coat. He pulled from it again his prized possession; the flask. He rattled it side to side; there wasn't much left. Without taking a swig himself, he uncapped it and handed it to Jong-sup. It struck Jong-sup then that Pigeon pitied him. He didn't even see Jong-sup as his superior at all. This thought brought a fiery rage from his gut, but the fire of the bitter liquid given to him was equally hot and quelled it and kept it in its place.

Why was he superior to this man? He thought. He had never once asked himself this but rather just assumed it was the case. Now though, he yearned for reassurance. He had made a small fortune during his life. What good was that now though, and, what good was it then. What good is money to a man who wants for little but the sweet embrace of Death. You can't take it with you, to wherever it is you go; he was pretty sure of that.

Then what did he possess currently that Pigeon did not? Nothing. In fact, he was quite envious of Pigeon's thick warm coat and pockets full of scrap and trinkets. Maybe, just maybe he wasn't superior to this man at all. Inferior? No! He wouldn't contemplate such an outrageous concept. He was much more intelligent than Pigeon, that was for certain. There was no way in hell that Pigeon could survive the corporate snake-pit as he had. On the other hand though, he had to admit that he wouldn't have been able to survive the streets as well as Pigeon. Discounting all that had come before these two men. Now sat in this ally. Around this fire. Eating the same food. They were just that. Two men.

Jong-sup looked over at Pigeon, and for the first time he felt not disgust but understanding. He didn't see a tramp, but a person. Pigeon gave one of his wide smiles and Jong-sup couldn't repress his reaction in time and the smallest inkling of a smile turned in the corner of his mouth. Pigeon nodded, seemingly understanding.

The two men retired to bed not long after, neither speaking another word nor bringing up the conversation ever again.

4

The following weeks were far different from the previous. The largest difference being the relationship. Jong-sup would have been hesitant to call it a friendship, but it was by far the closest thing he'd had in more years than he could remember. They continued to take turns on their "borrowing" excursions but occasionally they would go together. There still was little in the way of conversation between the two, except for nights they would manage to get their hands on some soju; then Pigeon would blabber on about mostly nonsensical things. Surprisingly, Jong-sup was content to listen to his companion's ramblings and sometimes found, though not often, that Pigeon would spout something truly profound and wise.

Mr Lee appeared less than before. He was more preoccupied with his shop than keeping the company of two down and outs. Jong-sup didn't blame him. He would stop to chat with him on days when Pigeon was off busy collecting rations and sometimes would sit (if he had had a bottom half of course) and listen to Pigeon's alcohol induced philosophy.

Jong-sup no longer felt the ache of starvation. After eating quite frequently and getting more regular exercise he could feel his muscles returning. He wasn't strong per say, but the pain of movement was minimal and that was satisfactory for now. The dramas and stresses of his old life seemed far away. He could recall them, but it felt as though he was someone else now. The thought of Jerry no longer sparked the rage that it once did. He no longer dreamed of revenge for the foiling of his plans at the hands of the tall, scruffy man in the green cardigan, and he was all the better for it.

The result of a stable routine and semi-good company was that time flew by; the days rolled past, and the weeks barely stopped to say hello. The winter deepened, dug in its heels and before long it was already the morning of Christmas eve. The holiday would have come and gone, and Jong-sup would be none the wiser had Pigeon not brought it up while they ate their breakfast in the morning darkness. He had grown accustomed to not paying any attention to any of the store fronts that would have surely been adorning lights and décor by now. When he left his ally, he saw the city streets as simply dangers and goals. They were his hunting grounds now, nothing more.

'Really?!' said Jong-sup 'are you sure?'

'Course I is. It's all up here,' replied Pigeon, pointing to his head, 'I never lose track of the date.'

Jong-sup grunted in affirmation and tucked back into his juk. He looked up at the sky and tried to visualise the route they would be taking to get to today's food store. They were going together today as stocks were running a little low. When he set his sights back to ground level, he saw that Pigeon was looking into his bowl with an expression of disgust.

'What's wrong? Cockroach?' asked Jong-sup.

'No not that,' replied Pigeon.

'Well, what then?!' asked Jong-sup, ever impatient.

'It's just, don't you think that we should be eating somethin a bit, well fancier?' said Pigeon.

'Why? you're normally fine with it,' replied Jong-sup.

'Fer the birth of the lord of course!' said Pigeon, looking incredibly pleased with himself.

'What the hell are you talking about?' asked Jong-sup, genuinely frustrated.

'That's mighty unlucky talk to be talkin at this time of year,' Pigeon laughed 'Christmas of course.'

'You're not a Christian,' said Jong-sup.

'Not really but my family still had our little tradition. Every year we'd have a great big feast. Odeng, gyerang bbang and manduguk,' said Pigeon, with every word his face took on a grotesque picture of pleasure. 'Oh and ttokpokki!'

'Ttokpokki gives me a bad stomach,' said Jong-sup.

'Ah but it's worth it,' said Pigeon, and Jong-sup couldn't disagree, 'besides, you were a Christian, right?'

'I *was* a Catholic, yes. To celebrate Christmas, we'd get an extra helping at dinner and we'd sing hymns, I guess. Oh, and the sister's wouldn't beat us so hard.'

'What's a hymn?' asked Pigeon.

'What's a hymn? How can you not know that? It's like a song about Jesus or god or something,' replied Jong-sup. Pigeon thought on this for a moment.

'Do you know any?' asked Pigeon.

'Hymns? Yes, a few,' replied Jong-sup.

'Go on, sing it then!' said Pigeon.

'No, you fool! I am not going to start singing at the top of my lungs and I'm not here for your entertainment,' spat Jong-sup, sounding more like his old self than he had done in a while.

'Go on, it'll be my Christmas present,' pleaded Pigeon.

'Drop it, I'm not getting you anything,' snapped Jong-sup but he couldn't suppress a chuckle. Pigeon took note of this, slapped Jong-sup on the back and stood up.

'Come on then, better get a move on. We'll talk more on this later,' said Pigeon.

'No, we will not you idiot!' Jong-sup didn't even try to stifle his laugh this time and he joined him in preparing for the morning foraging.

The two miscreants fled down the back roads of Seoul, pepped and fuller of energy than usual. It hadn't snowed this year so far, which was unusual. The streets, however, were iced over every morning. Today was no different. Every so often one of them would slip and pull on the other for support. They would start to laugh each time before simultaneously reminding each other to quiet down.

Leaving the sanctuary of the side streets, they came out onto a main road; an unavoidable moment of vulnerability till they reached the allies on the other side. Jong-sup scanned their surroundings to find that there were a couple of people silhouetted at the far end; probably cleaners.

He kept his eyes on the shuffling figures in the distance before his face came into contact with the crusty hood on Pigeon's coat.

'Why the hell have we stopped moving!' Jong-sup whispered loudly.

'Look,' said Pigeon, pointing across the road to where they were trying to get to.

His eyes found the subject of Pigeon's attention and locked into place. Out from the darkness jutted the pointed hood of Death. His ribs tightened to point of breaking and he swallowed the breath he hadn't known he was holding. It wasn't the sight of Death that scared him, he was long used to it, it was something else.

'How, how, how can you see?!' stuttered Jong-sup grabbing Pigeon by the arms and twisting him to look upon his equally twisted expression.

'What's got into you?' said Pigeon aghast.

'You can see that thing over there?!' Jong-sup pointed a shaking hand.

'I think "thing" is a bit harsh. We aint dressed any better,' replied Pigeon.

'You can see the black cloak?' asked Jong-sup acting as calmly as possible, betrayed by his shuddering arms.

'I can indeed. And aint I jealous, come in very handy come February, a strong raincoat like that,' replied Pigeon.

'I don't think you understand you fool!' snapped Jong-sup releasing Pigeon and turning to face Death.

'Hey! Leave him out of this!' Jong-sup called across the road ignoring the quiet protests of Pigeon.

Death moved.

Then Death moved again.

Her movements were less like Death herself and closer to the living dead. What was she playing at? She rocked this way and that, making little progress, till “she” fell into the streetlight. The old, hooded homeless man was the second most illuminated thing on the street; second only to Jong-sup’s blazing red expression of embarrassment. He had out crazy’d Pigeon, not an easy task and not an accolade he would gladly display on the wall of his non-existent home.

Feeling adequately foolish, he waited until the man across the road had disappeared around the corner before grabbing Pigeon by the arm and dragging him across the road, or at least attempting to. Pigeon wouldn’t budge.

‘What are you playing at now? We don’t have time to admire the scenery,’ said Jong-sup.

‘Change of plan, we aint goin to get no simple scraps,’ said Pigeon.

‘You can’t just go and change the plan just like that!’ said Jong-sup.

‘You seen that man there, what was the difference between him and us?’ asked Pigeon.

‘He had a raincoat?’ replied Jong-sup.

‘He was alone,’ said Pigeon.

‘Lucky him,’ said Jong-sup giving Pigeon another yank by the arm.

‘Say what you want but it’s Christmas.’

‘So what! you’re not Christian, this isn’t Rome and I’m not bothered,’ snapped Jong-sup.

‘So what? This is the perfect excuse to treat ourselves, eat well, get fat. What I’d give to be fat. Look, I know a place, a warehouse. I seen huge shipments of food coming off of boats. There is no way anyone is working there; not tonight,’ said Pigeon.

Jong-sup didn’t reply instantly but instead thought on it. It was true that they had hardly had any luxury food items and also true that this would probably be one in a handful of opportunities throughout the year to get in and out unseen.

‘How long will it take to get there?’ asked Jong-sup.

'Not much longer than where we're headin.' replied Pigeon.

'and you're sure that they'll have what we require?' asked Jong-sup.

'That and more my friend, that and more.'

Pigeon was not wrong when he said that it was not much further than their previous destination. They had passed it a little while back. Although he was tempted by his empty stomach and haunted by his false near-Death encounter to just call it quits, grab only the necessary supplies and head back to their alley. The determined look on Pigeon's face spurred him onwards.

Jong-sup could see cranes jutting out from the bank of the river Han. The neighbourhood surrounding the docks were rougher than his comparatively cushy alleyway. Graffiti tags decorated the walls and litter was in abundance, taxpayer money rarely visited this place. The few shady figures soon dissipated with the oncoming sounds of Jong-sup's and Pigeon's feet slapping the pavement as they rushed to their goal without pause.

'Are you sure that you can find the way back from here?' asked Jong-sup looking over his shoulder for potential threats.

'Of course I can, I is famous for bein able to find my way home no matter where I am. It's almost a fifth sense or somethin.'

'So that's why they call you Pigeon then,' said Jong-sup. Pigeon stopped dead in his tracks causing Jong-sup to bump into him.

'How do you mean?' inquired Pigeon curiously.

'Well, as you said. You can always find your way home,' replied Jong-sup.

'and?' asked Pigeon again.

'Pigeons, like homing pigeons,' said Jong-sup, but Pigeon's face remained contorted in a cartoonish expression of the very definition of lack of understanding. 'Pigeons can always find their way home you damn fool!'

'They can?' asked Pigeon seemingly amazed. 'Quite impressive for birds with such a small brain.'

‘I’m sure they say the same about you,’ said Jong-sup, giving Pigeon an incentivising push.

‘Just a strange coincidence I’m afraid,’ he said as he started again picking up speed ‘not far now.’

5

The dock yard was silent and poorly lit, perfect conditions for a light bit of thievery. Jong-sup and Pigeon were pressed up close to the surrounding wall, catching their breath before deciding their plan of action. Although the crate where he had awoken in agony a few months prior was located a couple of miles east of where they now stood, Jong-sup couldn't shake the feeling of unease that settled upon him being in such similar surroundings.

He pawed at his left side. The wound was completely healed, not even a scar remained. He wondered whether or not his kidney had grown back. He couldn't tell, there was a feeling of emptiness, but it was different than the emptiness that filled his entire being. Tired of longing to know more about how these things worked he decided to change the subject.

'Why do they call you Pigeon then?' asked Jong-sup.

'Wouldn't you like to know,' Pigeon said wryly.

'Fine, wish I'd never asked,' spat Jong-sup.

Pigeon's face twisted up in thought then unravelled as an idea entered his cluttered mind.

'How about this; that'll be your Christmas present from me,' said Pigeon with a sickeningly sweet smile.

'Keep your gift you fool, and you'll have nothing off me,' said Jong-sup, but his tone betrayed his harsh words.

'Suit yourself but after we get what in them crates, you'll be singin me hymns the rest of the day,' said Pigeon.

'What's in the crates anyway?' asked Jong-sup realising that he hadn't asked previously.

'All sorts of confectionery, Chinese mostly, some Japanese too though. Dried meats and wine from America I've seen come in before. I always wanted to grab a crate, but it's always been too busy, or no one has had been brave enough to come with me before.'

'What do you mean not brave enough? What kind of catastrophe are you attempting to pull me into?' asked Jong-sup.

'No, no, nothing at all. Just a bunch of cowards. Trust me, it'll be worth it,' replied Pigeon.

Jong-sup put his hands together to form a platform for Pigeon to place his foot. When Pigeon was in position, Jong-sup lifted with all his strength. Not all was needed though as Pigeon weighed about the same as a man half his size. He grabbed the top of the wall with outstretched arms and pulled himself up with surprising grace.

'Okay,' he called down to Jong-sup as quietly as he could manage. 'Now to find a way to get you up here.'

'How about I stay here and keep a look out?' proposed Jong-sup.

'Nonsense, we'll need two hands for this job,' replied Pigeon 'hang on, I have an idea.'

Then Pigeon adjusted himself so that he was on his knees carefully balancing, and did something that Jong-sup had not once seen him do before; he took off his coat. Jong-sup could immediately see why he weighed so little. Pigeon was extremely frail. He was wearing a thin vest that was once white and now a collage of different shades of yellow. He held one arm of the coat and hung it down towards Jong-sup who had to jump to reach the other arm. The moment he latched on to it he almost pulled Pigeon straight off of the wall, but he supported himself by leaning back over the other side. For such a lean man he was surprisingly strong. Then using every ounce of strength, he walked backwards down the wall, as if a professional cat burglar, hoisting Jong-sup up the other side as he went.

As Pigeon reached the ground Jong-sup reached the top of the wall. He could now see the vast compound stretching out before him. It was quiet but it wasn't empty. At the far end he could see figures stood at the entrance and he was sure there would be the odd patrol being conducted.

Below Pigeon outstretched his arms like a parent catching his child from a playground apparatus. Jong-sup accepted this invitation and he fell into the scrawny man in a heap on the floor. Jong-sup growled, untangled himself and dusted off.

'Thought you said this place was empty?' Jong-sup snapped.

'It is empty!' Pigeon defended 'Spare a few guards and a couple of dogs.'

'Dogs! Are you crazy man, you looking to get yourself killed?' said Jong-sup, pulling Pigeon by the collar of his disgusting vest.

'Relax, a couple of part time under paid workers will prove no bother,' said Pigeon.

'and the dogs?' interjected Jong-sup.

'Small and tied up, just used for intimidation,' explained Pigeon 'C'mon, aint much time till sunrise, let's get stealin (COUGH) I mean borrowin,' and with that he threw on his old battered coat and he sank into it like an extra layer of skin, and judging by the interior of the garment that wasn't completely inaccurate.

The place where they stood was completely shielded from potential onlookers by a wall of unmarked crates. Pigeon tapped his nose and began to peer round the corner. He pointed at the large foreboding warehouse in indication that it was their target. They braced to make a run for it but just as their muscles snapped into action a blinding light shone from around the corner. Luckily, they reacted quickly enough to stop themselves. Footsteps came into earshot and got louder but at a casual pace; their presence here was so far unknown. Jong-sup and Pigeon held their breath, silently praying that the security guard wouldn't decide to walk all the way to the surrounding wall and discover the unsightly pair.

It seemed that any gods (that neither of them believed in) were listening as the light disappeared when the guard turned down an aisle twenty-five meters from where they were stood. They didn't hesitate to take the opportunity and dashed for the next row of crates. Halting for a second to listen for footsteps, when none were heard they made their way to the next row over. They continued in this fashion weaving in and out of crates, pausing to listen intermediately.

Getting to the warehouse was quick and uneventful, there was barley a noise from the guards at the far end. The huge entrance to the warehouse was shut and sealed but the small door to the right of it was hanging slightly open. Pigeon cautiously stuck his head in the gap and had a look inside. He then squeezed through the gap and disappeared. Jong-sup didn't follow immediately but at the sound of an excited gasp from Pigeon he too squeezed through the gap.

The inside was dark and all too similar to the one Jong-sup had awoken in prior. Being here made him feel nauseous and the dull empty feeling where he hoped his kidney became more intense with every breath that he exhaled. He did not want to be here; he would have preferred to wait outside. As he turned to leave however, he was beckoned over to Pigeon who by the sounds of it had found something exciting. Curiosity clearly stronger than traumatic memories, he followed his ears that directed him to the dog-like panting of his crusty companion.

'We went lookin for food, but we found treasure!' yelped Pigeon.

'Keep your voice down you – genius!' said Jong-sup, spotting the prize of Pigeon's eyes. A single crate lay before them baring the insignia of Yamazaki and underneath were the words "Single malt".

'Have you had this before?' asked Pigeon licking his lips.

'Once, for my birthday a long time ago,' replied Jong-sup 'I'm more surprised by the fact that you knew what you had found.'

'I don't claim to know everythin but I know my whiskey!' Pigeon laughed 'I've never had this before though,' He licked his lips and clapped his hands.

They worked together to push off the lid of the crate and uncovered a layer of straw. Pushing the straw aside they saw the first delicately engraved beautifully decorated wooden box. Jong-sup lifted it out while Pigeon unravelled the bag from within his coat.

'Let's take it out of the box so that there's more room,' proposed Jong-sup.

'But it is so beautiful, it would be a waste to throw it away like rubbish,' wined Pigeon.

'You want to carry it all the way home?' asked Jong-sup.

'No but..' said Pigeon.

'But nothing, leave it,' said Jong-sup.

They took the bottles from the boxes and packed four into the bag. They were tempted to take more but thought they would save some room and have a look at what else this treasure trove had in store. It seemed they were in their very own cave of wonders as they browsed in glee. The sight of dried meats, whiskeys and chocolate filled their stomachs and warmed their throats with just the anticipation of tonight's feast.

Right at the back of the room were some unmarked containers. Jong-sup had a peek inside. Disappointment. It was filled with more dried squid; they had some already but this one had some kind of south Asian writing on it. Jong-sup picked out one packet to stuff into his bag but noticed something under it. A bright white gleamed from underneath the squid, so white that it was clearly visible even in this darkness.

'I know what that is?' gasped Pigeon appearing over his shoulder. 'That's cocaine that is. And good stuff by the looks of it!' Pigeon reached in to grab a bag, but his hand was swatted away by Jong-sup.

'Leave it!' he snapped 'We do not want to be getting involved with that! Who knows whose this is?'

'It's ours now is whose it is,' once again reaching in, quicker this time, out manoeuvring Jong-sup and earning himself a bag of the bright white drug.

'Pigeon!' yelled Jong-sup, his voice echoing throughout the warehouse.

'Keep it down you idiot!' hushed Pigeon.

‘Me the idiot, you’re the one who wants to steal from what is most likely a criminal organisation you bleeding fool!’

‘We’re thieves! We thieve things!’ yelled Pigeon his voice now competing with Jong-sup’s.

Jong-sup was about to defeat Pigeon in the ensuing octave battle but before his inhaled breath could be released the sound of the large door to the warehouse creaking partly open and the moonlight behind it cutting through the darkness killed it in his chest.

‘Who’s in here!’ came the voice of a silhouetted figure at the door. In an instant Jong-sup and Pigeon were silent and hidden. ‘Come on out! I heard you!’ bellowed the figure once again. ‘Right then,’ and with that the mysterious intruder disappeared and his feet could be heard as they slapped the ground, presumably heading for help.

‘We have to get out of here and quickly!’ said Jong-sup clutching Pigeon by the shoulder and pulling him to his feet roughly ‘Leave the cocaine!’ Jong-sup pulled the bag forcefully from Pigeon’s grasp, but he underestimated Pigeon’s grip and in a big cloud of white powder; the bag split in two.

‘Don’t breathe in!’ warned Jong-sup, but it was too late. The effect was instantaneous, it stung his eyes and his nostrils. His gums were numb, he felt them with his tongue, but he couldn’t be sure that he even had a tongue as numb as it was. He reached into his mouth to be sure, then looked over at Pigeon who must have been suffering the same fate, as his form mirrored Jong-sup’s. Although Jong-sup had seen many of his colleagues snort coke in many a toilet, he had never partook in the habit himself.

He had always been told it would help give him the confidence he lacked but that was not what he experienced. His fear had been intensified to sheer terror, an enormous overreaction for a man who cannot die. All senses were increased tenfold, he at least felt, that he could hear movement outside the walls and his tongue reacted to his every breath. His vision, which had been deteriorating over the years seemed sharper than he could ever remember. He spun Pigeon round by the shoulders roughly and looked at him for a moment. Pigeon was ugly, Jong-sup was already aware of that, but he never realised how ugly. His eyes scanned the creases in the professional tramp's face and the craters which covered most of his skin. He looked at his yellowed eyes that matched the teeth he had left. Although, for all this, he looked kind.

Jong-sup had always been too irritated by him that he never really noticed the aura of kindness that this decrepit man leaked from every pore. He stared in awe for what must have been only a few seconds and it calmed him, and the fear subsided. It was still present but had been pushed aside.

Only momentarily though, as a sound rung through the warehouse. Pigeon's ugly face became even uglier as it contorted in reaction. The sound came three more times before Jong-sup realised what it was. Barking.

Loud. Close. Louder. Closer.

There was barely enough time to react before three snarling hounds bounded through the entrance of the warehouse. The two thieves dropped what they were holding. All of today's takings, Pigeon even dropped the cocaine, survival instincts temporarily overriding greed.

The dogs sped down the right-hand aisle but their slippery prey ran down the left, circumventing the dogs and leaping through the door. Jong-sup and Pigeon slammed the door behind them, and Pigeon grabbed a chair and propped it making a makeshift, and flimsy, blockade. Jong-sup, knowing it would hardly slow the beasts down pulled Pigeon roughly by the arm and they disappeared around the corner.

Pigeon attempted to lean against a container for respite but was pulled on by the much wiser Jong-sup. He was trying to lead them to the wall where they had entered using only a vague sense of direction. He knew that it was the opposite end from where they had heard the guards earlier. All confrontation was to be avoided if possible.

'Are they really tryin to kill us? Sendin those damn hell hounds after us! For what?!' panted Pigeon between breaths.

'The kind of people their bosses are, it's probably us or them,' replied Jong-sup.

The noise of their pathetic blockade crashing into a shipping container and the door slamming open were followed by the patter of twelve feet and dread inspiring barking. The dogs were gaining on them quickly.

Jong-sup looked up at the height of the wall they had come in over. It was too high. It would take far too long for them both to scale it. One would be stranded while the other escaped. He could probably convince the simple-minded Pigeon to push him up and over first, he was definitely gullible enough.

The answer was simple; he couldn't do it. He did not know why.

'Quick Pigeon! There's no time, in here!' Jong-sup motioned to a bright green container. The hatch on the front was slightly ajar. He pulled it open, it was full of boxes of car parts leaving only enough space for one man to stand upright.

'It's no good!' cried Pigeon 'Let's try the next one!'

'No! Go on! Get in you fool!' shouted Jong-sup 'there's no time!'

'You would do that for me?' asked Pigeon, his voice quiet and cracked.

'Save your sentiment!' replied Jong-sup. With that he grabbed Pigeon intending to shove him into the crevice.

Pigeon though, pre-emptively swayed Jong-sup's arms and spun him round, leaving Pigeon at Jong-sup's back. Then, with force previously unseen by Jong-sup, Pigeon shoved him into the container, closed the door and lowered the bar to hold the doors in place. Right as the dogs came round the corner.

Momentary shock had silenced Jong-sup, but no more.

'Pigeon you stupid idiot!' screamed Jong-sup 'Let me out! You don't get it! I can't die!'

'and you won't have to, my friend,' said Pigeon his voice calm.

'No you idiot! I can't die! I can't die!' screamed Jong-sup summoning all the breath he could muster.

'Jong-sup, my real name, it's-'

The sentence was finished with a blood-curdling scream as the nearest dog, a Dobermann, jumped and bit down on Pigeon's neck, pulling him to the ground. Jong-sup used the little room he had to bash the container door with little avail. Now though, there was a gap big enough to see through, in time too to see the other two beasts bite into Pigeons flesh. One bit his leg while the other ripped through the flesh on the side of his stomach. Blood was gushing everywhere. Perhaps the loss of blood should have rendered Pigeon unconscious but still he screamed. His screams filled the streets of Seoul.

The awful wailing of his shabby companion granted Jong-sup strength despite his now slender and malnourished frame. He kicked open the door, fully revealing the pile of gore that, if he had not been such a stubborn man, he might have called friend. Pigeon was no longer screaming, he most likely lacked the strength, instead he whimpered. His leg was torn to pieces and part of the skin on his neck was missing. Worst of all some of his intestines lay on the ground and part of his entrails swung from the dog's mouth.

'Jong-sup,' whimpered Pigeon barely audible 'Help.'

Jong-sup roared at the dogs as ferocious as he could possibly muster. The dogs, to his surprise, stopped what they were doing, looked up at him, and with a whine they scampered off. He stood there in astonishment, until the spell was broken by the familiar icy chill he felt crawl up his spine. The dogs weren't reacting to him.

Jong sup spun around and sure enough, standing upon the container that had recently been his prison was Death herself.

'You stay away from him you bitch!' yelled Jong-sup at Death pointing an accusatory finger at her 'You are not taking him! So keep your hands off of him!'

Jong-sup turned his attention back to the wounded. From the look on Pigeon's face he was almost happy to see Jong-sup.

'Jong-sup are you alright?' asked Pigeon his voice quiet and cracked.

'Fancy you asking *me* that, you damn fool,' said Jong-sup, his voice unusually tender.

'I want to tell you my name before-' started Pigeon.

'You tell me when we get home, now save your energy,' he interrupted.

'I'm scared Jong-sup,' said Pigeon and he began to sob softly 'I don't have much time, my name is-'

Pigeon's eyes went dull and his skin a shade greyer. He was gone.

'No! Pigeon stay with me! Please! What was your name? What was your name? Tell me!'

A dark shadow passed over Jong-sup, he didn't need to be told who it was. He knew.

'Bring him back! Please!' he couldn't believe what he was doing. He was not a man who begs and surely not for the life of a scoundrel. It seemed even Death was surprised by this uncharacteristic outburst. There was no face beneath the hood on which to form an expression, but Jong-sup could somehow feel that Death was taken aback. She stood there silently for a few seconds.

'Please, bring him back, please,' Jong-sup pleaded, he was disgusted with himself, but he felt that he had no control. He dropped to his knees. Death's cloak swayed gently in front of him, degrading himself even further he reached out to grab it. He had never touched Death before. He half-expected his hand to phase through but he grasped the very-real fabric. It was a material of which he had never felt. It looked rough and tattered but felt like the softest silk imaginable. Just the touch of Death's cloak gave him a feeling of ecstasy. It reverberated through his body down to his toes and back up finally settling in his hands. It was too much to bear and quickly turned into searing pain. His hands froze, and then they burst into bloody chunks. Death drifted past him as he gaped at his gored stumps too astonished to make a sound. In a matter of seconds skin stretched over the wound and five little fingers no bigger than a new-born poked through. They were fully grown in less than a minute and no longer brought him pain.

Turning round to see where Death had gone and pushing himself up on his newly formed hands, he saw her standing over Pigeon. Jong-sup scampered over.

'Take me instead!' he begged reaching out to touch her but then withdrawing his hand not wishing to relive that experience.

No

'Why?' asked Jong-sup. Death gave no answer, she proceeded to crouch. Her hand slipped out from her baggy cloak and once again it was no longer skeletal but youthful and feminine. She grabbed Pigeon by the limp hand and pulled him into a standing position. For a moment Jong-sup thought Death had granted his wish and brought him back to life but looking to the ground Pigeon still lay there a dead mess of gore. Death had pulled Pigeon out of his body.

'Pigeon!' called out Jong-sup 'I'm sorry.'

Pigeon, it seemed, couldn't hear him. He gazed up at Death, his jaw agape stupidly. There was no look of horror upon his face though instead he looked, well, better than Jong-sup had ever seen.

At that point a surprising emotion flooded Jong-sup. Jealousy. It was him who longed for death, so why would a nobody like Pigeon be gifted sweet release while he be left here alone.

A glow emanated from Death and Pigeon, soft at first but then fierce. Jong-sup knew where this lead, she would take him to wherever or whatever happened next, if anything at all. Perhaps, he could follow them. He saw his opportunity and he took it, as was his way. Jong-sup lunged at Pigeon aiming for his arm. Before even slight contact he was blinded by the light and felt weightless and spinning.

Sight slowly returning to him he was immediately confused by what he could make out. Whether this was heaven or hell, it was disappointing as it all seemed too familiar. Giant structures of light spun round and round. Then it struck him. The blast had not carried him to another plane but catapulted him high over the buildings of Seoul. Then he was struck again.

This time by the ground.

분노

Part Six

Anger

1

The earth spun. Maybe it was the sweltering summer heat, maybe it was the bottle of soju, it was probably both. Another summer and winter had passed since Pigeon was torn apart by viscous dogs and although Jong-sup had long given up trying to die, he had certainly aged. His hair had grown past his shoulders with thick streaks of grey and a lengthy but wispy beard hung from his chin. He had always struggled to grow a moustache even now.

He sat on a street corner of the Dongdae-mun area of Seoul with a handkerchief on the floor in front of him. Pride had long since left him. Like a lot of the homeless in Seoul when he had first started his life on the streets he had kept himself hidden away, living off of scraps. Now though, begging was no longer beneath him. He couldn't actually conceive of anything that *was* now beneath him. Maybe worms? No, even worms were useful to a fisherman. Jong-sup was of no use to anyone.

He looked at his handkerchief, it had been a slow day. Barely enough money to buy another bottle of soju. He glanced up at the sea of faces that stomped past, most didn't notice him and those that did looked down their nose in disgust. When Jong-sup was a young lad, the war had left many Korean men and women without home nor food. He would look at them with sympathy not disdain. People had forgotten the struggles of the past; they lived a life of plenty, not scarcity and they were content to live in the present. The fact that Jong-sup had also hardened to the less fortunate in society went over his head; he was an expert at analysing all but within.

Deciding to give up and get up from the simmering pavement, he began to collect the coins from his handkerchief when a shadow was cast over him.

'Here you go, sir,' said a soft, sweet and all too familiar voice. Jong-sup's heart thumped loudly. He glanced up then instantly back to the ground. Could it be her? He risked another look. There was no doubt about it, though she had grown, there was no mistaking Mi-na. The last time he saw her she was wailing about not being allowed to his funeral. Her crying still rung in his ears and he was filled with shame.

She placed a lunch box in front of him. He waved his hand over his head to gesture that it wasn't necessary.

'It's fine, you need a proper meal,' said Mi-na rummaging through her backpack for something and pulling out a bottle of water 'This too.'

'Mi-na get away from him right now!' came a voice from an older woman. Jong-sup brushed his fringe in front of his eyes and peered up through the hair. He was terrified she would recognise him, and although she looked right at him without a hint of disgust, she didn't seem to. From Mi-na's face shone a beautiful smile, not an ounce of pity from her but an air of understanding. She bade him a low respectful bow and ran off to join what must have been her school mates as they were all wearing matching uniforms. Mi-na seemed to be getting chastised by the older lady who ushered her away, but it didn't seem to faze her and she smiled once again at Jong-sup before disappearing round the corner.

Something welled up inside him. An immense feeling of loss. His old life was long gone. His old apartment along with his accumulated material possessions. His job which although it would leave a bad taste in his mouth to admit, gave him a routine to follow, and of course the annoying young girl who lived next door. It wasn't as though his life had been ripped away from him but almost like he had been ripped from his life. Everything seemed to carry on without him, KSI still continued to operate and Mi-na continued to grow older and this fact somehow made him feel more worthless than before.

How long had it been? He wondered. Time was utterly lost on him with no way to measure it. Mi-na looked years older, though he knew that young girls grew quickly. He wasn't sure why, but he felt compelled to see her; perhaps just to look upon the last remnants of his old life. Putting the lunch and the water in his bag he scraped himself up from the floor and hurried to catch up with the troop of school children.

Peering round the corner proved fruitless; they were gone. Panic struck and his longing intensified. He ran in the direction they were heading, the crowds parting to let the dirty, putrid smelling man through. Some practically leapt out of the way as if poverty were an infectious disease. He did not care, if anything he was grateful in this moment for the advantage his odour brought him.

He crossed two intersections before he found them, he skidded to a halt and turned to face the opposite way in an awkward attempt to blend in with his surroundings. After checking that he had not caused a commotion he turned to stare at his old neighbour. The older lady must have been their teacher as she was the only adult amongst the relatively small group of about twenty girls and boys.

The teacher seemed to be giving a lecture on a large and old structure in front of them. From listening in Jong-sup learned that this was in fact the old west gate into Seoul from which the district was named. The children were listening intently, all accept Mi-na who was looking the opposite direction watching a bird in a tree. She gazed in that familiar glassy-eyed way that Jong-sup knew so well. She looked happy and healthy and Jong-sup felt a flood of relief for a concern he was not aware that he held. Watching Mi-na watching a bird, brought tears to Jong-sup's wrinkled eyes.

Convincing himself that he was only tearing up because of the wind and pollution he turned to leave; secretly satisfied that Mi-na was doing well. Before he left however, he noticed something odd. He was not the only person watching her.

The man, who from his tank top and shaved head was obviously bad news, was talking on his mobile and looking directly at Mi-na. It was the look on the man's face that scared him most, feral, like a wolf closing in on its prey. Jong-sup was filled with violent urges, he couldn't be sure of the man's ill intent but somehow, he knew.

Frantically he whirled round to see if there was anyone he could inform, anyone that would take him seriously. The inhabitants of Seoul often didn't take well to strangers approaching them out of the blue, let alone in the shambled state of Jong-sup. No, it would do no good, if anything he would be a repellent against any would be do-gooders.

His focus returned to the mysterious villain, but his eyes landed on empty space. He was gone. So were the children.

'Shit!' he expelled loudly, causing several people nearby to scamper. He scanned the crowds for a shaved head and found what he was looking for. The man was heading off down the street and not far in front, sure enough was the troupe of school children, their teacher and Mi-na, who was lagging behind the rest walking at her leisurely pace.

The group crossed a road and then passed an alley. Jong-sup kept the shaved man in his sights but then he did the unexpected; he took a turn. Jong-sup paused and wrestled with his plan of action. Should he pursue the shaved man or follow Mi-na's class to make sure she fairs okay. The decision was made for him though. As Mi-na was passing the ally she disappeared. If Jong-sup did still have his heart, it sunk. He reacted immediately, running into the road to avoid people potentially getting in his way. Cars beeped their horns, but Jong-sup paid them no mind; his mind was taken.

Rage fuelled his muscles and in a matter of seconds Jong-sup too was in the ally. A man had Mi-na restrained from behind, one hand holding her arms and another by the collar. Mi-na had a sack over her head and there were muffled screams coming from within. Her captor was too preoccupied with keeping her still to notice Jong-sup. He wasn't the man with the shaved head and from what Jong-sup could tell he was south Asian, though he was speaking in Korean.

'Get away from her!' roared Jong-sup, his voice possessed a strength that his body couldn't back up. Still restraining Mi-na's arms with one hand he used his free hand to pull a switch blade from his pocket. He didn't say a word he just cackled at Jong-sup. The fact that he had not tried to leave with Mi-na told Jong-sup that he was waiting for someone. There wasn't much time.

He flung himself into the man with all his weight. The blade dug into Jong-sup's chest just as he had planned. The pain tore through him but he wrapped his arms around the kidnapper as tight as he could manage and they fell in a bundle onto the ground. Unfortunately, Mi-na was also pulled to the floor but the shock of the recklessness of this tramp had released the kidnappers grip. Mi-na pulled the sack up and off her head. She saw the two men in a heap on the ground, blood pouring from one of them. She recognised the homeless man she had given her lunch to and the look in her eyes said that she knew that he had come to help her. She didn't want to leave him in danger, but he turned his head towards her and screamed.

'Run you idiot!' as he did so dark blood gushed from his mouth. Mi-na did as she was told and ran from the ally into the street where her class would hopefully still be. Jong-sup felt relieved regardless of the four inches of steel lodged between his ribs. The kidnapper managed to roll Jong-sup off him, got up and made to run after Mi-na, but stopped realising it was too late. He turned to face Jong-sup who had also managed to get back on his feet.

'You just made a huge mistake!' he yelled at Jong-sup, who seemed rather pleased with himself even though the front of his tattered clothes were now soaked a dark red.

'Don't you dare talk to me, you sick pervert!' roared Jong-sup and for the first time in a long time he didn't feel like the smallest and most worthless person around.

'Pervert?' said the kidnapper to himself, 'You don't know what you are getting yourself into old man.'

'I know your type, big tough guy likes to prey on the vulnerable!' said Jong-sup, his voice weaker most likely from the blood loss. 'Well not to-'

Cutting off his sentence was the feeling of Jong-sup's skull splitting right at the top in the middle. His legs gave way and his arms seemed unable to come to his aid and he toppled to the ground in a rag doll fashion. It seemed only his eyes were working as he lie there face up. He could see the kidnapper stood where he was, wearing the same facial expression that Jong-sup would be making if he could move his face. Then the shaved headed man stepped over him holding a plank of wood. He must have sneaked up behind Jong-sup while he was distracted.

'Where the fuck have you been?' yelled the kidnapper at the new arrival.

'You better save that attitude of yours for the boss, he'll want to know where the girl is.'

'It wasn't my fault, if you weren't so long I-'

'I was directing the van!' yelled the shaved head man. 'and if your excuse is that you were overpowered by a little girl and an old man you got trouble coming your way.'

'That guy is crazy, man, crazy,' said the kidnapper.

'The van is here now, let's get going,' said the shaved headed man.

'What about him?' asked the Kidnapper.

'The tramp? He's dead or just about, he aint telling nobody,' spat the shaved headed man, literally, onto Jong-sup's face 'we aint got time to finish the job at the rate he's bleeding anyway he's got minutes at the most, now get in the van!'

The kidnapper followed his orders and they ran through to the opposite exit that had Mi-na fled, much to Jong-sup's relief. Still unable to move even his eyes from the peripheral of his vision the dark shadow of Death crossed his way, apparently uninterested in him she made her way after the thugs. After a minute she was gone, he could tell because the ringing in his teeth subsided. Not only that but he began to get some feeling in his extremities. Within minutes he managed to wobble to his feet with the help of the nearby wall. He could feel that something was hanging over his ears, examining the top of his head he found that his scalp had fallen to either side exposing his bare skull to the world. He didn't panic, this wasn't the first time his head had been split open nor, he was afraid, would it be the last. He pulled himself together holding a hand to each side and trusting his healing abilities that his miraculously cursed body would grant him.

A siren sounded a few roads away. This *did* panic him, and he ran from the ally, through frightened crowds of strangers and into the building-scape of the city. He knew the lower street level better than most now and was confident that he could disappear once Seoul had swallowed him up.

2

Just three days later, nestled behind the wall that encircled the Rotte World theme park in a bed of leaves and in the shade of the trees was Jong-sup. The air was filled with excited screams and laughter, and every so often the woosh of the roller-coaster. Noise didn't seem to disturb the slumbering man though as if it wasn't for the gentle and infrequent rising and falling of his chest, he appeared dead. He had discovered this area yesterday and was rather pleased with himself. The small grove of trees reminded him of when he was young, and Seoul was far from the concrete jungle it was today. After his run in with Mi-na he wished to be away from the prying eyes of the city for the event it seemed had garnered quite a bit of attention. This place seemed like an oasis in the desert even with the constant, irritating noise of cheer.

Fate it seemed did not like the idea of Jong-sup's moment of respite and a sudden gust of wind blew through the trees. The wind would prove ineffective at waking him though, as he was quite snug in his bed of leaves. The wind was not finished with him just yet and on its breath blew in a piece of paper which settled nicely over Jong-sup's mouth and nose. There were a couple of deep attempts at inhaling, then a loud splutter and cough as the dead looking man sat up straight; rising like a zombie from the grave. He peered sleepily at his surroundings, his face the picture of irritation, for the first time in a long time his dreams hadn't been horrific. Just mildly unpleasant. Spying the bothersome rag that had awoken him he snatched it up from the ground beside him and stretched it out. It was a page from a newspaper.

SEARCH CONTINUES FOR HOMELESS MAN WHO SAVED MAYOR'S DAUGHTER

Would they never let up? Jong-sup thought. Surely if someone had not exposed themselves by now, they wanted to maintain their privacy. They didn't care though, not about him, not about the girl. A story is the only thing that they had feelings for. Story=money. He tore up the paper into an unnecessary number of smaller pieces.

'If I had known it would have caused such hassle, I would have let them take the damn girl!' he said to the surrounding foliage, though it seemed by the sinking feeling, that his stomach disagreed. He felt shame at this, mainly because he was not sure if his head or his stomach was right, or which was a harder pill to swallow. Jong-sup sat there for a good few hours, wallowing and feeling sorry for himself. Such an identity crisis had never plagued him before, and he despised being unsure of himself.

A soft pattering sound drew him out of his sunken state. He looked around at his feet and sure enough he saw droplets of blood dotting the ground and then disappearing a moment after landing. Raising his head backwards spread a rare smile across his face, which he suppressed quickly. Mr Lee hovered in the air in front of him, his lower intestine swinging freely. The picture was still grotesque, but Jong-sup felt relief at seeing him as he hadn't for over a year. He had kept the brick from Mr Lee's old shop all this time.

'Finally decided to show your face then,' said Jong-sup though it seemed that Mr Lee did not hear him as he hung there looking past Jong-sup with his mouth open, 'Hey!'

'Oh, I'm sorry boy,' said Mr Lee 'I was gone for a moment then.'

'Gone where?' said Jong-sup in a huff.

'I don't know, not really. It's all confusing, all this afterlife stuff. Sometimes it feels as though I'm still alive and running my shop as usual.'

Jong-sup had seen this before, sometimes Mr Lee looked as though he couldn't see him at all and sometimes, he would talk to him as if he was still a schoolboy visiting to buy some sweets.

'I haven't seen you in a while, is that right?' asked Mr Lee.

'Uh-huh,' replied Jong-sup in his best attempt at seeming nonchalant.

'I didn't realise until I was sweeping the floor and a newspaper blew in. I read the date and was shocked. Did you hear a homeless man fought off some kidnappers?'

'Do people just throw newspapers on the street! Have they never heard of bins!' raged Jong-sup feeling paranoid that the papers were out to get him.

'Calm down young man!' said Mr Lee 'Although I agree that society is in a sorry state if people are littering all over their homeland, and just after we've rebuilt it too. People are spoiled, they don't understand the hardships of the past, what our people went through, and so they don't respect it. That is why news like this hero-beggar is a sweet sound to dead ears. Maybe there is hope after all.' he looked at Jong-sup in way that said he knew more than he let on.

'He probably wanted the reward money.'

'Do you have to be so negative?' asked Mr Lee 'Is your mind really as bleak as your tongue?'

'Yes, and my eyes too, because I've seen humanity for what it really is,' he spat in reply.

'Not everyone is like you Park Jong-sup,' coming from Mr Lee this hurt, maybe it was because he always thought of him fondly as a boy. Perhaps it was also that he so rarely called him by name and it cemented what he said.

'No, they're worse!' snapped Jong-sup pulling up his shirt 'They stole my fucking kidney! Probably would've had the rest of me if I hadn't woken up so quickly!' no scar was there to see but not all scars are visible.

'They would have been disappointed when they opened your chest and found it empty!' said Mr Lee his voice raised for the first time as long as Jong-sup had known him. It quieted him, he pulled his shirt down and rolled over to face the wall.

'Is that why you're here?' said Jong-sup his voice no more than a whimper 'I'm not low enough already?'

'No.' replied Mr Lee. 'I'm just so disappointed. You had a spark in you when you were a boy.'

'Let's not talk of the past,' pleaded Jong-sup.

'No, we are. What happened to you, from the last I saw you while I still had breath till now. What went wrong? You could have been someone.'

'I was someone!' yelled Jong-sup finding his fire again and sitting up to face Mr Lee 'I made it. I had money. I pulled myself out of the gutter and focused on my career.'

'but were you happy?' asked Mr Lee.

'What kind of question is that?!'

'Were you happy?' repeated Mr Lee.

'No one is happy!' yelled Jong-sup. 'Happiness is a facial expression that people make. It's a lie!'

'You don't believe that,' said Mr Lee calmly, and he didn't, not really but lately he had wondered if it were true.

'Think back. Can you not remember a time when you have been happy? Have you been in love?' asked Mr Lee.

'I thought so once, I was wrong. I thought she loved me; I couldn't have been more wrong.'

'How can you be so sure?'

'Her tongue down an American's throat was a giveaway!'

Mr Lee was lost for words. 'I, uh, I didn't'

'She got what was coming to her in the end,' said Jong-sup but his temper had settled and the conviction in his voice was no longer there. His head dropped between his knees.

'I didn't come here to fight. I came here to ask you a favour,' said Mr Lee.

Jong-sup was in no mood to be granting anyone favours but it intrigued him all the same. He sat there in silence for more than five minutes before nodding his head.

'You've probably noticed from my absence that I appear to be losing myself. It's hard to explain but I feel I don't have long left.'

'You're dead, you have all the time in the world.'

'You'd think so. Sometimes though, I swear I'm still alive. I think I'm waiting for my wife to come help me close-up the shop. It's like a dream though, or a memory. I'm not sure but the longer I stay in that state the more of me I feel leaving.'

'What do you mean?' asked Jong-sup.

'Like I have a sell-by date. Like parts are rotting and falling off,' Mr Lee caught Jong-sup looking where his guts hung from his body, 'No, not like my midriff. My essence. I know I sound stupid.'

'Maybe you're just moving on,' suggested Jong-sup.

'No, I don't think so. I feel like I should be. Maybe this was my chance to move on. Maybe I was supposed to finish some business like they say. Whatever the case I think my time for reconciliation is running out. I don't know what awaits on the other side, but I'd rather take my chances than just cease to exist.'

Jong-sup thought on this for a while.

'So, what can I do about it?' asked Jong-sup in a huff.

'I was wondering if you could contact Death. I want him to help me. I think whatever it was that I had to do has-'

'No!' the mention of Death had flared up his temper again. 'Why would I call her? You know what she did to me!'

'But I-'

'Even if I called, it doesn't mean she would come. She only comes when she wants to watch me suffer.'

'Please Jong-sup.'

'Why are you in such a rush to leave anyway?' snapped Jong-sup 'I haven't seen you in ages and now you turn up just to tell me you want to leave!'

'Haven't you listened to a-'

'and not just that,' Jong-sup interrupted 'You want me to contact the thing that's put me in this position!' he felt betrayed. 'You don't have to make any stupid bullshit excuses if you want to leave!' Jong-sup reached into his bag and found Mr Lee's brick. 'If you want to leave then just leave!' He launched the brick as far as he could using the last of the little energy he had left. As soon as it left his fingers a deep regret consumed him. It was too late though. The brick soared through the air, between the trees and cleared the far wall.

'Oh no,' Jong-sup said to himself. Even with the sound of the roller-coaster whizzing overhead, it already seemed quieter than before.

He ran in the direction of the brick, scurried over the far wall and landed in an empty car park. He looked around frantically until his eyes settled on the reddish dust that splayed across the concrete. Apart from a few bigger chunks the brick had completely crumbled upon impact. It was an incredibly old brick. Made in a time after the war when the country was rebuilding, and things were made quickly and cheaply.

Jong-sup dropped to his knees and began to gather the little that remained and try to squeeze it all back together.

'Mr Lee!' he called out 'Mr Lee!' but no reply came. He had thought that he could not feel any more alone. He was wrong.

3

Jong-sup stayed in his bed of leaves and self-pity for another four days before his hunger forced him out to look or beg for food. It was early morning and the summer's sun was out in full force. Apart from the odd street cleaner, the only people that were around was the occasional businessman lying in their pricey suits on the ground, still drunk from the night before. He guessed it must be a Saturday or Sunday. He stared at one of the supposed "gentlemen" for a while, the man didn't stir at all, he was completely out of it. Jong-sup wondered if he had spent all his cash on last night's antics or if he had some left over. It wasn't worth it, if the man awoke Jong-sup doubted he could fend him off even in his hungover state. Plus, he wasn't that old, so he most likely uses a credit card most of the time and it would surely raise some questions if a man in Jong-sup's state walked into a shop with a credit card. Jong-sup preferred cash anyway, always had. Cash was freedom, freedom from snoopy bankers looking over your shoulder checking what you're spending. His way of thinking was becoming increasingly rare though.

Jong-sup trudged on reluctantly, looking for any leftover food. He spied an empty can of beer, the cheap kind, the kind people buy before they go to the bar so they can get a buzz without emptying their accounts. He scooped it off the floor gave it a little shake, there was weight to it, good. He tipped his head back, raised the can in the air, and then choked and gagged and spluttered it all on to the pavement. Someone had obviously been using the can as an ash tray. He threw the can against the wall and shouted obscenities forgetting momentarily his wish to keep low-profile.

'Will you keep it down!' came a voice from a stairwell to his right. He poked his head round to see whom had spoken to him so rudely. He was surprised to see a woman. A young woman. Wearing a puke ridden suit and lying on one of the stairs holding her head. Jong-sup attempted to retaliate but couldn't bring himself to. Such a young woman behaving in such an inappropriate manner. He was lost for words. He had drunk with his female colleagues before, something which took him a long time to fully accept, but never had he seen such outrageousness. Sure, men have been doing it for a long time, and it was not exactly "becoming behaviour" but to see a woman do the same was somehow worse. He could not explain why. It just was.

A sweet scent found Jong-sup's nostrils and pulled his mind from the muddy pit of outrage. It was as if the smell physically turned his head; the way he spun on his axis. Across the street a bakery had just opened its doors ready for the morning crowd. Fresh breads and pastries were visible, and the sight caused a pang in Jong-sup's stomach. He must have crossed the street somehow because he found himself right outside the entrance gazing in open-mouthed. It had been too long before he had tasted bread that wasn't stale, or mould ridden. A young woman behind the counter at the back eyed him suspiciously. Jong-sup took that as his cue to leave. He had not gone ten meters though, before he began to hesitate. Hopelessly he began to rummage around his pockets for change that he may have "magically" forgotten about.

Hunger trumps sense it seemed as he crept back to the entrance. The woman was now busy with some unknown chore beneath the till. An opportunity this good was all Jong-sup needed to convince him of his intent. He scurried in being much louder than he thought, grabbed a loaf of white bread and turned to flee just in time for the young woman to see him and scream for help. He ran. Fast, especially for his age and frail frame. He chanced a look over his shoulder, half expecting the woman to come after him. Worse, a man wearing identical uniform sprinted out the shop at full speed.

All the energy seemed to drain from him. His pursuer was a foot higher than he was and positively athletic. Jong-sup turned on his heels, held out the bread and screwed his face up in anticipation of the on-coming beating. But none came. He held his eyes closed just in case. What was going on? Could he now turn invisible and the man just ran past him?

'It's okay, sir,' came a voice. Jong-sup slowly opened his eyes and looked up at the man of no more than twenty-four.

'What do you mean?' asked Jong-sup.

'I think it'd be a good idea if you didn't come to the bakery again, sir,' said the man without an ounce of threat but a hint of kindness.

'No,' said Jong-sup looking down in shame.

'Look, we can't sell the bread now anyway. How about you keep it and I tell my boss you got away?' said the man. Jong-sup couldn't bring himself to reply, he knew the young man was trying to be kind, but it made him feel lowly. It almost wasn't worth the bread.

'If you try this again, I'm sorry but we'll have to get the police involved,' said the man. In reply Jong-sup shook his head and nodded simultaneously making himself look rather deranged.

'If you need food, I've heard there is a new religious group handing out food on Sundays to people who've landed on hard times near Children's Grand Park. You know where that is?' asked the man. Jong-sup nodded in reply, then without expressing his gratitude he ran from the scene taking care not to look back and wiping tears from his eyes.

Sunday came quickly, Jong-sup was thankful for that as he had not had a meal since the stolen bread. Knowing that he would be eating again so soon meant that the urge to scavenge or beg had subsided. His one concern was having to deal with some preachy religious nut-jobs in order to get the food. There was very little hope of converting him, he knew much more about the afterlife than they did.

From time to time he would hear of a government funded project to feed the poor, often coming with the requirement of registering or some nonsense. That definitely wouldn't do. Jong-sup's need to hide his identity surpassed even his need for nourishment. Hopefully these do-gooders worked on a need to know business, just as long as it satisfied their insatiable lust to "be a good person", or at least appear so.

There were few places more awful than Children's Grand Park in Jong-sup's estimation. The large square was home to a few playgrounds and an open-air zoo that was pleasing to the eye but painful on the ears. Nasty, rotten and spoiled children giggled and screamed. Young men guffawed, exaggerating the humour of their dates. The young women did the same but in a much higher, more annoying, pitch. It was all so sickeningly gleeful.

Luckily, he wouldn't have to venture into the manic torture park, as he spied the group of religious volunteers at the back on an adjoining street. He should have realised that there was no way they'd get permission to bring a load of bums into the actual park. No matter how good a cause.

Approaching cautiously, he noted that there was long line already. Word had definitely gotten far. Maybe he should have come earlier, he cursed himself, all the good stuff was probably gone. He walked about halfway down the line and pushed his way in, much to the protest of his fellow hungry men. He turned his head halfway and growled and they soon simmered down. The prospect of a fight wasn't worth being banished from the line. Still, there continued a whisper of resentment; not that Jong-sup noticed or even cared.

Ten long, agonising minutes later he was next in line and his stomach practically leapt in anticipation. There were two tables, one serving Budae Jjigae in a big metal cooking pot. It brought back memories of Jong-sup's brief military service, he had hated the dish then and had to practically choke it down. Right at this moment however, it was the best smell he had ever had the pleasure to come into contact with.

Behind each table were two rosy-cheeked, wide-eyed and naive looking volunteers. Just looking into their eyes told how proud of themselves they were that they were not completely disgusted by the homeless. This wasn't for the needy. It was for them, to signal their virtue across their social circles.

'Excuse me sir?' said a pretty young lady in her early twenties 'Would you like to take a picture with us?'

'Fuck off!' barked Jong-sup. She was visibly frightened, but she kept her cool, bowed and left his sight. Jong-sup was handed a Styrofoam container and a large, acne ridden boy dipped a ladle into the cooking pot and spooned some Budae Jjigae for Jong-sup spilling a large portion of it on his hand.

'Sorry, Sir,' said the spotty youth with no apology in his voice or on his greasy face. Jong-sup didn't flinch, he felt the burn but the joy at having these young virtue-signallers show their true colours was all the balm he needed.

The next table handed him a slice of bread, although he had seen the guy in front had been given three. They didn't even offer him any Kimchi but he stuck his hand in the bowl regardless and scooped a handful into his container. It wasn't much, but with the size of his stomach it would fill him up nicely.

Two minutes down the road Jong-sup strolled, taking large bites from his bread after dipping it in the container and he felt content. Then nervous. He had grown suspicious of contentment.

It never seemed to last.

He looked back at the line of homeless men. Jong-sup choked on his bread. It lodged in his throat and he gasped for air. Death stood at the front of the queue, as if waiting for her free food. None of the people around reacted to her presence. She hovered there with her scythe in hand. Jong-sup pounded on his chest desperate to swallow the morsel so he could ask her what the hell she wants now.

Before any dislodging took place, a white van stopped abruptly next to him and two men jumped out. Their tattoos told that they were low level gangsters. They grabbed him either side under the arm and threw him into the back of the vehicle. It all happened so quickly. Jong-sup had no time to even resist and the food blocking his airways prevented him from drawing any attention.

The men returned to their seats in the front and sped off so quickly that in the back Jong-sup rolled over twice. At last, his pipes were clear and he used them. Unfortunately, his screams were drowned out by the sound of children's laughter.

4

His surroundings were so dark, that the dazed and confused Jong-sup couldn't initially tell if his eyes were open or not. He realised that he had his mouth hanging open for some time when his dry crusted lips smacked into each other. How long had he been out? Thirty minutes? Three days? It was impossible to know by listening to his body; it ached and pained but that was no change anyway. He was however, getting real tired of being knocked unconscious.

He waited for his eyes to adjust but they wouldn't. He couldn't make out any shapes at all. He could just about tell that he was sat up in a metal chair with his arms on the rests. He was relatively calm considering his circumstance. That was until he realised he couldn't move his arms or his legs. Movement was often the last thing to return to him when he'd had some head trauma, but this was different. He could move his fingers and wiggle his toes. He was tied to the chair.

Jong-sup screamed. In rage and in fear. Struggling made no difference. He tried to rock his chair back and forth, but it must have been bolted to the ground. He screamed again. In fear and in desperation.

Before he could inhale to scream any further a chink of light cut through the darkness. The shape of a door was highlighted and a window in the top panel revealed itself and cast shadows around the room.

'Quiet down in there!' came a voice. Jong-sup listened for a second to see if he could recognise it. It was definitely male.

'What's going on here!' called out Jong-sup, he could hear the shaking fear in his own voice.

'Mr Park, don't make me come in there!' came the mysterious voice once again 'Only kidding, I'm coming in anyway,' there was a light hearted tone when he spoke.

He stepped into the room ducking under the doorway as he did so. He was tall and thin and although his face wasn't distinguishable in the darkness, it was his shabby green cardigan that gave him away.

'You!' gasped Jong-sup, shock preventing him from stringing together a full sentence.

'It's been a while old friend,' said the man as he switched on the light; a single bulb hanging from the ceiling. It was enough to burn Jong-sup's eyes regardless.

'Get me out of this you sick bastard!' yelled Jong-sup 'Have you not taken enough from me?!'

'I'm not sure, that's what we're here to see,' said the man nonchalantly 'now, you may want to be quiet and save some energy. I have a feeling you'll need it.'

'Is this some kind of joke to you?' asked Jong-sup.

'Look, I can't stay long I'm afraid,' said the man, 'I have a gathering to attend, I wish you could come but I can see you're all tied up.'

'You've had your fun, now let me go!'

'No, Park Jong-sup. The night is still young, and the fun is just beginning,' smiled the man 'Now, I spent a lot of money getting you here, so you owe me something. A present. And I know just what I want,' the man pulled out a pair of pruners and reached out to grab Jong-sup's hand. Jong-sup balled up his hand in a fist in defence.

'What are you doing! Stop!' screamed Jong-sup. Fire burned in the man's eyes behind his glasses and he drove the pruners into Jong-sup's hand. Some blood spurted out hitting the man's cheeks. Jong-sup's fingers splayed out and the man wasted no time in taking the opportunity to grab one of them. He put the blades either side of the appendage and with a loud crunch he cut it off.

Jong-sup's ears popped with the sound of his own screams.

'I have to go. I'll see you tomorrow!' yelled the man over the howls of pain and he slipped the pruners and the finger into his pocket.

Jong-sup didn't see him leave. He was too focused on the blood gushing from where his index finger used to be.

The man didn't come by the next day like he said he would. In fact, he didn't come back for three days. It was difficult for Jong-sup to tell the passage of time in this empty room with bricked up windows, but he had an idea how long he'd been sat there.

Once the blood had stopped running from his finger it wasn't long before the tip of a new one started to emerge from the wound. Jong-sup knew his ability to heal was incredible, but he had never had the chance to witness it this intimately. So, for the last couple of days he had passed the time watching his finger grow like bamboo. He now had almost three quarters of a full finger and the skin was pale, fresh, and sensitive to the touch.

Between watching the progress of his finger and looking around the room mindlessly, Jong-sup called for help. Sometimes for hours at a time. Nobody came. There wasn't so much as a noise in the building. It was impossible to know if he was on the ground floor or fifty floors up. He guessed from the windows, even if they were bricked up, that he wasn't underground.

Jong-sup was starting to think the wait was worse than actually facing the psychopath. That was, until he finally opened the door and walked into the room. Jong-sup immediately regretted his thoughts and wished he could go back to sitting alone watching his finger grow.

Without saying a word, the man came close and sniffed Jong-sup. It seemed to give him a kick as a wide smile spread over his face. In return Jong-sup could smell him. He stank. His green cardigan must have never been washed and it smelled like he used it to wipe his ass.

The man's face neared closer to him and Jong-sup knew an opportunity when he saw one. He leaned his head right back and swung it forward into the man's cheekbone. The man was able to pull away quickly though, so it barely did any damage at all.

'That was unnecessary! Do you know how long it took me to find you? And you repay me in this manner?' said the man. He pulled his hand back and slapped Jong-sup hard in the face. Jong-sup didn't make a sound.

'How did you find me?' asked Jong-sup once recovered 'How do you keep finding me?'

'Well, I am a private investigator you know,' said the man proudly 'You though, have proven particularly slippery lately.'

'What do you want from me?' asked Jong-sup.

'All that you are,' replied the man.

'What the hell is that supposed to mean?' asked Jong-sup desperately. The man didn't reply for a time.

'Watching you jump off a building, hit the ground and then walk away turned out to be the defining moment of my life!' yelled the man.

'Why?! I can't give you anything more! I have nothing! I have no value! You couldn't even ransom me, no one cares about me!' Jong-sup's throat was horse and stung with each strained word.

'You are so, so wrong my friend,' sang the man almost theatrically. 'Not about anyone caring for you of course, that much is obvious. You are, however, of tremendous Value.'

The man kneeled to eye level with Jong-sup, breathing heavily, before standing up and turning to face the wall dramatically. 'You see, I have always been full of such hatred, much like many others in this accursed city. Hatred for the government, for having bills to pay and especially for those around me. In time howe-'

'Shut it! I don't give a damn about your pathetic backstory you fucking psycho!' screamed Jong-sup. The man replied with a quick and powerful punch to his jaw, effectively silencing him.

'In time however,' the man continued 'I learned that what I hated most was myself. You see people consistently get in the way of the things I want. But it is me who lets them. I have always been such a passive coward. Afraid of what others think or how they'll react. That's why I admired you so much.'

Jong-sup looked into the man's manic gaze and wondered if he had misheard.

'No, it's true,' said the man 'I have been paid many times to investigate people. Sometimes for a legal matter and sometimes for jealousy or obsession. That's when you dropped into my life. I had been following you for two weeks and I was truly astonished by how little you cared what people thought. You never let anyone stand in your way and acted on all your impulses no matter what others around you wanted.'

'Who wanted you to follow-'

'And then, you took a tumble off the hotel roof. I was waiting in a car across the street for you to finish fucking that harlot and then, WHAM! You hit the floor. And I was awestruck. Here was this man who took life into his own hands and decided when he was done with it. I have often thought about killing myself, but I'd never have the balls to go through with it.'

'Who want-'

'And that wasn't all. The pile of mush re-assembled itself back into the man I have sat here before me. Amazing! Not even Death could handle the confidence of a man who knows what he wants and takes it.'

'That's not how it was.'

'Then I forgot about the investigation and I continued to follow you out of pure fascination.'

'You're sick,' said Jong-sup and was silenced once again by a swift punch, this time to his gut.

'No, we're the same you and I. Now, at least. When I saw you squirrelling away all your money and planning on faking your own murder,' the man bent over laughing, hands on his knees. 'my friend, you are such a bad-ass,' he said between hysterical breaths. Once he had collected himself, he continued. 'I watched you put yourself in this vulnerable position, and I thought to myself, what would you do if you were in my situation?'

Jong-sup wished he could defend himself, to declare that he had the moral high-ground, but he couldn't honestly say what he would've done.

'You sir, are my hero,' said the man.

Jong-sup felt physically ill.

'If I'm your hero then you should let me go. You've learned from me. You are a man who does what he wants and takes what he needs. I can give you no more.'

'No, no, no, sir. I have big plans for us,' said the man.

'What?' said Jong-sup, his voice weak and hopeless.

'No time for that my friend and mentor, I must depart for a have many pieces to put in place,' he spun around flamboyantly and made for the door but stopped right before exiting.

'Do you have any idea how much a liver will fetch on the black market?' he switched off the lights and left without another word.

5

The following week or so was a blur. The man's mental state seemed to fluctuate dramatically. He was cocky and arrogant most of the time, as he was when he had first met him. Other times he would burst in crying and wailing, punching walls and striking Jong-sup. The man's unpredictable nature made the situation all the more dark for Jong-sup. He never knew what to expect which made the waiting excruciating. Strangely, he found himself longing for a more stable captor, who would give him a beating, break some bones and leave. He could handle a beating, he had been through worse, but the man's comment about selling his liver on the black market gnawed at his thoughts.

Two days or nights ago, by Jong-sup's estimation anyway, the man rushed into the room with a long knife, he crouched in the corner for a while, covering his ears and mumbling to himself incomprehensibly. He then whirled round, and staring Jong-sup straight in the eyes, he pushed the knife against his stomach. Jong-sup winced as the tip of the blade scratched at his skin only slightly piercing him enough to draw just a droplet of blood. He tensed in anticipation for what was to come. When nothing happened, Jong-sup forced his eye lids to separate just a crack and as his gaze met the loony's, the man screamed loud enough, it felt, to burst an eardrum. He then pulled the knife away ferociously and cut at his own arm three times in quick succession and then fled from the room, his shrill screams still audible through the corridors.

Last night was worse still.

The man entered rather calmly in comparison with his previous performance. He walked over to where Jong-sup was tied and knelt down in front of him. His head was bowed to the floor and he made what sounded like a gentle sobbing noise. Jong-sup thought he saw a teardrop hit the floor, but his vision was hazy and unclear.

'I've changed my mind,' said the man.

'What?' asked Jong-sup sounding much older than he actually was.

'Your free to go!' yelled the man 'Pack up your shit and get out!'

Before Jong-sup could even respond the man brought his face close and kissed him hard, forcing his tongue deep into Jong-sup's mouth. Jong-sup pulled his head back as far as he could manage, gasped for air and swung in for the headbutt. The man had already turned around however and was heading out the door.

'You fucking pervert!' bellowed Jong-sup, 'Is this all some sick fetish, you sick bastard!' but if the man heard he didn't react.

Now, Jong-sup sat and waited for what today had in store.

Only, the man did not come.

Jong-sup sat with his head lolling to the side. Tapping his foot repetitively helped him keep a mental note of the passage of time, it wasn't accurate, but it was a necessary distraction. A loud groan came from inside him; he had not been given any food since his capture and from the pain it seemed as though his body had decided to make do with eating itself.

Worse still was the thirst. His mouth was dry, his lips were cracked to the point of bleeding and it felt as though his very breath on its way to fill his lungs snagged on the crispy flakes of skin that lined his throat. He had been given a few sips of water but not for days now.

A bang echoed round the room making Jong-sup immediately tense up and lose count of his foot movements. Then after a moment of silence the familiar squeak of unoiled wheels travelled down the unseen hallway towards the door.

The man entered the room in reverse pulling with him a trolley similar to the ones used for hospital food. Upon it was a television and on the lower compartment a video player. Smiling for an instant at Jong-sup the man scurried out of the room. Noises of rummaging and things falling to the ground and faint swearing were heard, before he came back into the room unwinding the cable of an extension cord from its circular case. He plugged both devices in and the television immediately burst into crackly static life.

'Hey Park Jong-sup,' said the man, awkwardly kicking his foot and looking at the ground 'apologies for my emotional turmoil being so overtly visible. It was unprofessional of me. I am going through a hard- sorry, one moment,' he ran out of the room, down the corridor and it was near three minutes before he returned holding a videotape in his hands, 'left this in the car ha,' he said mockingly hitting himself on top of the head with it and pulling an idiotic expression.

Jong-sup made a mental note that his prison couldn't be that big if his car was a minute's sprint from this room. He tried to scrape some feeling of hope from this fact, but hope had long left him.

The man switched off the light in the room, so the only source of illumination came from the television. The man looked longer, thinner, more spider-like with his shadow cast out around the walls hiding from the unnatural light.

'I know that as your keeper it is my responsibility to show my dominance.'

'I'm not your pet sic-' Jong-sup was silenced with a swift hit to the face. His lip, being so devoid of moisture, tore like paper and blood began to drip onto his lap.

'As I was saying, I owe you an apology, as your superior I should show an image of continual strength. I have not done that. I am sorry,' the man bowed low to Jong-sup the sight of which made him sick with fear, 'I don't want you to think that I don't have what it takes to go through with all this. I am dead serious about this. I want to become like you. Take life into my own hands, grasp it so tight that even Death won't be able to snatch it away.'

'I would never do any of this,' said Jong-sup his voice cracked and weak.

'Perhaps, but you do what you desire. You take and take. This is what I have desired for so long but was too afraid to enact. I want to show you exactly what you have inspired in me, as thanks,' The man waved the tape playfully, 'this is all thanks to you,' he inserted the VHS into the player and pressed play.

The screen quality was poor and grainy, but Jong-sup could make out a single bed with pink sheets in a dingy room with tattered wallpaper and next to no decoration. Next the man came out and sat on the bed, placed his head in his hands and began to breath heavily.

'Sorry, I'll just skip to the best bit,' said the man and he began to fast forward the tape. On screen, the man's shoulders heaved mechanically in the sped-up motion. Then he got up to the door and walked back holding the hand of a young woman who joined him sitting on the bed.

'Time for the real show,' said the man and he resumed playback at regular speed.

The man and the mystery lady were now kissing. From her body language Jong-sup could tell that the woman was not into it. The man however, seemed totally oblivious to this as he passionately kissed her.

Jong-sup was not a man who was inexperienced with prostitutes and he could tell from her dress sense, mannerisms and, although the picture wasn't clear, something about her face radiated "desperation". This girl was definitely pay for play, not some poor girl from the bar he had convinced to come back with him.

The woman stood up and in one, well-practised motion pulled her dress over her head, revealing a slightly fat and unappealing body.

'What the fuck is this?' cried Jong-sup 'More of your sick perversions? I don't need to see you fuck some whore.'

The video was paused. The man sighed deeply. Taking two steps towards Jong-sup he lifted his foot off the ground and with considerable force planted his heel into Jong-sup's crotch. There was a distinct noise, halfway between a crunch and a pop, and a sensation of liquid trickling down his leg. The pain was intense. In all his misadventures so far Jong-sup luckily had avoided testicular damage and the feeling was something you could never grow accustomed to.

He did not cry out in pain. He would not give this man the satisfaction. He did vomit onto his own lap though. Not being able to curl up in a ball made everything so much worse.

‘Every time you interrupt the film or I feel that you’re not concentrating, you’ll get another one of those,’ stated the man coldly ‘now to rewind to before you started talking over everything.’

Jong-sup sat there watching the video of the man lying naked on top of the woman with her legs wrapped around him for twenty minutes. If this was to instil some respect for the man it was doing a poor job. The way the man flopped up and down on the poor woman while burying his head into the pillow looked pitiable at best. Even at Jong-sup’s age he was sure that he could do much better. Perhaps the only positive to come out of this was that after that poor performance the woman might go home and rethink her life choices.

At last the man’s shunting became harder and less rapid. It seemed the show was almost over, and Jong-sup could go back to waiting for the next horror. Surprising himself he found that the worst part of it was that he was completely and utterly bored. Maybe try a new position? How about the girl on top?

On screen the man was still going at it with his hard, drawn out pumping when a flash of silver shimmered into view. It took a second for the object to register in Jong-sup’s mind but once it had horror ran from it into every part of his body. He wanted to call out to the lady. To warn her.

But it was too late.

The man had pulled a knife from underneath the pillow and plunged it deep into the girl’s chest. There was no sound from the television but from her expression Jong-sup could tell she was screaming in agony.

Jong-sup flinched and looked away. He forced his eyes shut tight as he could muster but it was too late. The girl’s face would forever be etched into his mind. The silent scream would forever ring in his ear.

Jong-sup's reaction was not good enough though it seemed, as the man walked behind Jong-sup's chair and locked one arm under his chin and with the other hand he ripped Jong-sup's lids open. Jong-sup lost all power to fight back once his eyes focused in on the display.

The girl was no longer screaming. All life had left her. Jong-sup felt grateful for that, at least her suffering was at an end. This did not deter the man however, as he cut madly at the girl, swinging his arms in wild excitement. Worse still, he continued to thrust himself inside her.

If Jong-sup's arms were not chained to the chair he would have ripped out his own eyes so he wouldn't have to look at the vile display. His eyes watered profusely, and he begged silently for it all to end. Eventually he couldn't take it a moment longer and began to sob violently.

His tears streaked down his face and landed on the man's hand. The man whipped away his hand in disgust and examined it.

'I expected better from you,' said the man, surprisingly softly. Jong-sup winced expecting to be struck across the face, but no punishment came. Without another word the man turned off the television and wheeled the trolley out of the room turning off the light before closing the door.

The darkness that surrounded Jong-sup for the first time in a while, along with the mental anguish of the night exhausted him and he fell into a deep sleep within minutes. A sleep so deep that he couldn't sense Death standing over him.

6

He woke, as he had many a time now, with a back-handed slap across the face.

'Rise and shine,' said the man in English spreading out his fingers and shaking his hands in mock excitement.

'Today is a big day. A very big day indeed,' said the man 'today, I open up my people farm.'

Jong-sup's stomach sank and the now spotless part of his body in which his kidney had been cut out by the Yuk Sung Pa lurched and twisted.

The man walked out and came in with the trolley he had used for television, only now it was a set of knives and surgical tools.

'Please, you don't want to do this. Please,' begged Jong-sup.

'Begging only deepens my disappointment in you Park Jong-sup, it won't work.'

'What you're planning won't work. If you take anything out of my body. Anything at all. I will die. Then your plan falls to shit. What will you do then?'

'Oh, I really, really very much doubt it,' laughed the man 'you see your finger? There's nothing whatsoever wrong with it. In fact, it looks healthier than the ones I hadn't cut off. If your finger can grow back, then I'm sure some intestines or even your heart will be just fine.'

'That's not how this works.'

'Even so, unfortunately for you my needs outweigh yours. Now, there are a couple of guys coming tonight. I have promised them organs in exchange for a generous amount of money. These are not the kind of guys you fuck with Park Jong-sup. They will be leaving with organs tonight, and I intend them to be yours.'

'Please.'

‘Don’t worry, I’m planning on taking something you can live without first as a test. Your Kidney. But perhaps I’ll chuck in one of your eyes too as a good will gesture,’ laughed the man.

Jong-sup released a loud whine and tears drenched his cheeks and lap.

The man turned to browse through his collection of pointed, metallic, pain inducing utensils.

The next tears that hit Jong-sup’s lap were ice cold. Two more slowly streaked down his cheek hit his lap, bounced off and smashed on the floor. He exhaled and his breath was visible in the air. The man also exhaled large clouds of condensation, but he did not seem to notice. The icy fear that consumed Jong-sup thawed instantly, being replaced by a searing pain in Jong-sup’s wrist. His jaw hung open as the chains that bound him to the chair flashed bright red and cooked the flesh underneath. The chain then fell around Jong-sup’s feet, the links fractured in several places.

The chain hitting the concrete floor did not go unnoticed though and as the man whirled round with a look of shock and horror on his face he dropped the scalpel he had decided on being his first instrument of pain, and it slid across the floor and hit the wall opposite of the door.

Jong-sup thought about tackling the man, hesitated, then fled for the door. The man was younger and quicker though, and he reached behind him and threw one of the knives at Jong-sup with the precision of a circus act. It spun twice in the air and then buried itself three inches into Jong-sup’s shoulder, making him crash to the floor.

The man walked over to the bundle that was Jong-sup, put his hand on the knife handle and his foot on Jong-sup’s back and yanked the blade from its new home. The room was filled with Jong-sup’s howling. He raised the blade high above his head ready to strike, but Jong-sup’s taste of freedom had filled him with new vigour and he kicked the man in the testicles; he was sure he had lodged one of them inside. The older man tackled the younger one to the ground. They punched at each other, some hits connecting, most not. Every time

Jong-sup found himself on top after laying down a couple of hits, he would try to get up to escape and would get pulled into the fray once more.

It was the younger of the men, as it often was, who came out on top. The energy had been punched out of him. The man kicked him hard in the chest. Jong-sup felt his ribs crack. The man heard them. He laughed, delivered another swift kick to the old man's stomach, then pulled him up away from the door and threw him across the room putting himself between Jong-sup and escape.

'How the fuck did you do that?!' laughed the man manically 'See the Park Jong-sup that I respect is back. For all I know you could have got out anytime but were waiting to see what happened next. Amazing!'

Jong-sup was too winded to respond.

'It was no use of course, but I appreciate you trying though. I am going to have to find a new way to contain you. Those chains were brand new. Too badass for the laws of physics, yeah?'

He glanced around the floor for his knife but gave up, not wanting to take his eyes off of the winded old man for too long. He reached behind himself, maintaining eye contact, and grabbed what looked like a pizza cutter.

'Time for you to go to sleep for a little while!' hissed the man.

He raised the serrated circular cutting tool above his head and slashed down aiming for Jong-sup's throat. It cut instead into Jong-sup's collar bone. The man readied himself for another attempt. Jong-sup flailed and in doing so his hand clasped round the scalpel that the man had dropped and without even thinking he reacted. He jumped up from the ground, his arm fully extended, the scalpel pointed with deadly intent.

The man went stiff and the tool dropped from his hand. Jong-sup must have caught the man's jugular as blood showered out in every direction splashing over his face. An image of Jerry covered in Jong-sup's own blood flashed through his mind.

As the pressure was released, the spray was reduced to a heavy pouring of blood from the wound in the man's throat. Jong-sup was surprised that he was still standing there holding the source of the flow, swaying slowly. He tried to speak but all that was heard was a thick gargle and splutter. Jong-sup felt the bile in his stomach rise at the sound.

The man lurched forward in what could have been another attempt at reclaiming his prize or what was more likely a pitiable cry for help. Fear and anger were Jong-sup's reaction and he stabbed at the man's abdomen six, seven maybe ten times, he wasn't counting. The man looked at Jong-sup one last time with an expression of admiration, before collapsing on the ground. A dark red puddle leaked from the lifeless corpse.

Taking a life was much more of a shock than Jong-sup had ever thought it would be on the occasions when he had pondered such things. He had ruined lives, so surely the difference was little? This *was* different, however.

Jong-sup cried loudly and deeply, his body convulsing horrendously. He stared at the hands that had carried out this awful and unnatural deed. They felt as though they were someone else's. Movement in his peripheral caught his attention. It was the shadow of his hands. They flickered as if they were made of fire. He spread out his hand watching in fascination and turning it slowly. The shadow hand spasmed and the flesh fell off it, revealing bone. Jong-sup checked his hand, panic stricken but no effect had been replicated in reality.

Then the shadow spread up the wall and detached from it. Jong-sup understood. It was Death.

She slowly solidified into her usual form.

Murderer

The accusation seemed to not come from her, but from his own memory of that night on the rooftop.

'That is not quite fair,' Jong-sup defended 'I had no choice!'

There is always choice

'But....but you accused me of the crime long before any was committed. Surely if that is true then choice itself is only an illusion?!'

Death did not say anything but started moving towards Jong-sup.

'Your silence says it all. If you have come to finally take me to hell, then please do so!' Jong-sup spread his arms wide, but Death passed through him, an experience that no mortal would ever grow accustomed to.

Death stopped at the body of the man, reached down and pulled the spirit from him.

'You can't be serious! Him?! I killed in self-defence, he out of a sick fantasy and you decide he is worthy of moving on and you're going to leave me in this awful place?'

Death did not answer.

'I won't have it!' Jong-sup lunged forward to grab Death's wrist, to knock the spirit from her grasp or to show her he wasn't to be ignored. He wasn't sure what he planned to do; in truth he didn't think it would work. Death must not have expected it though as he actually made contact. His fingers locked around Death's wrist and he yanked hard. She did not move an inch. Her cowl however began to move as if in high winds. Anger emanated through the room and through Jong-sup's body.

A fear so primal Jong-sup had not felt since that night when he had first been introduced to Death and she had buried her Scythe into his skull. He let go in an instant, pulling back as if he had touched something hot for the very first time. It was too late.

Staring at the fingers his skin turned black and shrivelled. All the way to the elbow before stopping. Death's hood turned towards him. The endless void exposed. A dreadful noise coming from within his cranium threatened to cook his brain.

He had spent so long looking for Death. Now he ran from her.

He didn't look back.

고통과 죄책감

Part Seven

Pain and Guilt

1

In a quiet suburban area of Seoul, a car raced through the night. Lights were switched on as it passed; the residents not used to loud reckless noises in the early hours of the morning. Some came to their windows, but the vehicle was already out of sight by the time they stuck their nosy faces out from within their homes.

Jong-sup paid no mind to inconveniencing the neighbourhood. As the car ran through red lights and took the side off of a corn dog vendor who'd closed for the night, Jong-sup's mind was only on one thing: getting as far away as possible from Death.

As he had predicted, the exit from where he was being kept was not far, and it led to a garage where the man's car was stored. It was a lower end Sundai model and although it was only a couple of years old it wasn't in great condition. The interior was worse still. Evidence of roadside binge eating littered the floor of the car. A discarded drink can was wedged under the clutch and it was harder to find a part of the seat the wasn't stained with mustard. Jong-sup wasn't feeling fussy though. After rooting around frantically for the keys that he desperately hoped the man kept in the car he had found a pair in the glove compartment.

He didn't stop driving till he had left Seoul behind. He had had enough with that cursed city. Even before Death had ruined his death, it had been a long, long time since he last felt happy. There was a reason that all his life events had led him to that roof top on that night.

He was happy once.

Those thought weren't helpful right now, so he quelled them and concentrated on his loathing for Seoul and its citizens and used it as fuel to keep his foot down on the accelerator.

Gradually the buildings became shorter and the roads less well lit, until he was driving in near darkness. The tall corporate buildings and apartment blocks were far behind him.

With each mile travelled with Seoul in the rear-view mirror, his stress seemed to evaporate equally. He took a deep breath, held it, and exhaled slowly. For some reason he was overcome with an intense feeling that this was the best decision he had made in a very long time. The sky was beginning to lighten in colour and his surroundings were becoming clearer. There was nothing but fields and trees now, not a building in sight. No people; with their hypocritical judging eyes and pretentious attitude. Things, at last, were going to be okay.

The sun suddenly broke over the hills in the horizon, beaming directly into Jong-sup's eyes rendering them useless. He did not ease up on the accelerator however, since he felt he was starting a winning streak he threw caution to the wind. By the time his vision returned to the road, it was no longer empty. A cat was stood in Jong-sup's path, startled and unable to move. Jong-sup was reminded of the cat that had been bothering him that night he sat with Death and who was ultimately responsible for the young bartender's untimely end. Jong-sup did not waver, but attempted to line up his wheel with the beast. The thrill of cruelty invigorated him, as he justified it with avenging a soul that he could not care less for.

It was further away than he had initially thought. Jong-sup drew closer and the cat grew bigger. Big enough to cause some damage. Jong-sup swerved hard. The world slowed to a crawl. As he passed the beast he glanced out and couldn't believe what he was seeing. It was no mere domestic cat but a full-grown leopard; teeth bared, staring right into Jong-sup's eyes even as he passed at high speed.

Attempting to right himself back onto the road proved impossible, so he released his foot from the accelerator and slammed it onto the brake and braced himself for a quick stop. The car barely slowed however, Jong-sup stepped on the brakes repeatedly in frenzied panic and averted his eyes far too often, returning them just in time to see the front of the car wrap itself around a tree.

Jong-sup, never the seat belt wearing type, flew through the window screen, hit the tree and landed in a crumpled pile on top of shards and pieces of broken glass. His body stung all over and he felt the now familiar sensation of blood trickling from several orifices. His bowls emptied and so did his consciousness, his fleeting thought of the leopard melting away.

2

His eye's opened and he felt pain, as he always did, as he had come accustomed to till the point of hardly feeling it at all, but there was something else. Something different. Something that made the continual suffering wrought on his body so much more noticeable. Comfort.

He was not in a hospital bed, thank god, they would ask too many questions, demand his ID and charge him for the privilege. This was a bedroom, a young lady's bedroom by the décor. It was feminine but had a touch of tradition that Jong-sup appreciated. In the corner stood a wicker chair with a teddy bear sat upon it. No other toys littered the room, so it was probably a daughter who had left home for university.

He could tell just by lying still what was broken; his right arm and leg and a couple of ribs as well as plenty of bumps and bruises. Nothing he hadn't been through before; he would be able to walk in a day. He got off lucky, he could have been eaten alive. The leopard.

'Hey! Hello!' Jong-sup yelled 'Hello!'

'One moment!' came a voice from below.

The muffled sound of footsteps and the soft clatter of a tray sounded from the other side of the door before in stepped Jong-sup's host. A woman in her mid-forties stepped in with a tray, two cups, a pot of tea and a pot of water. She placed the tray down on a small bedside table.

'Hav-' started Jong-sup.

'You shouldn't shout,' she said sternly.

'Huh?'

'Your throat. It must be sore. Keep your voice low in my house, please,' said the woman during which she had gone over to the wardrobe, and from behind it slid out a fold-up chair and unfolded it next to where Jong-sup rest. She poured one cup with hot water and held it out to Jong-sup.

'Can you use your arm, or do you need me to feed you?' she asked matter-of-factly.

'Uh, no that's fine,' said Jong-sup 'Thank you.'

He took the cup and sipped it. The warm water coated his throat and soothed to an extent he had forgot possible. He looked at the water and felt for the first time how much of a privilege it was. He felt grateful to this kind stranger.

'How did I get here?' asked Jong-sup.

'That was my tree you damaged. On my land. On a private road,' said the woman.

'I'm sorry.'

'Dragged you in myself, and no mean feat that was, slight as you are. You have a lot weighing on you, and not all physical I sense,' the woman smiled.

Her stern face was made beautiful in an instant. She smiled with her eyes as well as her mouth and though she had a youthful appearance her eyes wrinkled. A single streak of grey ran through her black hair that was tied back into a ponytail and she wore a plain pastel pink t-shirt and jeans. She radiated simplicity. Simple beauty.

Jong-sup's relief at his newfound situation compared to his last one made it impossible not to return her smile. Though he wished he hadn't as he felt ugly and old in comparison and found that he had to avert his gaze.

'I hope this is good enough for now. You should be in hospital,' Jong-sup made to protest but she spoke over him 'but, the phone lines are dead since the storm three days past. So, it's best you rest here for the time being. I've checked you over and I don't think anything is broken.'

She was wrong, but Jong-sup was in no hurry to correct her.

'You'll be having a lecture on driving safely from me, you can be sure of that, but it can wait till you've rested.'

Jong-sup nodded and looked down ashamed and rightly so, as if he were back in the orphanage being scolded for some matter or other.

'Soup is nearly ready I will bring it up in a little while,' She got up from the chair and turned to leave.

'Wait, I'm sorry, who are you?' asked Jong-sup.

'Jung Mi-sook,' she replied, 'and lucky for you that I am, others around here may have left you for dead rather than near break their own back pulling you from that wreck.'

Not long-ago Jong-sup would not have let anyone patronise him so who wasn't paying him, not least a woman. Had his mood been particularly sour he may have even struck them. Her tone, however, was far less disrespectful than Jong-sup had grown used to of late.

Once she had left the room with the door ajar, Jong-sup laid back staring at the ceiling. He could feel his torn tendons fastening themselves together, though he noted that it was taking a lot longer than it used to.

The door creaked slightly, and a man's head filled the gap. He then stepped into the room and nodded his head in greeting. He was perhaps ten years older than Mi-sook; his skin was dark and sun weathered and he had a hunched posture; signs of a life of labour, most likely farming given the land. He smiled but there was little happiness in his eyes. Jong-sup felt all of a sudden like an unwanted guest.

'Are you Mi-sook's husband?' asked Jong-sup. He nodded, before motioning Jong-sup to rest and left without a word. Jong-sup could feel that perhaps there was a disagreement about whether or not to allow him to stay. The thought made him uncomfortable so he focused on healing as soon as possible; he wouldn't want to burden these people any longer than he had to.

3

Over the next five days, Jong-sup was fed and cared for by Mi-sook very well. He hadn't felt so content in years, long before his run-in with Death. He enjoyed a different delicious meal every day. Breakfast generally consisted of a bowl of rice with an assortment of banchan, simple but Jong-sup looked forward to it every morning. One evening, when asked if he would like some tea after dinner he asked if he could have something a little stronger. He was told rather harshly that she does not allow drinking in the house, and that he was eager enough for a drink that she would drop him off at the nearest town, he could find a bar there and that perhaps they would look after him. He dropped the subject immediately.

'Mr Park?' called Mi-sook from the other side of the door. 'Are you decent?'

'I don't know about decent, but I am not exposed or anything,' replied Jong-sup.

Mi-sook slid in, holding a pile of clothes.

'These clothes belong to my husband; they should fit you. I was thinking you are probably well enough now to get up longer than just to go to the toilet.'

'Yeah, I guess so,' Jong-sup replied. In truth he had been well enough for three days but didn't want to arouse suspicion.

'Good. Maybe you should eat dinner downstairs at the table tonight.'

Jong-sup nodded.

'Here,' Mi-sook handed him a razor. Have a wash and a shave before you come down. I don't mean to be rude, but the room is starting to stink.'

Jong-sup smiled coyly.

'It'll be ready in about an hours' time. See you!'

Jong-sup stood in front of the mirror in the bathroom trying to build up the courage to look himself in the eye. He could not do it. He couldn't be sure why, but he was terrified of what he may see.

He focused instead on the parts of his face he could look at. His beard was matted, greasy and mostly grey. His hair had started to become one big unified cone. His skin looked grey and sagged from the bone. He had stopped being presentable years ago but now he was truly repulsive.

He put the blade to his skin and started to shave away his beard vigorously, taking little care for nicks or cuts. Hair fell into the sink basin in clumps and clusters and with each section of newly exposed skin; Jong-sup felt lighter and relief washed over him. Once his face was free of his wiry facial hair he looked and felt immensely better. He then looked up to his disgusting tangled hair with disdain.

Mi-sook's hand flew to her mouth and she giggled loudly upon Jong-sup entering the room.

'You know, a trim would have sufficed,' said Mi-sook.

Jong-sup face reddened with embarrassment. His head was shaven smooth. The only hair on his head was his eyebrows. He had felt much better until Mi-sook's reaction to his new look.

'Is it unsightly?'

'No, no not at all!' laughed Mi-sook. 'Come sit down, please.'

Jong-sup sat down at the table, fidgeted with his fingers and looked around the kitchen nervously. It was a fairly standard Korean kitchen, rather sparse of ornamentation but spotlessly clean. It was a fair size, much bigger than what you would typically find in Seoul, big enough to have two Kimchi refrigerators. On the wall hung an empty picture frame, Jong-sup thought it odd but knew it was better not to ask.

'We're having chicken,' said Mi-sook 'wait, are Buddhist monks allowed to eat meat?!'

Jong-sup didn't find the humour in her remarks but Mi-sook evidently did as she smacked the table with her palm and chortled loudly. Her mannerisms were quite a contrast to her lady-like feminine appearance and somehow it put Jong-sup at ease.

Jong-sup noted that she only laid two bowls and two sets of chopsticks on the table. From the window he could see her husband tilling the field, quite late for farm work as there was little daylight left. Perhaps their marriage was bad, he thought, or perhaps her husband was avoiding him.

Dinner was delicious as usual, and the kitchen was silent apart from the occasional slurping or coughing on Jong-sup's part. The moment he had finished Mi-sook whipped the bowl from under him and replaced it with a plate of dragon fruit and apples. She sat opposite from him just watching him eat.

'Maybe if you are feeling up to it after, you could wash the dishes?' asked Mi-sook playfully.

'Sure,' replied Jong-sup. 'Mrs Jung, may I ask you something?'

'Of course.'

'Why are you helping me?' asked Jong-sup. Mi-sook paused for a moment.

'We all need a little help sometimes.'

'But I crashed into your tree, I could have hurt someone.'

'Yes, we have been over that, and thank god you didn't,' said Mi-sook sternly, 'I can't and I won't try to justify your actions, but I know that you are a good man who would help others in need.'

'I wouldn't be so sure of that Mrs Jung,' said Jong-sup, shame and sorrow evident in his voice.

'I won't hear of such nonsense. Are you not the man who defended that girl and stopped her being kidnapped by thugs?'

'How ca-'

'I am familiar with you. I was there that day in Seoul, I saw you run into the ally after them while I and others around stood there and did nothing!' her voice was raised but the anger was not directed at him, 'I have been ashamed of myself since that day! Then I find none other than you in my garden in need of help. It was as if you were sent by god to help me repent.'

'I am afraid it was not god who sent me, Mrs Jung.'

'Well, regardless I wasn't going to make the same mistake twice,' said Mi-sook, 'I figured that since you never came forward when the papers were looking for you, that you must be a private man and I could tell that you had fallen on some hard times.'

'You could say that.'

'So, I thought that you would refuse hospital treatment anyway and that you were better off with my help.'

'Look, I am grateful for your help. Truly I am. With all due respect though, I think you have done enough. I am feeling much better now, perhaps I should leave tomorrow.'

'You are a free man you can do as you please, but I feel that you are in no position to decide that now and you should wait until the morning.'

'Okay,' said Jong-sup.

'I'm sorry for shouting, it's just I've never shared this out loud. You must think me awful.'

'Not in the slightest, Mrs Jung. The fact that you have dwelt on it so, is a far greater testament to your character. You were one of hundreds who didn't act. I bet my life that most sleep soundly in their beds.'

'Thank you for saying so, but I hope you don't truly think so little of people.'

'I am people,' replied Jong-sup 'that is all the evidence I need.'

4

Jong-sup arose early the next morning. The sound of a steel-capped shoe pressing down on gravel came from his back as he sat up. He swivelled, placed his bare feet on the ground and scratched deep into his bald head. He could do with a few more nights on the comfortable mattress but he couldn't shake the feeling that he didn't deserve the help he was receiving; he was probably right. He was ready once he had his clothes on, as he had no possessions to his name. He opened the door slowly and, slinky as a feline, he made his way silently down the stairs. The door to the next uncertain but most certainly painful chapter in his life. Next to the front door the keys were hung on a little wooden hook. He reached for them, but his hand never made it. His attention was drawn to a little ornate trinket box on a shelf near the door. Jong-sup's stomach sank when he opened and confirmed what he suspected was inside. A roll of won. Not a lot, but enough for transport, a meal and a night in a hotel. He cursed himself and wish he never found it, then he slipped it into the pocket of the clothes that had been so generously donated to him.

'I really am a despicable piece of shit,' he muttered under his breath. He wasn't angry at what he was doing, but rather the fact that he didn't feel as guilty as he thought he should do. It really was too late for him.

A delectable waft came from the kitchen and Jong-sup's stomach responded violently. He may as well take some food for the road, he thought. As he approached the kitchen, he could see light spilling out from under the door. Perhaps she had left the light on, he thought. He opened precariously, just enough to squeeze his head through.

'You're up early,' came a gruff voice. Mi-sook's husband was sat at the table, cigarette hanging out of his mouth, looking down at a Janggi board.

'Good morning,' Jong-sup said giving a slight bow 'didn't mean to disturb you.'

'Nonsense. Please sit down,' he smiled.

'Apologies, we have not yet been formally introduced I am Kim Jong-sup.'

'I know. Jung Kwang-su,' he said.

'Thank you for letting me stay in your home.'

'You should thank my wife, had it been me, I would of left you in that wreckage,' he laughed loudly and banged his fist on the table. Jong-sup winced at the thought that it might wake up Mi-sook.

'Sorry,' said Jong-sup pathetically.

'Ah well, what is past is past,' said Kwang-su cheerfully 'I trust you know how to play?' he said gesturing to the board.

'Of course,' replied Jong-sup.

'Good, I haven't had anyone to play against in a long time.'

'Were you playing against yourself?' asked Jong-sup confused. Kwang-su took a deep drag on his cigarette, held it and blew the smoke out into the air.

'Don't be silly, I was waiting for you.'

It seemed that neither man was big on small talk nor were they particularly talented at Janggi. Jong-sup briefly considered letting his host win as a polite gesture but once Kwang-su had more pieces, Jong-sup noticed the corner of his mouth rise in a nearly undetectable smirk. Jong-sup felt rage and tried to gain ground he had frivolously given away. Twenty minutes later it was all for naught.

'It seems I have won,' bragged Kwang-su.

'Seems you have.' said Jong-sup through gritted teeth.

'I guess you haven't played in a while, am I correct?'

'That's right,' replied Jong-sup jaw still tightly clenched.

'Would you care to play again? This time with stakes,' said Kwang-su cheerfully.

Jong-sup thought about declining but who was he kidding, he was a gambler at heart. The last match Jong-sup would have been victorious had he not been so gracious as to give his host a head start.

'Fine, but I have little to no money on me,' said Jong-sup, but Kwang-su waved his hand in the air dismissively.

'I never play for money,' he laughed 'My wife would kill me.'

'Then what?'

'If I win then you will do me a favour of my choice. If you win, I will do the same in kind.'

'Doesn't sound that interesting.'

'Please, humour me' said Kwang-su gesturing to the board once again.

Jong-sup had made a terrible mistake. The next seven minutes were a frustrating blur. He could barely move a piece before Kwang-su swept in and took it from him. He seemed to think ten steps ahead of Jong-sup, and several times Jong-sup had to fight the urge to flip the table. The two men sat staring each other down, one smirking in arrogant victory, the other defeated and emasculated.

'You bastard!' roared Jong-sup in a hushed voice 'You played me!'

'I played the game,' smirked Kwang-su 'The board and pieces are only a part of that game.'

'Call it what you want, I didn't expect such slippery behaviour from a country boy.'

'Underestimation is the folly of many men,' said Kwang-su 'now then, you owe me something.'

'I'll consider it, what do you want,' spat Jong-sup his voice full of venom. Kwang-su sat in silence for a moment, his aggravating grin was nowhere to be found. His expression was dark.

'I want you to go upstairs and get back in bed.'

'What?' asked Jong-sup gob-smacked.

'If you leave first thing in the morning, like you were planning on doing,' said Kwang-su.

Jong-stomach sank, had he really been so transparent?

'then my wife will worry about you. Now, I personally think that that is a pretty poor way to repay someone who so kindly took you in, right?'

Jong-sup grunted in shameful agreement.

'Stay today, convince her that you are completely healed, she will probably ask you to stay one more night so that she can be sure; she's kind like that. The next morning, I want you gone. Thank my wife for all she has done and then leave like a gentleman. Do we have an understanding?'

Jong-sup grunted once again in agreement and then stood up from the table suddenly and went to make his way back to the room.

'One more thing,' said Kwang-su 'Put back the money you stole.'

Jong-sup paused, didn't turn round nor did he answer, he was much too ashamed. He put the money back, went upstairs and got back into bed.

Jong-sup only left his room once he heard the clanging of Mi-sook making breakfast downstairs.

'You're up early,' she called cheerily, as he walked into the kitchen and found himself relieved that Kwang-su was not present. The morning sun splashed across her face from the kitchen window and she flashed him a wide smile. She was truly beautiful, Jong-sup thought. He was lost for words.

'What's wrong? You feeling worse?' she asked, her face changing to genuine concern.

'Uh- no, I'm fine, I am actually feeling a lot better,' spluttered Jong-sup.

'Glad to hear it,' she responded, her face returning to a glowing smile and rendering Jong-sup silent once again. Two dishes that Jong-sup had never seen before were placed on the table, some kind of spicy lettuce omelette.

'Does it look awful?' she giggled; she really was in a very good mood, 'It's supposed to be good for healing and plenty of protein.'

'No, it looks great,' lied Jong-sup. It tasted much better than it looked though, and he tucked in as if he was still starving. They were eating in silence as usual till Jong-sup broke it.

'I am very grateful to you for taking good care of me,' said Jong-sup.

'You don't have to say-'

'Unfortunately, I am not in a position to pay you back right now,' explained Jong-sup, his eyes in his lap.

'You stupid man. You think I was going to hand you a bill when you leave?' she said genuinely offended.

'No, I didn't mean-'

'You don't help people to get something in return, right? When you saved that poor girl, you didn't ask for a reward.'

'Of course not I-'

'I want nothing of you but to help you get back to health and send you on your way in the best condition possible.'

'That is very kind,' said Jong-sup. 'now that I am fully recovered, I think it is time for me to leave. I hope I can repay you some day.'

'Oh right, okay. Is it not too soon?' she was trying to sound fine, but she couldn't disguise the hurt in her voice.

'You have been a wonderful host. I should leave before I get too comfortable,' Jong-sup smiled and from the discomfort in his face he was reminded that it had been a long while since he had last pulled this expression. It wasn't pretty, but with his shaved face and scalp it was a lot less hideous than usual.

'You know, that is the first time I have seen you smile,' she said sounding simultaneously happy and sad, 'I guess you are recovered. If you are ready to go, then do me a favour. Help me out around the farm and leave in the morning with a full stomach.'

'Very well,' agreed Jong-sup 'Thank you.'

Jong-sup was not used to country life in the slightest, but he didn't mind it; well, he didn't hate it as much as he thought he would. He spent the day tilling the soil of a small vegetable patch and helping Mi-sook empty out and organise the barn. There were no animals inside, just a load of tools, scrap metal and a large American pickup truck. Mi-sook told him that her husband had visited America while serving in the military and that he fell in love with the vehicle there.

Getting a better look around the farm Jong-sup had to wonder, what did Kwang-su do all day? It was unkempt, there was junk strewn all about the place. Did he just lean against walls and lay in the grass? There were empty enclosures that at some point must have housed chickens and other animals. He always looked busy, but was he simply wasting time? Was this why they weren't happy with each other?

At the end of probably the most physical labour he had done in his entire life, he had a shower and sat in his towel on the end of the bed. He felt great. His muscles ached but not in the usual way. Best of all, he no longer felt stressed. Physical work had been a lot better for the mind than his old job. Sat in an office all day looking at paperwork seemed such a silly choice right now.

There was a knock at the door, but Mi-sook did not wait for an answer before barging in. Jong-sup bolted to his feet; hand tightly gripped onto his towel. Mi-sook yelped at the sight of the naked man.

'Sorry!' they both shouted simultaneously. Mi-sook didn't leave but faced the wall and held out a rucksack behind her.

'Here,' she said eyes not leaving the wall. 'I hope you don't mind. I packed a few things for you. Just some clothes and some food for the road. I want you to take it.'

'Thank you,' said Jong-sup rather abruptly.

'Well good. I wanted to know if you wanted to come into town with me for a drink, before you leave.'

'Yes.'

'OK great. Get dressed. We'll leave in twenty minutes,' and she left, not looking back but Jong-sup could see her flushed cheeks from her profile.

Jong-sup sat back down looking at the rucksack, feeling paranoid that he hadn't sounded grateful enough for this kind gesture. Then he thought about the money he had been caught stealing and he was once again filled with shame, and an anger at Kwang-su for being up so early.

5

Jong-sup left the house in some more of Kwang-su's clothes that had been left neatly folded on the edge of his bed. Mi-sook was waiting for him in the driver's seat of that American pick-up truck they had fished out of the barn. Laying down in the back was Kwang-su. Great, thought Jong-sup, he would have declined, or feigned illness had he known they would be joined by that lazy untrustworthy bastard. Begrudgingly, Jong-sup strapped himself into the passenger side and smiled awkwardly at Mi-sook.

'It's a little way into town,' said Mi-sook. 'About fifteen minutes or so.'

'Do you drink there often?' asked Jong-sup, not knowing what to say but feeling that he should try to converse.

'Me? Don't be silly. I haven't been out in a long, long time. I'm not much of a drinker, that won't change tonight either. I have to drive us home after all,' as she spoke they drove past the psycho's car that Jong-sup had wrapped around a tree. Mi-sook didn't even glance at it. She had made no attempt in getting the vehicle removed or scrapped and she seemed content on leaving it where it was. A scar on an otherwise picturesque backdrop.

Houses became more and more frequent as they got further into town till, they pulled over in what Mi-sook had told him was the centre. There were a few people walking here and there as well as a few dogs running around ownerless. The shops only had a single floor and were all closed, most had apartments above them but the highest was around four stories. There was a Japanese style pachinko parlour and next-door, a bar advertising chicken and beer. Kwang-su jumped out of the truck and without comment headed towards the bar.

'So, is that the place?' asked Jong-sup.

'That place? No! I wouldn't go in there. It's dirty and to be honest the chicken tastes like shit!' Mi-sook replied, she flung her hand to her mouth, 'I am very sorry,' she bowed 'I forgot my company.'

Hearing a lady speak in such a way did make Jong-sup uncomfortable, but for some reason she still seemed elegant and beautiful. It was as if it were impossible for her to appear crass.

'There's this place that does really good barbecue, and the drinks are cheap,' she said grabbing his arm and leading him down the street.

Mi-sook was right. The barbecue was excellent. Jong-sup and Mi-sook sat on a table for four opposite each other, the grill between them. Mi-sook planted a giant glass of beer in front of Jong-sup.

'What's this?' asked Jong-sup shocked and slightly intimidated

'The owner just returned from a trip to Europe. Apparently, this is called a stein, popular in Germany or something.'

'Are they big drinkers?'

'I wouldn't know, I have never left Korea. I guess they must be to make glasses this big.'

'Do you want to travel?' asked Jong-sup.

What was he doing? Since when was he so loose lipped. He really did not give a shit about her unfulfilled aspirations. It must have been the four beers prior to trying to tackle this foreign monstrosity. The beer was pretty weak and didn't taste brilliant but after so long without drinking, for him at least, he was starting to feel buzzed already.

'Um, I hadn't really thought about it. I don't speak any other language so I would be pretty scared,' said Mi-sook 'What about you? You travelled much before?'

'My company would always try to send me to China, Japan or America,' replied Jong-sup.

'And how was it?'

'I refused,' stated Jong-sup.

‘What? why?’ asked Mi-sook taking a large swig of her stein while turning her head to the side and covering her mouth with her hand as was standard etiquette.

‘Foreigners. You can’t trust them. They’re bad enough when they come to Korea. I won’t go there to be surrounded by the bastards.’

Mi-sook attempted to halt her laugh before the beer shot from her mouth, but the liquid found an alternative route in her nose and sprayed through her nostrils onto the already sticky table in front of her and worse still; in front of Jong-sup.

‘I am so, so sorry,’ she gasped snatching a paper towel from a slide-out cutlery drawer under the table and wiping frantically. Usually such an unfeminine display would have repulsed and insulted Jong-sup but looking at her face full of shame he was instead filled with a strange mix of pride and desire to protect.

‘It’s fine, absolutely fine,’ he smiled ‘Honestly, it barely splashed me. What was so funny anyway, just out of interest.’

‘Well… um… you just sounded like such an old man,’ she said giggling.

‘Sadly, I am an old man.’

‘You’re not *that* old.’ she said pleasantly gazing at him. ‘Although, you are still, thankfully, still *my* elder. I should have been more careful. Honestly, I can be so uncouth sometimes,’ she was beginning to slur slightly now.

‘I would say, more charming than anything,’ he cringed hard at his own words and prayed that she had miraculously gone deaf for a second.

‘Mr Kim! Are monks allowed to flirt?’ she said, mocking appalled shock and then laughing loudly. Jong-sup noted mentally that normally he would have felt embarrassed and reacted in anger, but here and now, he felt nothing of the sort.

‘For that, I really am too old,’ laughed Jong-sup. Could it be, just maybe, that he felt for with this woman? Christ, he must be more drunk than he had thought.

A couple of hours later, Jong-sup and Mi-sook were sat on a low wall in the centre of town talking much louder than either of them realised. The few people who were still out steered well clear of the very obviously drunk pair.

'So, you don't have a favourite film?' shouted Mi-sook in exaggerated surprise.

'No, I don't,' laughed Jong-sup.

'Really?' she pressed.

'I don't, seriously. I have hardly seen any films ever,' their speech was barely recognisable Korean, but they seemed to understand each other perfectly.

'How is that even possible?' she asked louder still, 'You saw The Godfather, right?'

'What is it?' asked Jong-sup.

'You have got to be fucking joking,' she laughed but the anger sounded real, 'Suddenly at Midnight?'

'What are you saying?' asked Jong-sup looking down at a watch that did not exist.

'Suddenly at Midnight! The film. I love that film.'

'I get it, but when I was a kid there was still a couple of Japanese propaganda films around and people generally detested them after the war. I tried to watch a couple of those cowboy films the westerners brought over. Spent a week's wage on em too.'

'Well, did you like em? What were they? Good bad and Ugly? Shane?'

'I don't know, I couldn't understand a word of it, and I was the only kid in our group that couldn't read the subtitles quickly enough,' the words stuck audibly in his throat and he choked on them. Even in this intoxicated state Mi-sook could tell that she had broken down a wall of this poor man. This was obviously painful for him to admit. She linked her arm round his and rested her head on his shoulder. Jong-sup's heart was immediately aflutter, and his head shot around for any on lookers, in particular, her husband.

‘I was a slow reader too,’ said Mi-sook with an expression she swore was sympathetic but looked more like a sad cartoon clown.

‘I wasn’t slow. The words were too fast,’ defended Jong-sup.

‘True, I’ve always said they were too quick for human minds to read,’ she lied.

‘Exactly, *you* understand.’

‘Well anyway, my personal favourite is Casablanca.’

‘Is it good?’ asked Jong-sup.

‘Is it good? I should slap you,’ she said as she slapped his arm, ‘It’s a masterpiece.’

‘It’s American right?’ he asked.

She nodded.

‘Can’t you pick a Korean film as your favourite?’

‘You have too many hang-ups Mr Kim. It’s the ultimate romance film.’

‘Well then. I won’t like it. I can’t stand all that mushy stuff,’ he said adamantly.

‘Come on, everyone likes romance. It’s the one universal truth, something all people of the world can relate to.’

‘Not this people of the world,’ he said pointing his thumb at his face.

‘Seriously. Have you never been in love?’ she asked.

‘I have,’ he answered, ‘just once.’

Mi-sook’s mouth was agape. She had not anticipated that answer. She fully expected him to sweep all past loves under the carpet and bury the thoughts deep inside. So, she pushed further.

‘Tell me about her,’ she demanded.

‘No. Sorry but no,’ said Jong-sup firmly.

‘That’s fine don’t worry. Was she pretty?’ she laughed.

‘She was beautiful,’ answered Jong-sup without missing a beat, his eyes became distant.

‘Well, how did you meet?’ she asked

‘We used to work together but let’s change the subject, please.’

'I want to talk about this!' she stomped her foot playfully coming off bratty.

'There is nothing to tell. Man and woman meet at work. Man becomes completely obsessed with woman. Shortly after marriage man catches her going into a hotel with a US marine,' Jong-sup put his hands over his ears, his head in his lap and exhaled lengthily. He was a fool. Alcohol had made his lips loose in a way it had never done before. This woman, who was no more really than a stranger, and here he was just spilling memories that he had never even said aloud. Mi-sook was stunned, perhaps she had pushed too hard. Her hidden curiosity and her mouth disagreed and conspired against her.

'So, you left that bitch, I'm sorry, that woman, right?' she asked wincing as she did so and wishing she hadn't drank so much.

'No,' he replied, the corner of his mouth lifting in an unsuccessful attempt at a smile, 'I didn't.'

'Then, where is she now?'

'She's dead,' he answered, and, in his eyes, she could see a wound deep inside of him that was still wide as the day he had earned it. At first, she felt a flash of fear that he was trying to confess to something atrocious but looking at him she felt nothing but pity. The fun of the night and thrill of discovering more about her mysterious guest had left her. She decided that the conversation should be nipped in the bud finally.

Jong-sup sat looking up at the pitch-black sky for near ten minutes in silence. Mi-sook was getting very uncomfortable and was about to give him some time alone when -

'I hated her. I hated her so much,' he said finally, eyes still fixed to the sky.

'Oh,' she muttered; she could think of nothing else to say.

'The night I had caught her with that disgusting American, she had told me she was going to visit her family in the country. She didn't see me. I watched her go into the hotel from the other side of the road and I tried to build up the courage to barge down the door and confront them but- the guy was huge. I took so long that I was still there when they came out. I'm a coward.'

'And they saw you?' she asked tentatively.

'No, they were far too enveloped in each other,' he answered.

'So, what did you do?' she asked unsure whether she wanted to know.

'I waited at home till she came back. Three days later mind you. With each day my rage elevated. I was scaring myself with thoughts of what I may do to her. It got to the point where I was hoping that she'd never come back through that door for her own safety.'

Mi-sook said nothing.

'Of course, she did come back,' he continued 'I invited her to sit down. She could tell that something was off. I was about to unleash my pent-up fury when she collapsed to the ground.'

'Why what happened?!' asked Mi-sook.

'I thought at first that she was doing it for attention,' said Jong-sup.

'Of course she was, right?'

'Well, I ignored her but then she started to have a fit and all the anger evaporated. I was suddenly worried that I would lose her, so I rushed her to hospital. After some tests and two days waiting around, she was diagnosed with a brain tumour. She was given less than a year.'

'Oh god that is awful. I'm sorry. So, when did you get round to confronting her?'

'I didn't,' he sounded as though his throat was closing and that each word was a fight to emit.

'What do you mean?' she looked up at him and could see tears streaming heavily down his cheeks.

'Once I brought her back from the hospital, I couldn't bring myself to say anything. She was going through enough. So, I did what had to be done. I took time off work and became her carer.'

'So, you forgave her?'

'No. A real man would've. A real man would have been true to himself and either told her the truth and got someone else to care for her, or he would have forgiven her and loved her whole heartedly till the end of her days. Instead I hated her quietly. I fulfilled my duty, but she left this world not with the warm embrace of love but the frosty front of resent,' he was sobbing heavily now, 'I will never forgive myself for that.'

'To be feeling how you do now, you must have loved her,' said Mi-sook placing her hand over his trembling clenched fist.

'Maybe, but if I did, I made sure she never felt it. Even now I still hate her so much.'

'I think you've been holding on to a lot of anger for a long time. That's not healthy.'

'Forgive me, but I'm not sure you would understand,' he said trying not to sound dismissive or rude. Mi-sook looked around and fidgeted uncomfortably.

'I understand more than you would think,' she said eventually 'the night my husband passed away we had a huge fight,' she too, began to sob.

It took Jong-sup a moment to realise what she had just said. His stomach sank once he had.

'You don't mean Kwang-su?' he said, his voice trembling.

'How d-' she started.

'I think I saw his name somewhere at your place,' he explained.

'Oh, right,' she replied, suspicion in her voice 'well, yes, Kwang-su. I have never forgiven myself for leaving so much unsaid and for some of the things I did say,' she began to weep heavily. Jong-sup said nothing but wrapped his arm around her and she buried her face in his chest.

Jong-sup looked up across the square. Stood outside a convenience store glaring at him was Kwang-su. There was hatred in his eyes that Jong-sup could feel even at a distance. He whipped his arm from around her roughly and stood up.

'I don't know about you, but I actually feel lighter having shared that with you,' he said.

'I'm glad,' she said wiping her eyes on her sleeve.

'I have never been one for moping around though, perhaps we could find some bread to eat. I think we need to sober up if we're going to get home,' he said looking over his shoulder.

Kwang-su was no longer there.

'Oh, I will not be driving us home tonight,' she stated firmly 'we're not all as reckless drivers as you, you know?' her mouth curled into a wry smile.

Jong-sup smiled back weakly.

'So, what shall we do?' he asked.

'There is a budget hotel not far from here,' she said 'now don't get the wrong idea,' she stood up and poked him hard in the chest.

'What idea?' he laughed.

6

Jong-sup had looked over his shoulder for Kwang-su the whole way, but he hadn't appeared. That sly bastard, thought Jong-sup, tricking him like that and telling him to leave. He was quite embarrassed that he hadn't realised Kwang-su was dead. He was not afraid of ghosts, he had spent enough time with them, but something in the way Kwang-su had looked at him filled him with tremendous guilt.

The hotel was a narrow four-story building. Dingily lit and no signs of life. There was no one manning the reception simply placed on the counter was two baskets. One for keys and one for money. The small towns of Korea held very trusting people. Jong-sup could not imagine this happening in Seoul.

'Problem,' said Mi-sook dangling a key in front of her 'There's only one room left.'

'Oh right. Maybe I should sleep in the car then,' said Jong-sup.

'Well it's up to you. It wouldn't be very comfortable though. I'm okay if you want to share with me,' she said, going red even in the dim lighting 'if you're uncomfortable with it, that's alright.'

'No, no, I'm okay with it, if I'm not intruding of course,' he said tripping over his own tongue.

Lying in bed, fully clothed and looking at the ceiling; Jong-sup and Mi-sook were both feeling incredibly awkward. The room was tiny and cramped but the bed was big enough for them both to lie in without touching. Jong-sup tried to focus on going off to sleep but whenever he closed his eyes the world spun out of control making him nauseous. He guessed that Mi-sook was feeling the same way.

'What we spoke about earlier,' whispered Jong-sup.

'Huh?' said Mi-sook disturbed from a daydream she was trying to turn into a real one.

'The things we spoke about earlier,' he repeated.

'What about it?' she asked.

'I hope I need not remind you that you shouldn't repeat it to anyone,' he said.

'Don't worry, I won't,' she said turning on her and facing away from him sulkily.

'I mean,' he put his hand on her arm 'thank you.'

'For what?' She turned back round to face him.

'For everything. Saving me. I feel that a huge weight has been lifted from me. I mean I can still feel it there, but it's lighter somehow.'

'Well, you're welcome,' she pulled herself into him, pushed her face into his breast and embraced him. Jong-sup was startled but he let his body sink in. His whole life, he had not been held in this way, with such warmth. He wondered if his mother had held him like this before she passed, and he caught a tear before it fell from his face.

'If you think this is leading to sex you've got another thing coming,' she smiled cheekily.

'Of course not,' he smiled 'besides the topics of today's conversation haven't exactly put me in the mood.'

'Sure, you men are always in the mood,' she laughed 'Like dogs.'

'You're not wrong,' he replied 'but in this instance, I'll abstain. Can I ask you something? But if it's too personal or upsetting don't worry.'

'Sure,' she replied, her eyes shut.

'How did your husband pass away?' he winced. He knew he was overstepping the mark, but he was riddled with curiosity about how the man, who had probably cheated him at Janggi, had died.

'Car crash,' she said, as though she was tired of talking of it.

'Oh right,' he understood now why she was so harsh with him about reckless driving and felt the sharp pang of guilt. He tried to picture Kwang-su to see if he had any indicators of a crash, Mr Lee's spirit was missing his lower half and his intestines were hanging out, so why did Kwang-su not have broken limbs or a steering wheel protruding from his skull. He scratched at his head; he did not understand the dead.

'You may have read about it a few years back,' she said 'the whole Sundai scandal. Parts of one of their models were poorly manufactured and went unchecked. Kwang-su was one of the victims of that whole thing,' her voice was steady but although her eyes were still closed, she was welling up at the corners.

Jong-sup tried to talk but he could not. He wanted to ask more questions; to disqualify himself as perpetrator. It could have been a different model. A different scandal that he had nothing to do with. It was as if his voice wouldn't allow him the opportunity to talk his way out of the weighty responsibility.

It was him. He was responsible. He wasn't the only one in the wrong, but he was as far away from innocent that it made very little difference.

Mi-sook's head and arm began to feel very heavy as though they were pinning him to the bed. His body was still but his mind was racing. Beads of sweat appeared on his forehead.

'I tried to get justice, but eventually you get to the point that you cannot fight any longer. There is no winning against big corporations. I even paid a private investigator, but he took my down payment and I didn't hear from him again. He stopped answering his phone and I've visited his office numerous times and he has never been in. That was what I was doing in Seoul when I saw you,' she stopped 'Jong-sup are you OK? Your heart is pounding.'

She turned over to look at him and it was as if a boulder had been lifted off him. Mi-sook's eyes staring into his was an altogether worse sensation that made the night's alcohol rise into his throat.

'I'm fine,' he stammered and spluttered 'just beer sweats,' he wiped his forehead with his sleeve and it came away damp.

'Okay, are you sure?' she asked, 'It's not something I said I hope.'

'No, no of course not,' his eyes were drawn to the window. There, looking straight at him. On the outside of the window, four stories high, was Kwang-su. His stomach fell through the floor and the floors beneath them. He stifled a scream to an audible whimper.

'I'm sorry, I must go to sleep if I'm to feel better in the morning,' he turned away to look at the wall and tried to force the image of Kwang-su's face from his mind.

'You are sure you are okay?' she got no response, so she too turned on her side to face the opposite direction.

After a couple of hours, when Mi-sook was quietly snoring away, Jong-sup who had had no sleep whatsoever, rose from the bed. He didn't look at the woman who had pulled him from the car, fed him, gave him clothes and a place to recover. He did, however, look at her bag. After rummaging through as quietly as possible not to awake the woman. He left with her car keys.

In her sleepy hungover state, she thought she could hear tires screeching through the night. It would not be till she awoke she'd discover who they belonged to.

충격과 거부

Part Eight

Shock and Denial

1

Kwang-su's pickup truck had made it to Seoul after a couple of hours with Jong-sup at the wheel. He had arrived in a much less reckless manner than he had left the city. He took Mi-sook's feelings about dangerous driving seriously, apparently much more serious than her feelings about her possessions. The thought of her waking to the disappearance of not only Jong-sup, but also her husbands prized vehicle hurt him. She would probably understand though had she known the full story, he hoped, in fact she would probably want him to disappear as quickly as possible.

Morning rush hour boxed him in as he travelled at a snail's pace. Time wasn't exactly a factor here, but he wanted to get it over and done with, the sooner the better. Decisions had been made but they were in no way set in stone. Battles raged in his mind and he was constantly talking himself out of it.

It is impossible, he thought once again, what are the chances? Out of all the trees in Korea I crash into the one owned by the woman who set that psychopath on me. If she knew what she had caused me she would probably hand me the keys herself. Death must be behind this somehow; he had seen her possess a dead body and conjure a boat. Manifesting as a widow was surely within her capabilities? Or maybe she steered him into the tree? Either way he was tired of being an ant under her magnifying glass; burning him just enough to put him in excruciating pain but not enough to kill him.

The journey had been strangely uneventful. His eyes flickered from people to shop windows to the tops of building keeping an eye out for Death. There had been no sign of her nor had he felt her presence in any way. Still, he knew that somewhere she was probably watching.

Arriving in his old neighbourhood he was filled with a sense of foreboding; most likely because he could see his old apartment block jutting out of the landscape. It was a rural area so there were few tall buildings, so it was always in the periphery of his vision. There was no way he was going to set foot on his street, it was risky enough being this close to it considering the last time he left was in a body bag.

Pulling over in an empty side street he hopped out of the car, leaving the keys in the ignition and the engine running; he didn't plan on staying long. At the end of the street was a large wall which Jong-sup had some trouble clambering over and landed hard on the other side. Twigs and leaves cushioned his fall slightly but it still winded him.

Between the trees he could see his destination: Mr Lee's shop.

As he approached the dilapidated building, he felt hesitant to enter and face the truth. Ever since smashing Mr Lee's brick into dust he had been worried that he had killed his ghastly friend, if it was even possible to kill a dead person. He had been trying unsuccessfully to convince himself that without an anchor to our mortal plane, Mr Lee had been free to move on to the next stage, whatever that was. Either way his own existence had been all the more painful and lonely without Mr Lee's voice of reason.

He peered round the doorway and his fears were confirmed. It was quiet and still. Maybe he was able to move on? Jong-sup wasn't fond of kidding himself and decided to focus on the task at hand. The sun shone through the large hole in the wall and highlighted all the dust in the air.

This time, for reasons unknown to him, standing in the shop at the counter that Mr Lee used to busy himself behind, took him back to being a child once more. Back when he was filled with mostly innocence, naivety, and a dash of mischievousness. Although times were hard, and his future was uncertain he longed for those times again. He had always blamed the way he was now on his tough childhood in the orphanage but this time things were different. He knew that he didn't have to become what he had. He could feel that deep in his gut, that young boy still existed but with each choice in his life he had caked him with greed and selfishness.

It was probably too late to change who he was now the damage had been done. It was also impossible to take back the pain he had caused to others too, but he might be able to help them heal.

He tore his mind away from the enticing nostalgia of the past and made for the broom closet. The trap door was wide open and the niggling feeling of doubt began to prod at his brain.

'It better still be here,' he said aloud to himself.

Ducking under the floorboards and catching a face full of spider webs he saw the safe. He approached tentatively. He loudly exhaled; it was still locked. He crouched down in the dirt and twisted the dial. 18-08-18. There was a clunk, and the door swung open creakily.

There was no money in the safe. That psychopath had seen to that. Resentment flared up in him once again at the thought. He wasn't here for money, however much it seared at his mind. His reason for travelling to this cursed city lay right there at the bottom of the safe.

A purple binder.

His prize claimed, he hurried out of the basement but stopped dead in his tracks as something splatted on the ground in front of him, blood. He raised his head reluctantly, but relief and joy washed through him.

'Mr Lee!' expelled Jong-sup louder than he meant 'It's good to see you.... I was worried that... never mind.'

Mr Lee was busying himself dusting the upper corner of the ceiling, making no impact whatsoever and noticing about as much. His shredded flesh and hanging intestines swung rhythmically to and fro. He carried on with his chores for nearly three minutes before looking down.

'We're not open yet!' he snapped sternly, then realisation hit him. 'Young man, it has been a while,' he floated down as if he was descending a ladder that did not exist and looked Jong-sup straight in the face 'you don't look so good young man,' he said, 'you been eating alright?'

Jong-sup struggled to find words. It was Mr Lee who did not look so good. Not that he ever looked great, being torn in half, but all things considered he looked much worse than when they had last seen each other. His skin clung to his bones like loose fitting clothes. His hair had large patches missing but it was his eyes, or lack of that was the greatest change. Two dark sockets took the place of the kind caring eyes he once owned. He stepped back. Perhaps Mr Lee's life force was more intertwined with this building than he had realised. So, by destroying part of it he had, no! He could not bear to face it.

He turned away from the ghoul who at one time had been his only companion. Not in disgust but shame.

'I'm sorry Mr Lee.'

'Sorry for what?' asked the spectre, 'It hasn't been that long, and although times are hard, I don't rely on your custom alone to keep running.'

'I'm sorry for how I spoke to you last,' he said sniffling 'I shouldn't have been so disrespectful.'

'What in the heavens are you talking about lad?' he came a little closer and placed a thin and rotting hand on Jong-sup's shoulder 'Are you in some kind of trouble?'

It seemed his mind as well as his image that had faded away. He did not seem to remember anything. It was too much for Jong-sup to take right now. He rushed out of the door frame without turning back, his eyes we're grieving him far too much, his ears would give him no respite though.

'You were always a good boy,' he heard Mr Lee say softly in a sad tone that was almost whispered into his ear.

Making it to the alley that led to his old road, he squatted down, pushed his eyes into his knees and scratched at his bald head till he could feel skin under his nails. He wailed through gritted teeth and wished he could do it all again. All of it. His whole life. Dying now would be no reward. With such a path of destruction left in his wake, he was sure he could think of nothing else till the end of time.

The crushing weight of the realisation of living in a world of his own making was like drowning. Hopeless. Claustrophobic. Alone.

Preparation for a long stint of self-pity was cut short by the sound of people. Lots of them. He realised the yelling and clamour had been going on the whole time on the periphery of his hearing, but he had been too wrapped up in his own failings to notice.

The only way he could put an end to this internal struggle was to put things right. He got up, dusted off his knees and set in the opposite direction of the noise of potential curious eyes.

One sound, among all the others, stopped him in his tracks. Sobbing. Familiar sobbing. Not being able to place the sound irritated and worried him, so grudgingly he turned round and sought the origin.

Sprawled out on the steps wailing loudly and dramatically flailing, Mi-na's housekeeper didn't notice Jong-sup's approach and she most likely wouldn't recognise him if she did. Jong-sup however, recognised her immediately, and he was washed with dread.

'Catrina!' called Jong-sup, his fear of being recognised or exposed left him completely, or more accurately was replaced by a much greater fear of an outcome he couldn't bear to think about.

Head snapping up and eyes flicking open, her face painted a picture of confusion and fear through flooded eyes.

'Who is that?' she sobbed.

'Catrina! Where is Mi-na?' asked Jong-sup crouching down to her level and clasping her shoulders.

'You no see the TV?' she snapped in broken Korean. She pushed his hands from her and thrust her arm in the direction of where the rest of the noise was coming from.

Jong-sup for the first time took note of the crowd. Before he had seen them merely as a loud obstacle, warning him to avoid at all costs. Piece by piece the situation stitched itself together however, and true realisation of the horror crashed into him.

The crowd, apart from a couple of bystanders and policemen, consisted of reporters and camera crews. Representatives of all major networks in South Korea were here. All the cameras were pointed at a podium placed upon a make-shift stage, and on that podium stood Mi-na's father.

He had not yet spoke, he was fingering through some papers and occasionally reorganising them.

Jong-sup had no time for politicians, this was a time for action not words.

'Catrina, what had happened to Mi-na, is she alive?'

Catrina just shook her head; she couldn't understand Jong-sup's panicked rambling. He breathed deep and slowed down.

'Where is Mi-na?'

'She gone.'

'Gone where?'

'I don't know!' she wailed.

'Is she lost?'

Catrina shook her head and spoke in English but seeing that Jong-sup was not following a word of it switched briefly to Tagalog before exhaling exasperated.

'Bad men come,' she said 'take Mi-na,' the name was forced through her lips by loud cries.

'Catrina!' said Jong-sup, firmly but gently 'Who were these men?'

'I don't know but I see them before,' she sniffled 'Sometimes they come to the house.'

Jong-sup's mind swept over his memories for anyone in the neighbourhood who might have even looked at Mi-na in the wrong way. It was impossible, Mi-na was special, the type of person you meet once in your life, someone who brings joy to everyone they meet. Well, nearly everyone, he thought, remembering some of his past interactions with her. Christ! He hated himself. He did not deserve to be her neighbour. He slapped himself in the face, Hard. Now was not the time to fall back into to self-pity and scorn.

Jong-sup thought of the last time he had seen Mi-na. His mind flashed back to the night he had seen her father being harassed by Young-jin.

'Catrina! Was it the Yuk Sung Pa?'

'Yes!' she screeched. 'The people try to take last time. They shoot the reception man. They come to my boss house. Only me and Mi-na,' she howled so loud at that point that a couple of people from the crowd started looking her way. Jong-sup blocked her from sight by kneeling before her.

'Calm down Catrina,' he said softly. 'Is it money they're after?'

She nodded her head vigorously.

'They tell me tell my boss they want 50,000,000 dollars or they send Mi-na back in small piece,' her body shuddered all over at the thought of it.

That's a lot of money, thought Jong-sup, they must know that Mi-na's father doesn't have that kind of money.

'More,' said Catrina 'my boss say police he don't know them but I see them before.'

'Your boss said he doesn't know the police?'

Catrina shook her head.

'Your boss told the police that he doesn't know why they took Mi-na, but you have seen him with them before?'

Catrina nodded.

Jong-sup began pacing. He knew what he had to do. Even if he did not realise it yet, his mind had been made up as soon as he saw Catrina in such a state. He had a responsibility.

Strewn unknowingly on the floor was his other responsibility. He must have dropped his folders at some point. Luckily, none of the documents had blown away and he quickly collected them and dropped them into Carina's hands. She looked at them Dumbfounded and went to pass them back.

'Listen Catrina. I think I can help Mi-na. At least I hope so. Do you understand me?'

She nodded.

'First I need you to send these folders to this address. Right?' she nodded again. He then whispered into her ear the next instructions. She looked at him and her eyes shone with fear but also hope. They held each other's gaze for a few seconds.

'Trust me, please,' he said.

'What? How? Mr…….Mr Park? Is this you?'

'I don't have time to explain, I am sorry Catrina,' he said sweeping around and sprinting down the street, leaving Catrina to draw crosses in the air and mutter blessings and prayers.

Jong-sup knew where they might have her. It was somewhere he never ever wanted to return to again. He held his lower abdomen, feeling the pang of remembrance as he ran.

2

There had been a large influx of guards since his last visit, or more accurately, escape. They patrolled the perimeter in groups of three. Some were decked out in full security gear, most dressed in typical dock-worker attire of grey overalls. Jong-sup could tell from their manner that they were all one and the same. Yuk Sung Pa.

From Jong-sup's lookout; the fire escape of a closed down administrative office, he had a wide scope of the whole complex. Directly in front of him heading north back to the city was a wide road; perfect for getting lorries and cargo trucks to and from the loading stations. Either side of which, stood two separate complexes each full to the brim with shipping containers and poking out from behind were four warehouses. On his right: 25 and 26. On his left 24 and the all too familiar 23.

The horrors he had seen in that building would stay with him the rest of his hopelessly unnatural long life. He would give almost anything to never set foot there again. However, Jong-sup's reasoning was that it would be foolhardy to spread all your evil doings to any more buildings than was absolutely necessary. The thought that it was possible that all those warehouses could be full of dismembered and dissected bodies briefly crossed his mind, but he forced it back to whence it came. He had no time for hesitation.

The fact that security had been bolstered to such an extent around 23 and 24 and was virtually non-existent at its twin, reinforced Jong-sup's theory. There was no doubt about it; something big was happening, and what is bigger than the kidnapping of a Mayor's daughter?

It was Ji-sung's first day in the big league. Well, kind of. He was still a very small fish in a giant pond, but he could feel that he was nearing ever closer to the time when he would prove, finally, that he was in fact a shark.

The last couple of years he had been working as a low-level drug dealer for the Yuk Sung Pa. Cocaine mostly; in the toilets of night clubs around Gangnam. His connections always made sure to remind them that although he was selling for the gang, he was not part of the gang. They treated him like scum, berated him, constantly cut his margins and took every opportunity to emasculate him. But, god, he wanted to be like them. All the shit he has had to deal with these last couple of years, all of the built up anger and frustration, he couldn't wait to take out on the next low level dealer trying desperately to get with the gang. His dreams of being able to lord over the weaker were all that had kept him going.

Finally, an opportunity had presented itself. Brother Dong, also known as snakeskin, had been there to receive the Yuk Sung's cut instead of the usual riff raff that he usually dealt with. They had a couple of drinks together and was told about this job they needed doing that was top priority, all the big players were going to be there.

After walking on air all the way to the port he had to admit he felt a little deflated. It seemed they had invited every piece of shit from Gangnam, Itaewon and Uijongbu to this little gig. It didn't matter much, he rationalised. Once they had seen that he was more cut-throat and more deserving than any of these losers they would welcome him with open arms.

Slowing down to separate himself from the others that were preventing him from truly standing out, he began to dream about what his new life as a gangster would be like. He was so engrossed that he didn't hear the whistling from across the road next to the administration building. Something flying past his vision and hitting the wall next to him quickly snapped him out of it. A small stone rolled by his feet. His eyes darted to bushes across the road the most likely source judging by the trajectory.

Ji-sung was about to call to his temporary comrades but decided against it. He felt for the knife in his pocket and rushed headfirst to check it out. The time for him to shine was now.

About ten minutes later Jong-sup walked out from the bushes wearing Ji-sung's garb. He pulled his cap down over his eyes, flipped his collar up and made his way to the entrance.

'Ji-sung!' called one of the guys Jong-sup had seen his victim walking with previously. He was one of four about seventy-five meters away. Jong-sup turned his head the opposite way and walked through the gates.

Out of the shadows a big burly half Korean emerged and placed a hand on Jong-sup's chest.

Jong-sup tensed his fists ready to fight his way out of the situation if he had been compromised.

'Not waiting for your friend,' he said eyebrows raised. Jong-sup didn't reply. Not because he thought that was the best course of action but because he wasn't quick minded enough to think of a response.

'Ji-sung, where'd you go?' came the voice again from behind the wall. Jong-sup once again did not react.

'What's the matter?' asked the man obstructing his passage into the grounds 'Lover's quarrel?' he laughed until he saw Jong-sup's emotionless reaction. 'I don't give a shit, just keep it down. One more peep out of either of you and it will be your ass. Understand?' Jong-sup nodded in response.

'What's your name?' and by his tone he wasn't asking.

'Uh Ji-sung.'

'Okay old timer, you do a round of the eastern containers. Go.'

Jong-sup didn't need to be told twice and he made for east of the compound.

After doing two laps of the containers to dissuade any suspicion Jong-sup made his way to the daunting hollow building where he had painfully awoken in a crate what seemed like a lifetime ago.
His instincts screamed in his head not to go anywhere near there, but the memory of sweet and kind Mi-na's voice flushed them out and compelled him onward.

The large opening to the warehouse was flush with traffic; people pushing trolleys piled high with crates or pallets. The big boat was nowhere to be seen, and he hoped neither was its owner. The second, man-sized door, was being guarded by two heavily tattooed brutes. They didn't even acknowledge Jong-sup's presence as he passed right by them his cap pulled low over his eyes.

He latched on to an oncoming trolley and pretended to guide it inside. The crates were being stacked in a pile in the middle of the floor where some other men were cracking the tops open. Every now and then they would find something they were after (Jong-sup assumed drugs, well he hoped it was drugs) and motion for someone to cart it off into the back room directly below where Jong-sup had awoken to the bodies hanging from hooks.

He was in. There was no time for respite, however. The next step was to find out if Mi-na was here. Jong-sup had not planned for the possibility of her being in another warehouse. The Yuk-sung pa owned at least three on this port. Perhaps she wasn't even in a warehouse but in a van or at a club or brothel. The voice he had overheard saying that they keep all the most valuable stuff here echoed in his mind and he used it as wind for his sails, driving him onward. That was a while ago however and things change. If he did find her here, he had no idea how he was going to. Catrina had let him down, his distraction had fell though. If he had taken time to think this through properly, he would have jumped overboard and swam for shore.

To his left was the small administration office with the stairway that led to the staff room and dissecting floor upstairs. The window told that it was empty for now and since a better opportunity seemed unlikely, Jong-sup rushed straight in and closed the door behind him. Scanning the desks for clues as to if Mi-na was here bore no fruit. He did not know what he was looking for regardless.

Just as he placed his toe on the bottom step of the staircase, a voice echoed from above. Instinctively Jong-sup scuttled, cockroach-like, under the desk closest to him. Just in time too as multiple pairs of footsteps came rushing downstairs. Jong-sup could only see their feet as he tried to make himself as small as possible. He counted around ten men. The door flung open and an exasperated man fell into the room.

'What the hell is going on?' demanded a familiar voice.

'The boss wants a word, Young-jin,' replied another man.

'Well where the fuck is he?' snapped Young-jin.

'Right the fuck here,' came a low voice from behind the door.

Jong-sup knew that voice. Jong-sup could still see the scarred man stomping Uncle Eung to death, before tying him to an anchor and dropping him in the Han.

The messenger made way and bowed low, as the boss entered, and all the other men followed suit.

The boss walked slowly over to Young-jin's lowered head, scooped him up from under his chin and slammed him into the wall; hand clenched around his throat.

'Do you know what's going on outside?' said the boss; his voice calm with bubbling rage 'cause it's your fucking job to know what's going on. You're supposed to be coordinating this little circus. Do. You. Know. what's. Going. On. Outside?' he wasn't asking, or if he was, he was not loosening his grip to allow a reply. The other men all shifted uncomfortably but stayed silent. Jong-sup focused on keeping his breathing as low as possible, but his heartbeat was pulsing in his ears so loudly that he thought that someone was bound to hear it sooner or later.

'Right now, the police are searching through my warehouse in the western wing. Why have I heard this from this piece of shit,' he motioned behind him to the man who had announced his entrance 'and not you, my eyes and ears? Why?!' with his question he administered a swift but strong punch into Young-jin's stomach, 'Why!' Another hit, 'Why!' Another. All this time Young-jin barely uttered a groan. Finally released he slid down the wall pathetically.

Jong-sup could now see Young-jin's face. Which meant that Young-jin would be able to see Jong-sup in turn. Young-jin lolled on his shoulder, eyes closed however, Jong-sup held his breath and envisioned all possible means of escape for when his eyes finally opened. Perusing his chances, getting out alive did not look good for Jong-sup and he twitched in anticipation; spring-loaded to move.

'Look at me when I am speaking to you!' bellowed the boss, 'Get up.'

Young-jin's body moved instantly not taking note of whatever, or whoever was on the ground. Jong-sup parted his lips ever so slightly to allow his captive breath to escape slowly.

'Now, fortunately there is nothing particularly incriminating held in there at this very moment but who knows where they'll search next.'

The door swung open again and yet another person rushed into the room. It was so crowded in here that the people at the back had to stand on the stairs. The more eyes present the greater the chance that one of them would spy Jong-sup. A bead of sweat trickled down his bald head.

'Don't just stand there panting, dribbling on my floor. Spit it out!' snapped the boss.

'It's Lieutenant Park sir, he's here,' said the bumbling man.

'About fucking time! Send him in!'

People shuffled about to make more room. One of the thugs sat on the desk his feet hanging next to Jong-sup's face. Lieutenant park? Thought Jong-sup. Could someone so high up really be in co-hoots with this band of wanton criminals? After a couple of minutes, the lieutenant stepped through the door.

'Hello boys,' said the lieutenant, nonchalantly putting a cigarette to his lips and lighting it. He offered the pack to the boss who refused.

'What the hell do I pay you for? Huh? To prevent shit like this happening.'

'Or to get you out of sticky situations,' countered the lieutenant exhaling a big plume of smoke 'and you, Dai Tau, my friend, are very much stuck.'

Dai Tau thought Jong-sup. Sounded like a nickname.

'Get on with it,' commanded Dai Tau.

'And if you could shut your mouth a minute then I could offer you salvation,' snapped the lieutenant.

At hearing such disrespect aimed at his boss, Young-jin lunged at the lieutenant but only made it a couple of inches before he was frozen in place by a slight flicker of Dai Tau's hand.

'Listen,' continued Lieutenant Park 'a call came in approximately an hour ago. Anonymous female, Mexican perhaps, claiming that she knew the location Dong-wook's daughter. Now I know your boys took the girl. Now, please tell me she's been taken to one of your locations around the city and you haven't stored her in your main fucking base of operations.'

Dai Tau sighed, 'She's upstairs,' he groaned, one hand gesturing to the stairway and one pressed tightly to his temple in stress.

'Fuck! You don't make my life easy do you,' snapped the lieutenant. He put his cigarette out on the wall next to him and flicked the butt onto the floor. It bounced twice and then rolled under the desk, stopping right in front of Jong-sup's face. 'I can't stand around here all day,' he continued 'I can hold my lads off for a time, but it won't take long till they're banging on this door.'

Thank you, Catrina, thought Jong-sup. She had come through. He told her to send the folder first to give him some time to get here before they arrive. He knew that if the police found the girl before he did, the Yuk Sung Pa would have killed her to stop her speaking out.

'In the meantime, boys,' said Dai Tau 'let's sneak the girl out of here.'

'Not until I tell you it's safe,' interrupted Lieutenant Park. Dai Tau scowled at him but kept his mouth shut. 'Right now, we've got people patrolling the perimeter. They'll stop any vehicle coming out of here. I'll think of a way to keep them busy then I'll send word.'

'Fine!'

'And pull you all your men outside the wall, inside! It looks suspicious as hell,' with that last word he put another cigarette to his lips and walked out of the small and crowded office.

'Big teeth!'

'Yes boss?' came a voice from the back.

'You go round up our security and bring em inside the walls. The rest of you idiots grab any drugs or weapons and take them right into the back room and into the corner. I'll be having a chat with each of you later till we find out who told their little Mexican girlfriend.'

The room emptied in unorganised fashion till the only one remaining were Young-jin, the boss and Jong-sup.

'Listen here Young-jin. Have I not always treated you as a son?'

'Yes boss. Forgive me.'

'I am extremely disappointed in you.'

'I'm sorry it won't happen again.'

'No, no, it won't. Cause the next time you'll end up strapped to something heavy and thrown with the others.'

Jong-sup's head filled with the memory of his time at the bottom of the grimy river. His throat filled with the sensation of drowning again and from the look on Young-jin's face he was feeling the same.

'I understand,' he said.

'Now who's watching the girl?' asked Dai Tau.

'Fat Tang,' replied Young-jin.

'Fat Tang? You left her with that animal. You *are* cruel, Young-jin,' smiled Dai Tau.

'Should I send someone to watch him?' asked Young-jin.

'No time,' said Dai Tau 'you go organise the others.'

'Yes boss,' Young-jin turned to walk out of the room.

'Before you go,' said the boss 'aren't you forgetting something?'

Young-jin sighed. He walked over to the boss who grabbed his face and pushed his lips onto Young-jin's.

Their wet kisses filled Jong-sup's ears and he covered them from the sound of their tongues sliding into each other's mouths. Thankfully for Jong-sup's sake they were in a hurry and it did not last long.

'Now then,' said the boss 'I must go be diplomatic with some pigs.'

Both men left the room.

3

Waiting only seconds to see if the coast was clear, Jong-sup rolled from underneath the desk and sprung to his feet. A short dash to the steps and he began his slow creeping ascent up the stairs. Stealth would be everything; he did not want to alert Fat Tang to his presence in case he called the rest, or worse, hurt Mi-na.

He listened as he climbed, he could hear the gruff grunting in the mix of what sounded like a young girl sobbing. It must be Mi-na. Those monsters. She must be terrified; how could anyone do this to a poor girl? No matter what happened, Jong-sup was going to get her out of here.

Three-quarters to the top, a step creaked loudly. Jong-sup stopped dead. So did the noise. Jong-sup prepared himself mentally for any heavy footsteps coming towards the door. If they did Jong-sup would have no choice but to rush Fat Tang and he prayed that his nickname was ironic, or he did not stand much of a chance. No such thing happened, however, the noise continued.

Reassured that Fat Tang had not been made aware of him, Jong-sup continued his creeping. The door at the top was open thankfully, well, at least enough for Jong-sup to stick his head through. Which he carefully did once he made it to the top. He eyed the room. It was exactly how he remembered, large with windows on one side to look down into the warehouse floor below. However, it was filled with tables upon tables, and boxes upon boxes upon those tables. So cluttered was the room that it obscured any sight of Mi-na, but he could just make out the very tip of what looked like Fat Tang's fat head. Jong-sup crept closer, his eyes darting around for signs of the girl. The boxes seemed to form a maze-like corridor that weaved its way towards where Fat Tang was standing.

Slinking from place to place, always taking the utmost care not to reveal himself, he moved closer and closer. Fat Tang was slowly revealed as his bulbous grotesque form was flashed between objects that concealed Jong-sup. His back was turned away. His head bald but patchy and spotty. He was morbidly obese wearing a sweaty stained white vest. Jong-sup could not see his legs but thought he looked around six foot three inches tall. Much too big for Jong-sup to take down.

When Jong-sup was a mere ten feet away, he spied a plank of wood with a couple of rusty nails sticking out of it. To reach it he would have to expose himself which was too risky. He looked round for something he could throw to distract the blob of a man. Nothing. He had no idea how he was going to get her out of here. Perhaps he would need to hide her somewhere until the police searched the warehouse, and then when the time was right expose themselves to the officers. Yes. That's the correct course of action.

A cry audible but weak came from behind Fat Tang before a loud unmistakable sound of knuckles meeting skin was heard. Jong-sup pushed his head out from his hiding place giving up notion of remaining hidden.

Jong-sup almost fell to the ground in horror, but his rage lifted him up. Fury consumed him elevated him till he was larger than his prey. Fat Tang was shocked, but Jong-sup could see into his heart that he was also ashamed. This only fuelled Jong-sup's wrath however and before Fat Tang could even pull up his trousers, Jong-sup grasped the plank and jumping; dug it straight into his head. The wood split in two, one half pinned to Fat Tang's skull while he lulled there for a moment, before his heavy form thudded to the ground. Jong-sup looked down at the disgusting putrid man. There was no sign of movement. Jong-sup kept his eyes on the man a few seconds more, not because he was checking for signs of life, but because he could not bear to raise his head. He forced himself. She needed him.

Mi-na was lying on a pile of pallets. She wasn't moving. Her expression was vacant, and her eyes rolled in their sockets. Her school uniform was ripped and stained with blood at the bottom. Her arms were wracked with dark bruises. A popping sound was coming from her throat.

'Mi-na,' cracked Jong-sup.

No reply.

'Mi-na, can you hear me?' he said gently tapping her face.

No reply.

'Mi-na. Please wake up. Please. Please. Please. Please' he begged.

There was still no response.

Park Jong-sup was too late.

He looked at her slight form lying there. The shell that once housed the kindest, purest most innocent person he had ever met. She didn't deserve this. No one deserved this. The world was evil and cruel. No place for such innocence. How could Death forbid him from leaving this plane but allow her to die in such a horrible manner. He let it all out. He cried out loud; not caring if he was heard.

Placing his forehead on her stomach, sobbing uncontrollably, his experiences with her washed through him.

She was moving in next door. He felt irritated at the thought of having a loud child ruining his peace and quiet.

She was telling off the other kids in the block for chucking stones at his car. Although he had seen the whole thing he had come outside and scolded her in front of her peers, and she ran away upset.

She had asked if he could walk her home as she was scared of being bullied. He said he didn't have the time.

She was bringing him food. He was unappreciative.

She was unknowingly helping him kill himself. He took advantage of her naivete.

She gave him food when he had none. He had thought that he had done her a kindness by protecting her. Well he hadn't protected her. She had suffered more than he could imagine. He turned his head on his side to look up at her face. Thump. A noise. Thump. He stood back astonished.

'Mr Park,' she said gently. He looked at her through tear-filled eyes. His lip tremored. She raised slightly and forced a broken smile, 'You came.'

Jong-sup had no words. He embraced her tightly. Hard at first and then he melted into her.

'Am I …. am I dead?' she asked quietly as if it was a secret they should keep from the living.

'No, you lovely girl. You're alive,' he replied, 'I can't believe you're alive. I'm so glad that you are.'

'You heard me call?' she asked weakly. Her eyes closed and her head lowered.

'Hey!' said Jong-sup 'wake up. I am so sorry. I know you must be tired, but this is no time for sleeping,' he tapped her again, 'What were you saying about me hearing your call?'

Mi-na opened her eyes. 'I called out for you,' she said after a moment 'for some reason I knew you would come. I felt it. Even though you're dead.'

'Of course I came. I wasn't about to sit around and let anything happen to you.'

'That day in the alley with those guys. That was you back then too, right?'

'It was.'

'See. I knew you were good.'

Her head flopped to the side and her eyes closed again. Jong-sup tried to keep her conscious but there was no stopping her. She was still bleeding. If she did not receive medical attention soon, she would be a goner.

Jong-sup was not going to let that happen.

He scooped her up in his arms. His determination making him strong.

'Let's go,' said Jong-sup; more to himself.

4

Fat Tang was not where Jong-sup had left him. He froze. The pool of blood remained, but the source had disappeared. He moved suspiciously quiet for such a large man. Perhaps Death had taken him. No, she left the physical form. Perhaps she was just messing with him. She had done it before. He eyed his surroundings carefully for any signs of movement, while he stayed still as a deer in headlights.

'Death?' he whispered, 'Is that you?'

'Oh, it's death motherfucker!' roared Fat Tang emerging from his hiding place like a cockroach. He charged at the old man cradling the girl he had victimised. Jong-sup's anger fired back up in his chest at the disgusting blob of a man and swiftly dodged out of the way making sure to keep his foot tactically placed to trip his hefty weight.

Satisfying as it initially was to send this pervert back to the ground it quickly turned to horror as the unmistakable sound of smashing glass rang out loudly. The window looking down into the warehouse was nowhere near strong enough to hold Fat Tang and it gave way immediately, sending him screaming down to an audibly squelching death.

The men in the room; about thirty or so including Young-jin, stopped what they were doing and looked up at Jong-sup silhouetted in the window of the upstairs office. For just a moment everyone froze not knowing how to react.

'Stop that bald prick!' yelled Young-jin.

A rallying cry bounced around the large room, and about ten or so men pulled handguns; ready to fire at the old man and young girl.

'Put down the guns you morons!' screamed Young-jin 'You want the cops banging on our door! Knives, metal bars whatever you can find, kill him!'

There was only one way down; the stairs. Any second now it would be flooded with thugs. He would have to get there first. Darting across the room as fast as his body would move proved useless however; opening the door revealed that the stairway was already packed with men. Jong-sup lashed out with his foot kicking the closest face dead on sending him and everyone in his wake tumbling backwards. Jong-sup wasn't about to hang around. There was only one other place he could run to, and he struggled to think of a place he would like to avoid more.

His side ached as he approached the door. He checked to make sure Mi-na's eyes were closed. She did not need to see this. He prepared himself for the horrors that lie beyond. The sound of footsteps pushed him through. He looked around the room he had seen in most of nightmares ever since he had awoken here cold and in the company of swinging corpses. Shock and relief filled him.

The room was bare.

It had been stripped clean of any bodies or gore. The blood on the walls had been scrubbed off or painted over. It was now packed full of crates and pallets. A few meat hooks hanging from the ceiling were all that was left of this room's barbaric history. Jong-sup integrated himself into the wooden maze just mere seconds before thugs poured into their old chopping grounds.

Jong-sup crouched low; no easy task as Mi-na seemed to be getting heavier by the minute. He could see a couple of men through the gaps between crates. They looked confident, as if they knew for sure that he would never make it out of this room alive. They were probably right. He looked down at the unconscious girl in his arms. No. There was no way she was dying here. Not while he drew breath; it would take a lot to make that happen.

'Hey you!' someone shouted. Jong-sup froze, surprised that they had spotted him so easily.

'You! Big guy!' continued the shouter, 'You stay by the door. So that bald rat doesn't scurry out.'

Jong-sup sighed in relief. However this did present a new problem, it was indeed his plan to sneak around them and out. He searched his brain for a new strategy. All options were torn from his grasp however.

'I see him!' screamed another thug, 'over there!'

Hiding was no longer going to work it seemed, so Jong-sup did the only thing he could think of; he charged. The first man in Jong-sup's wake was stunned at the sudden outburst and could not react fast enough. Jong-sup's fist hit him square in the jaw. The impact wasn't strong enough to knock him unconscious but it knocked him off his feet and that was good enough for now.

An iron bar swung past his face, smashing some pallets into splinters. Jong-sup looked at his assailant; a scrawny man with a ferocious expression. Jong-sup swung at him but the little guy was too quick and ducked under his arm. He swung his bar once again this time aiming for Mi-na. Jong-sup pulled out of harm's way, but only just. Targeting the girl was a mistake he wouldn't get to repeat however, as Jong-sup swept his legs from under him, and while he lay flailing on the ground Jong-sup jumped on his skull silencing him instantly.

A war cry sounded from nearby as four men ran at Jong-sup and he took the only sensible option; he ran in the opposite direction. Weaving in and out of crates and boxes did little to slow his pursuers. Jong-sup turned a corner, stopped and pulled a large stack of pallets that crashed onto the floor. One thug tried to climb over the debris but was soon tangled up in it; the others tried to find an alternative route.

Jong-sup knew he couldn't keep this up. He had zero chance of taking them all out, especially without Mi-na coming to more harm. If they were going to get out of here alive, then they would have to get past the big guy blocking the door, and time was of the essence. He weaved his way through the maze simultaneously trying to get closer to the door and avoid bumping into anyone whom would wish to cause them harm.

Finally he stepped into the middle aisle that led straight down to the exit as well as his largest obstacle. Unfortunately, Jong-sup was joined by a number of men that spilled out into the aisle a little further up. They didn't hesitate to charge, herding Jong-sup towards the door and the ogre of a man.

The guardian of the door could see Jong-sup sprinting his way, girl over his shoulder, followed closely behind by his comrades. This was the perfect opportunity to trap the old man and even claim the glory for himself, so he stomped to meet them. He held his arms out wide giving them no chance to evade, but the old man took action he hadn't even considered. He jumped and grabbed onto a meat hook with one arm and swung. He prepared himself for what he predicted would be a relatively ineffective kick; the kick never came. The old man instead released his grip as he launched the hook with so much force that the guardian didn't realise what had happened until the hook was buried into his face from under his chin. His legs gave out but he did not hit the ground. He hung there; a warm sensation flooding down his front and a cold sensation rising from his toes. Men roughly pushed and bumped past him but not one person stopped to help him. His seemingly lifeless body spun slowly just enough to see the old man slip out the door, girl in arms, before everything just, stopped.

A relieved Jong-sup practically fell into the room and he slammed the door behind him pulling the security bar down. Frantic banging from the other side ensued. Jong-sup attempted a well-earned inhale. A flash of silver on his periphery cut it short however, as a knife aimed straight for the girl. Jong-sup spun just in time; the blade carved a deep line down his back, just left of his spine. Jong-sup stumbled forward and turned to see two men, knives and grins bared approaching steadily. They lunged out, not caring who they cut; young girl or old man. They seemed happy as long as they were separating flesh and drawing blood. Jong-sup wasn't quick enough to dodge any of the blows but he made sure that none even grazed Mi-na. He met each strike with whatever part of his body he could move between Mi-na and harm in time. His blood trailed on the ends of their blades and splattered the walls. A loud sound of gears crunching stopped them in place. Jong-sup looked around for the source. A portion of the floor was lowering. He recognised this platform from his last visit. His back hit a corner; he had been herded in next to the window Fat Tang had fallen through.

The platform returned from below now carrying Young-jin and a couple more men. One of them pulled up the security bar letting out the men from the butchery room. From the stairway came more men still. The small room was crammed with bodies.

'Bald guy,' called Young-jin calmly 'look around. The game is over.'

'I'm leaving,' said Jong-sup weakly.

'I am sorry,' Young-jin chuckled and was joined by several others in the crowd 'you *are* going to die here. Before that happens though. I need to know how you knew we were here and what connection you have to the girl.'

Jong-sup shook his head.

'Look, I am *not* asking here. I got to tell you, I have a lot of respect for you, old man.'

'Seems like it,' spat Jong-sup bitterly.

'No, no, really,' said Young-jin holding up his hands theatrically 'it takes some huge balls to try to infiltrate the Yuk Sung Pa!' he laughed, 'Stupid, but brave. So, I tell you what. I will kill you quickly. A warrior's death. And since you care so much about the little bitch, we'll finish her off humanely too, how about that?'

'Why do you need the girl?' asked Jong-sup 'She is innocent! She doesn't deserve this!'

'What she does and does not deserve is irrelevant,' replied Young-jin his temper flaring slightly 'it's just business. Her dad owes the Yuk Sung Pa and we will get our payment.'

'Don't you have enough money already?'

'First, we decide what counts as "enough money" and secondly this is about something much more valuable, respect.'

'Respect!' laughed Jong-sup through bloody lips 'You boys know nothing about respect. You will never become men. You will die as boys.'

'That's a real shame old man,' sneered Young-jin 'You're chance of a quick death has gone.'

Jong-sup peeked through the smashed window. Fat Tang's large form splayed out cartoonish below. There were only a few men in the warehouse below, it seemed most of them had rushed up to witness the kill. They crept forward, like a pack of wolves closing in on a sheep. Young-jin realised what Jong-sup was planning but it was too late. Jong-sup tucked Mi-na into his chest and jumped backwards through the large whole in the window; cutting his ankles as he did. The shocked expression of the all the men in the room were frozen as the adrenaline in Jong-sup's veins slowed the world.

The fall took much longer than Jong-sup had expected and yet didn't seem long enough. He closed his eyes, squeezed Mi-na into himself and prayed that he had aimed correctly and Fat Tang was directly below them. His prayers were answered by a squelch, several crunches and snaps; some were Fat Tang's, some Jong-sup's. Blood shot from Fat Tang's orifices and it was as if their bodies melded into each other; becoming one being. Mi-na slipped from his grip and rolled onto the floor.

'He's dead! Kill the girl!' came a command that stirred Jong-sup out of his daze. He pulled himself out of the Jong-sup-shaped dent he had left in Fat Tang. He rolled over to Mi-na, making it right on time to shield her from an oncoming assault. Bats, bars and planks of wood were smashed into his back neck and head nearly crippling him but he would not go down.

'Mr.....Park,' came a weak voice, Mi-na's cracked one eye open 'leave me.'

'Shush girl, you need to rest,' said Jong-sup between hits.

'Don't die here for me, Mr Park,' she managed again '*leave me please.*'

'Some people are worth dying for.'

'They can't...... do anything more to me Mr Park, there....there is no point us both dying.'

'You are not going to die Mi-na.'

'It's not your fault Mr Park.'

'What?' asked Jong-sup taken aback.

'It's not your fault,' she repeated.

'No Mi-na, that's what I have been telling myself for years, but it is my fault. If there was something I could have done and didn't then I am responsible,' said Jong-sup barely audible with the wind stricken from him 'it.... It's about time I take my responsibilities seriously. I can start by getting you out of here.'

At least ten men stood around him not even pausing for breath as they brought their weapons down; bones broke, skin tore, blood splattered but he would not go down. Jong-sup peered out between the legs of the man punching him on top of his head. The large opening to the warehouse was closing slowly. It was now or never.

There was no strength in his limbs, so he looked deeper. He looked at Mi-na's face and dug deep down into his core. He tapped right into his life force itself and drew from it. His body was on fire. He tucked his forearms under the girl and placing his head between the legs of the man in front he stood with all might flinging the man over his back. The men stopped. A couple dropped their weapons; their grips loose as their jaws. They couldn't believe what this man could endure.

Jong-sup put one foot in front of the other. He couldn't run. He didn't know how he was managing to move at all. Light from the exit warmed his face as he approached. An obviously forced and afraid war cry came from behind him as someone ran at him and plunged a knife into his shoulder. Jong-sup didn't react. He did not even slow. The attacker didn't follow up, but joined the ranks of agape men.

Jong-sup passed through the exit. The sun exposed how much Mi-na had been through. Jong-sup winced. A movement to his left. Jong-sup turned his head to see the half-Korean man who had stopped him on his way in. He tried to stop him once again this time with a machete. Jong-sup didn't attempt to evade; he knew it was useless. He held up his hand. The blade went between his fingers and cleaved his hand in two like a knife through butter. It hit his radius, which proved too tough for it and it bounced from the attacker's grip and hit for floor with a clang. Still, Jong-sup didn't brake stride.

The outside of the complex was rather empty thanks to Dai Tau pulling his men inside. Not a soul stood now between him and the gate. Hope filled him, and was magnified by the colour blue. He never thought he would be so happy to see the Seoul Metropolitan Police. His eyes flooded with tears at a promise almost fulfilled.

'What the fuck are you doing!' screamed Young-jin who must have just made it downstairs.

'You there! Put the girl down!' came the tinny voice of a police officer from a megaphone.

Jong-sup took another step.

'Why the fuck have you let him just walk out!' screamed Young-jin.

'I repeat. Put down the girl and step away or we will have to neutralise you!' sounded the megaphone again.

'Do you know what he could tell the police?!' screeched Young-jin.

Jong-sup took another step.

'This is your last warning!' cried the officer.

'Fine I'll do it myself!' cried Young-jin.

Jong-sup took another step.

There was a deafening bang.

All was dark.

출생

Part Nine

Birth

All was shrouded in fog around Jong-sup. There were objects in his periphery but when he turned to focus on anything in particular, they flittered away into the mists, leaving only the knowledge that they were once there. He had not long gained consciousness. He did not wake, however, as he had not been asleep. It was as if he had only just begun to exist, materialised in the air perhaps, and that before he had not existed at all.

Before? What had he been doing before? He could not remember, yet it did not trouble him. He felt remarkably at ease with the fact that he did not know where he was, where he had been nor where he was going. He knew that the collection of thoughts, memories and emotions that he had once considered Jong-sup would have been frantic with where he had found himself.

The fact that he knew this meant that he still had some semblance of who or what he was before, but he could tell that it was drifting away, pulling apart and scattering as it did so. He cared not in the slightest at seeing it go.

He breathed deeply and sat thinking for quite a while. Not about anything in particular, in actuality about nothing at all. Solely thinking for thinking's sake. It was pleasant really. Peaceful.

Carried on a wind he could not see nor feel was a feint melody. He couldn't hear it, but he could feel it. It was a song he had never heard and yet had known his whole life. It was sung by his mother. He didn't know how or why he knew, but he knew regardless.

He looked around for the mother he had never known but the mists were tricky and kept what was in the distance veiled. He realised that he was sitting and attempted to stand up but no strength found him. The ground beneath bore him no sensation whatsoever as if he floated just a fraction of a millimetre above it. There was no fear at his newfound immobility, so he decided to sit and wait a little more.

In front of him way off in the distance, the fog washed aside to reveal a tiny figure getting slightly bigger. Although it was the only animated feature in this place, still he found it difficult to focus on it and each time he glanced back the figure was closer. Or perhaps, it had just grown in size. It was difficult to tell. That was until it was close enough that features were noticeable.

A woman. Wearing a pastel blue and cherry hanbok, she strolled leisurely to Jong-sup with a pleasant smile on her face. Her hair was tied up in Jjokjin meori style and walking with weightless grace she was incredibly beautiful. Emotion welled up within Jong-sup and exited in the form of tears that streamed endlessly down his face.

She knelt to meet his eye level.

Hello Park Jong-sup she smiled.

He wanted to respond but no words felt worthy enough to leave his mouth and expose themselves to her ears. By her sweet chuckle, she knew this and planted a delicate kiss on the top of his head. An almost electric surge of energy rippled through his body from the epicentre of the kiss and was felt in the physical world as the woman's hanbok fluttered as if it had been hit by gust of wind.

Come with me she smiled and grabbed him by the hand.

His body suddenly had the strength to move and he rose although he could still not feel the ground.

Walk with me a spell if you would she said and took him by the arm.

They strolled together arms linked tightly. Neither of them said a word. There was hardly any scenery at all, as behind the mist seemed to be more mist. Still, he had not felt this content since he had last been sat in his mother's lap long before he could even hold his own head upright. Another thing he knew but could not remember.

This reminded him. There was a question he needed to ask but in doing so would move this moment on to another, and he was content to hold on to it for as long as possible.

However, the realisation of time as something that exists or had existed brought questions. How long had he been up? How long had he been out? How long had they been walking and how little time did they have? With questions came doubt, or perhaps it was the other way around. It was unimportant. He had spoiled the moment for himself now.

What is wrong she asked in a tone that exposed that she knew exactly what was wrong.

'Are you,' he began but coughed out of habit as there was no itching in his throat what so ever 'are you my mother?' for the first time since he had awoke he felt something other than utter content; embarrassment. The pieces of the Jong-sup he had become used to, began to pull closer together at the familiar feeling of shame.

No she replied.

'Why?' asked Jong-sup, his heart piecing back together and breaking again.

Why am I not you're mother?

'Then why, why do you look just like her?'

The better question is, what do you think your mother looks like? she said.

Jong-sup stopped and thought about this. The first clear thought since he arrived here. The ground rose up to touch his feet and he felt gravity press him against it again.

'May I ask who you are then?' asked Jong-sup.

You know who I am

Jong-sup did know. He had known since she was a speck on the horizon, only he had just realised that he had.

'Death?' he asked, the answer already set in his head.

Death only nodded and smiled gently. The confirmation did not upset him; however, he began to feel more himself. The bits and pieces of his memory and mind were starting to reconnect. Something did not return but he couldn't know what it was.

'Why do you appear in this form?' asked Jong-sup.

I do not appear

'You are only perceived,' interrupted Jong-sup with a smile.

Death matched his expression and took his arm and continued walking into the unknown. They walked for some time while Jong-sup battled with the noisy thoughts and questions bouncing off the walls of his head. He almost wished to return to thinking of nothing at all. Eventually the questions won out.

'So, why do I perceive you like this now?'

How do you perceive me? asked Death.

'Well, so lovely, so beautiful,' he replied.

Is the answer not in front of you?

'No,' he looked around in confusion 'I don't understand.'

You no longer fear death

'I'm not sure that's quite right,' he said 'I never really feared death.'

Death smiled knowingly.

'If I feared death why would I have tried so hard to kill myself?' he continued, 'If anything, it was life I was afraid of.'

There is no difference

'There is a big difference, they're completely opposite of each other.'

Big only exists if there is a small. If there was no small, then big would cease to exist. Life and Death are the same way. One cannot be without the other

'Well, for the last, for however long, I have been living but not dying so that's not quite right either.'

Were you not dying? Or were you not living?

'Both I guess,' he shrugged.

Correct

'but before you cursed me, how was I not living?'

You were empty. There was nothing left of the young bright-eyed boy called Park Jong-sup. You lived only for yourself. So when you stopped caring about even yourself enough to jump from such a height there was nothing left of you at all. An empty husk without a soul

'Is that why you cursed me? So I could find my soul?'

I do not have motive

'You must, you surely have action, so there must be a motive.'

Death is beyond human reasoning Park Jong-sup

It wasn't quite the answer he was looking for, but he accepted it as he knew he wouldn't be getting better.

'Well, I guess I am still without a soul, as I still don't give a shit about myself.'

That's not true

'It's not?'

You hate yourself

'Is that better?'

It makes you a better man now than how I found you on that rooftop

'I don't understand.'

Living for the light of others has cast a shadow over you and highlighted who you really are and more importantly, who you want to be

'Is wanting enough?'

It would be a start if it was not the end

'The end? You mean I'm dead?'

Yes

Jong-sup did not feel how he thought he would have. He should have felt overjoyed about his long suffering coming to an end, but he felt numb, if not a little sad. Why? What was he missing?

'How did I die?' he asked.

You were shot

'Surely that wouldn't have killed me,' he said almost offended 'I've been through worse.'

Perhaps the Jong-sup who was not alive, but the Jong-sup who lived for others if not himself was not so robust

Jong-sup stopped and wondered what kind of situation he could have been in to be murdered in such a manner. He was doing something important, he could feel it. If he could only remember what it was.

'You heard my call,' rang a sweetly familiar voice, parting the mists and then disappearing again.

'Mi-na!' he cried out 'Death, where is Mi-na? Is she alright?'

She is right there said Death, and so she was. It wasn't as though she had appeared there suddenly, but she had been there all along; six feet away from where they stood. He just hadn't noticed.

Mi-na was sat on the ground with a man's head in her lap. Her head was turned up towards the sky, her face stricken wild with grief. A police officer was trying to pull her away from the corpse but she was having trouble as Mi-na had her arms fastened tightly under the man's chin. They moved as though they were immersed in tar. Jong-sup had to look closely to see that they were moving at all.

'Is that me?' asked Jong-sup pointing towards the dead body.

Yes

'I've forgotten what I looked like.'

You have forgotten what your flesh looked like

'I guess I won't be needing it where I'm going.'

No

'She looks so sad,' said Jong-sup 'I guess she really cared for me.'

She cares for you still

'I have no idea why,' he pondered aloud 'Can I say goodbye?'

She will not hear you said Death *but if you wish*

Jong-sup knelt down next to her and looked in great detail at the young girl. He reached out to touch her, to comfort her if possible. A static like shock zapped his finger when it was about an inch away. He put it to his mouth, he was surprised that he could feel pain.

The scene around him suddenly sped up becoming highly animated. The officer still trying to pry the girl away gently. Officers and a paramedic emerging and disappearing into the mists. Mi-na's cries became audible. It lasted a mere second and things slowed to a snail's pace again.

Jong-sup looked back at Death who did not seem at all surprised.

He tried again this time grabbing her by the arm. The world burst into movement again. The officer managed to prise Mi-na's hands away and pull her two feet kicking and screaming before slowing to near stillness.

'Could she feel me?' asked Jong-sup looking at Death.

No

'I felt certain that she had,' he said deflated 'so, is she going to be okay?'

I don't know answered Death *she is not ready to die if that is what you mean*

'That's good at least,' he said relieved 'I thought you knew everything!'

Did I ever tell you that? smiled Death

'Wait!' snapped Jong-sup 'Is that why you wouldn't let me die? To save Mi-na? is she supposed to do something amazing in the future? Was that your purpose?'

Calm down Park Jong-sup said Death, crouching down and taking Jong-sup's hand she lifted him to his feet.

'But, I remember, you guided me to this end.'

Did I?

'You did, you broke my chains that time in the Han, and you helped me escape that psycho's chair,'

Stop trying to rationalise death she said, *to understand is to control and to control death is neither the role nor responsibility of men*

Jong-sup didn't argue. It didn't really matter. He had a feeling that Mi-na would go on to do great things. However, no matter how she turned out he was just relieved that she was out of that hell hole. He hated to see her so distraught. If she really knew him, she wouldn't have wasted the tears he thought, well maybe she would have. She was a sweet girl. Yeah, if he had to die this is the way he would like to go.

'Death?' he asked 'Where am I going?'

I do not know she replied with an expression that said she wish she could tell him more.

'You don't?' he asked surprised 'I mean, there is a heaven and hell, right?'

I am not sure

'How can that be? You are Death herself!'

I exist solely in the realm between the living and the dead. Death is just the transformation of one mode of being to the other

'How about reincarnation?' he asked.

I am sorry Park Jong-sup she said sweetly, *I do not know what lies beyond only that it is your turn to go there*

'It's time?'

Yes

'Okay. Just let me say goodbye.'

Jong-sup bent down to face the distraught Mi-na. He prepared himself, then wrapped his arms around her. Energy shot through his body and it took all his will power to keep himself locked around her as time returned to the world and she was squirming to get out of the officer's grip.

Then the strangest thing happened. She settled. She stopped resisting. Jong-sup could have sworn that he could feel her bury her head into his shoulder. As painful as it was resisting the force vibrating throughout him, he held on tight to her.

'You are such a special young lady Mi-na. I am sorry I didn't realise it sooner. I'm so sorry.'

The increasing pressure pushing them apart became too much to bear and he was blasted nearly five feet from her. Mi-na seemed unaffected. She stood up, turned, took the officers hand and they began to walk away together before almost freezing in place once again.

'She recognised me,' said Jong-sup dusting himself off and standing tall.

If believing that makes you content said Death, *then I think you've earned the right*

'Oh, that's right, I nearly forgot,' said Jong-sup, 'Mr Lee, wanted me to tell you-'

I know she said, *you need not worry, I will take care of your friend*

'I hope that Mi-sook receives the binder,' said Jong-sup aloud, to himself more than his present company, 'the woman deserves closure, and maybe Kwang-su will be able to move on.'

Maybe

Death stretched her small, delicate hand out to Jong-sup who took it.

'You know what?' said Jong-sup 'I hope there is something after this. It would be nice to see Pigeon again, and In-sook,'

In-sook? I am surprised to hear you say that

'I need to tell her something,' said Jong-sup 'she needs to know that I don't hate her. Never have, not really.'

Then for your sake Park Jong-sup I hope that you get your chance Death said, linking his arm.

Are you ready?

Jong-sup looked at Death as if an old friend.

'Ready.'

About the Author

If there is anything that Shayne Meissner really hates, it is writing about himself. Especially in the third person. However, it seemed from examples from his own bookshelf that it was the done thing, and always one to admit that he has no idea what he is doing he decided to follow people who did.

Hailing from the great city of Bristol has gifted him the extra challenge of trying not to sound (or write) like a cross between a farmer and a pirate, especially since he decided to teach in Hong Kong. However he considers it one his greatest contributions that many a child is fully equipped with an inner lexicon of Bristolian slang.

Spending most of his adult life abroad, experiencing many different cultures and meeting many incredible characters has inspired him, taught him about life and given him plenty of writing material.

In his free time he enjoys spending time with the greatest thing that has ever happened to him; his daughter. She won't be able to read this book for a good number of years yet, but one day he hopes she does and hopes that she is smiling while reading this.

Sometimes escapism is necessary and the best way to escape is a good book. Shayne has read many. If he has written one is yet to be seen. They say everyone has one good book in them. So if anything, this could be seen as some kind of experiment.

Please feel free to reach out to me at:
smeissnerbooks@gmail.com
All feedback is appreciated.

Printed in Great Britain
by Amazon

57894231R00148